Euphoria Lane

TINA SWAYZEE McCRIGHT

ISBN: 1523260351
ISBN-13: 978-1523260355

PRAISE FOR TINA SWAYZEE MCCRIGHT

Winner of the Desert Dreams Contest

Winner of the Hot Prospects Contest, Contemporary Series

"A surprising twist in every story!" —Tia Dani

"[She] . . . has a true gift for writing sympathetically and insightfully. Even her villains are compelling and three-dimensional . . ." —*The Long and the Short of It*

"[*Liquid Hypnosis*] has such a twist to it that when it happens you wonder how you didn't see that coming." —Fallen Angel Reviews

This book is dedicated to the memory of Shirley Mays, a positive influence in many lives. She helped me realize I had finally found my writer's voice. She is greatly missed.

ACKNOWLEDGMENTS

I would like to thank my beta readers for their time and insight: Rosie Mays, Jeanette Lyons, Pat McCright, Kathy Froncek, and Mari Dominguez. A special thanks is due to Kathryne Kennedy, Tia Dani, Carol Webb, my husband, and my daughter, Jackie, for their advice, support, and assistance.

ONE

Andi Stevenson stood in front of a two-story condominium building on Euphoria Lane, clutching a shiny, gold key in one hand and a copy of her mortgage papers in the other. Relief mingled with an overwhelming sense of pride. No more apartment leases for her. No more drunken college students stealing her assigned parking spot while wearing underwear for hats. No more landlords repairing ancient appliances with duct tape and bailing wire month after month. And no more neighbors screeching out rap songs at all hours of the day and night. She'd truly bought a piece of euphoria and she wouldn't allow anyone else to ruin her portion of heaven on Earth.

The rented moving van, parked at the curb, reminded her of the work ahead. Basking in the glow of homeownership, she walked down the cement path leading to her ground-level home. The spring breeze fluttered the fuchsia-colored petals on the bougainvillea next to her front door. She slipped the key into the lock and wondered if she should say a few words to commemorate the momentous occasion.

TINA SWAYZEE McCRIGHT

"You having a stroke?"

The familiar voice belonged to her sister.

"What?" Andi turned to find Jessica, nicknamed Jessie, carrying a box too big to handle alone.

"You have that vacant look that says nobody's home."

"My mind wandered for a moment," Andi confessed. "Let me help you with that." She reached out to assist, but her sister stepped out of the way.

"I got it. Just grab the door." Jessie struggled to hold on to the box while walking. A jerky movement sent her Diamondbacks baseball cap flying off her blonde hair.

Disappointed that she wouldn't be the first person to carry her belongings inside, Andi quickly unlocked the portal to her new life and pushed the door open. She scooped the cap up off the cement and followed Jessie into the foyer.

The sisters had been roommates since Andi had become a teacher six years ago. The arrangement had allowed her to save money for the down payment on the condo. Jessie was also saving for a down payment—on a detective agency. After ten years as a police officer with the city of Glendale, Arizona, the eldest Stevenson sister now wanted a career with fewer rules, no boss, and better hours. Two more paychecks and the agency would be hers.

Andi tossed Jessie's cap onto the kitchen counter and surveyed the room. Brand new, stainless-steel appliances reflected the morning sun shining through the window. She couldn't wait to try out her cookie creations in her brand-new oven. Since the counselor at her school told her she needed a hobby to release the tension brought on by teaching in a gang-infested, poverty-stricken neighborhood, she had poured her creative energy into baking.

Jessie entered the kitchen and dropped the oversize

2

cardboard box next to the wall with a resounding thump. She stretched and grinned. "Hope your mixing bowls weren't breakable."

"I hope I don't accidentally drop your collection of lava lamps," Andi teased.

Jessie narrowed her eyes. "You wouldn't dare."

"Try me." Andi chuckled and followed her outside for another load. Her mixing bowls were stainless steel and her sister knew it since she'd licked the frosting from them countless times. "When we're done here, I'll pick up something to eat."

"Anything but pizza. Five days in a row is my limit." Jessie jogged ahead of her to the back end of the moving van.

Twenty boxes later, Andi's shoulders ached from the strain. "Are you ready for a break? I know I am." She snatched empty Styrofoam cups and water bottles from the countertop. "I'll make coffee after I throw out the trash."

"Sounds like a plan. I'll search for the filters and coffee pot." Her sister tugged open a box labeled "Essentials."

Carrying the lumpy plastic trash bags outside, Andi walked the quiet residential street toward the dumpster. She tilted her left arm to check her digital watch. The salesman at the store had promised the new sofa would arrive between noon and two. She still had time to grab lunch before they arrived.

With her hands full, she used her pinky finger to flip up the latch on the gate to the fence surrounding the oversize trash bin. She poked her tennis shoe beneath the wood and tugged the gate open with her toes. Tossing the first bag of garbage into the dumpster, she noticed an adorable wooden dollhouse resting on top. It must have taken someone days, perhaps weeks, to assemble and paint the three-foot-by-three-foot toy structure.

Why would anyone throw it away?

Next to the dollhouse, a red-and-white sock stuck straight up in the air.

What? Socks aren't usually stiff. Not without a ton of starch . . .

She stepped closer to get a better look. Under the sock, visible above the mound of trash, she saw a white, plump, hairy leg. Screams erupted from Andi's throat. She couldn't stop. Each explosion of sound bellowed out longer and louder than the one before.

Memories of zombie movies flooded her mind. Dead souls walking about in dirty, shredded clothing with their arms outstretched. Each one craving a live person to devour. She dropped the remaining trash bag and trembled.

Please don't climb out of the dumpster—if you're dead.

From behind came the sounds of doors opening and people shouting, but Andi couldn't turn from the horrid sight of death. Terror seized every cell of her body.

The rhythmic pattern of someone running over the asphalt grew closer. Jessie stepped into her line of vision. "What's wrong?"

Andi tilted her head in the direction of the dumpster. Even that simple movement took all her will to complete.

Her sister placed one hand gingerly on her shoulder, then leaned close to the metal container to glance inside.

"Great housewarming gift." She reached for the body.

"No! Don't touch it!" Andi grabbed hold of her sister's arm like a drowning woman gripping onto a life preserver.

"Calm down," Jessie cooed. She patted Andi's arm, then casually leaned toward the mountain of trash as though finding a dead body in the dumpster was an

everyday occurrence. Perhaps in her line of work, it was.
"I need to move the trash bags to see if she's alive."
"It's Bernice," a teenage boy yelled. He balanced one
foot in front of another along the top of the brick wall
surrounding the complex. "She's dead, all right. I can
see her face on this side of the dollhouse. She's all fat
and gray."
"Her face is always fat." The raspy voice belonged to
a woman wearing a leopard-print, spandex jumpsuit. She
ambled over next to Jessie and the dumpster. Judging by
the lines fanning out from her heavily painted eyes, she
had been celebrating her fortieth birthday for over
twenty years.
"Now it's gray." The teenage boy, sporting a
Mohawk, stood on his toes to get a better view from his
perch several yards away.
The crowd closed in around Andi. She had no idea
where everyone had come from and, frankly, she didn't
care. People on all sides of her spoke at once.
"A dead body?"
"Who is it?"
"Bernice. She must have fallen off her patio."
"Where did the dollhouse come from?"
"It's part of her *Wizard of Oz* collection. That's the
house that fell on the wicked witch."
"Another case of life imitating art."
"Maybe she lifted the house, lost her balance, and fell
into the dumpster. That's her condo up there."
"I was about to throw my trash out. I could have
found the body."
"If I had found her body, I would have passed out."
With her sister close by, Andi found she could now
breathe easier. She glanced up at a patio overhead.
Foliage from a healthy plant occupied the corner near a
chocolate-brown wicker chair. Nothing appeared odd or
out of place. A broken porch railing would have

5

explained the situation.

The spandex-clad woman lit up a cigarette and blew smoke rings that floated up and over the dead body. "Pretty ironic, if you ask me."

Andi studied the amused expression on the stranger's aging face. "What's ironic about someone dying?"

The woman gave her the once-over. "You're new, so I'll fill you in. Bernice was a bigger gossip than the Hollywood paparazzi. Since she was the president of the homeowners' board, she had the goods on everyone. Her tongue never stopped flapping. What's ironic is that finding a dead body in a dumpster is the most exciting thing to happen around here, and she's not alive to spread the news. Life is sweet." With that, the woman lifted the cigarette back to her dry, chapped lips.

Andi's jaw dropped. *Who are these people?*

An attractive blonde wearing violet-colored medical scrubs and a hospital badge indicating she was a nurse stepped from the crowd. "Speaking of the board, you're going to receive a warning for parking in a fire lane."

"What?" Andi gestured toward the rented van. "I'm moving in today."

"Doesn't matter." She pointed down the road. "You have to leave the van in guest parking and unpack from there."

Andi studied the area indicated. "That's a building away."

"The board doesn't care if it's a mile away. The rules—"

"Are the rules," the crowd finished in unison.

The teen shook his head with obvious disgust. "But, Mom, the Wicked Witch is dead."

The nurse shook her head. "Doesn't matter. Her flying monkeys are still alive and they'll send a report to the property manager."

The crowd murmured their agreement. Andi

furrowed her brow in confusion. She waited for her sister to snap her cell phone shut before asking, "Do you think she fell off the patio?"

Jessie shrugged. "We won't know 'til after the investigation."

This woman's death had to be an accident. If it wasn't, that meant murder.

****

The next morning, Andi woke to furious pounding on her front door. Squinting, she peered through the peephole to find her scowling father. She twisted the deadbolt with a low, guttural moan. If the marines needed a few good men, why had they let her dad retire? He could still bark orders with the best of them—and often did.

He barged in the second she tugged open the door. "I heard about the dead woman. It's all over the news." He marched past her and inspected the boxes lining the walls. "I see you haven't finished unpacking. I think you should come home with me until the murderer is caught."

Andi had no intention of running home to Mommy and Daddy. She didn't care how many nightmares she would have from finding the dead body. "Dad, I'm not going anywhere. This *is* my home."

"Then I'll bring you my shotgun. Keep it handy."

Andi shook her head. "Jessie has an arsenal that would make an arms dealer jealous. I wouldn't be surprised if she had weapons of mass destruction hidden behind the television set."

"What about bullets?"

"She has a few hundred of those, too." Andi planted a quick kiss on his cheek. "I need a pot of coffee. How about you?"

7

"Sure. And while it brews, you can tell me what's going on around here. Jessie must have talked to the detective in charge. I want the facts, not the flimflam-coated media."

"I'll share what little I know." Andi shuffled her pink slippers into the kitchen as her father followed close behind. Since she made a habit of wearing oversize T-shirts and shorts to bed, she had felt no need to grab a robe. She checked to make sure the coffee maker had been properly prepared the night before and pushed the "On" button.

Her father leaned against the counter and folded his tan, hairy arms across his thick chest. The salt-and-pepper hair only added to his commanding air of authority.

"The woman's death was most likely an accident." Andi opened the refrigerator and searched for her flavored creamer. "The dead woman probably leaned too far off her porch, fell, and hit her head on something hard in the trash." She found the bottle nestled behind a gallon of low-fat milk, cashew chicken leftovers, and cherry pie.

Her father's grimace said he wasn't satisfied. "Is the detective in charge *convinced* it was an accident?"

She debated whether or not she should tell him the whole truth, then figured he'd know if she didn't. "Jessie didn't speak to him." Before her father could respond, Andi added, "But she said there's nothing to worry about."

Or did she say not to worry unless she told her otherwise?

"According to the neighbors, the entire community hated the woman who died. If it wasn't an accident, it was an isolated incident."

He scowled. "You think she deserved to die?"

"Of course not. I'm trying to tell you *I'm* not in any

danger. There isn't a serial killer out there randomly selecting his victims." If this conversation continued, she knew he would pack up her bags and drag her home. She needed a diversion. With a glance over at her new white-linen sofa and matching pillows decorated with a red leaf accent pattern, she changed the subject. "Thank you again for paying for the moving van and buying my new living room sofa."

"It's my pleasure, sweetie. I know you can't afford nice things on a teacher's salary."

He was right, but hearing the words spoken out loud made her cringe. "I could always become a police officer like Jessie. Not that they're paid a lot more than teachers," Andi added.

"You, a cop?" Her father laughed. "I don't think so. Besides, your mother would have a heart attack. It's hard enough for her to handle Jessie's career." He released a slight sigh. "I am so glad your mother is out of town with your other sisters visiting Grandma Shirley right now. They would all be worried sick if they knew about the stiff in the dumpster. That's the last thing I need."

A hissing sound signaled the completion of the brewing cycle. Andi poured the steaming coffee into the ceramic mugs and handed one to her father. "You can sit at the dining room table. Just toss the empty boxes onto the floor."

While he proceeded to judge the contents of the mug and walked into the other room, she poured flavored creamer into her cup and then joined him. He wore a huge grin on his face.

"Did I miss a punch line?" Confused by his change in mood, she eased down onto the closest chair, careful not to spill.

"No. I just wish I had been here to watch your sister work the crime scene until the officers on duty arrived. That must have been quite a show." He drank from the hot mug and then nodded his approval.

"You didn't miss anything." Jessie sauntered in wearing red sweatpants and a matching Cardinals football jersey. Her disheveled, shoulder-length hair hung over one eye. "I couldn't help. I'm working undercover. The department needed a woman to pose as a waitress."

He turned to his oldest daughter. "What's being undercover got to do with a death in your condo complex?"

"It means I can't let anyone in the community know I'm a police officer. My undercover assignment is only a few miles away."

Andi had heard of the Nighthawk Diner, but never ventured inside. The parking lot full of motorcycles made her nervous. "Jessie's working at one of those eating establishments where they exploit their female employees. She is required to wear tiny skirts and necklines that plunge so low you can tell her belly button is an innie, not an outie."

Jessie poured herself a cup of coffee. "The restaurant has a reputation for peddling more than hash browns."

"Drugs and prostitution," Andi clarified before sipping from her mug.

Their father shrugged. "I guess you have to work where you're needed."

Andi stared at him in disbelief. "Let me get this straight. I find a body, no murderer in sight, and you want to haul me home. Your other daughter is cavorting with perverted men while pretending to be a drug-dealing prostitute and you shrug it off? Jessie is your daughter, too. Why isn't she receiving the overprotective-father routine?"

"Your sister is a police officer. She can take care of herself." He looked her straight in the eye—his way of making sure she paid attention. "When Jessie draws it's with an automatic, not a red grading pen."

Andi knew there was no point in arguing. First, he was right. Jessie was better equipped to take care of herself. Second, Andi would always be considered the baby of the family. She was lucky he still didn't remind her to look both ways before crossing the street.

He set down his mug, snatched the newspaper from the table, and headed down the hall.

"Life's not fair. Get used to it," Jessie teased while returning to the dining room table with a mug of coffee. The doorbell interrupted their conversation. "I'll get it. You never know when an armed kindergartener might follow you home to raid the place."

"Very funny," Andi answered. "If that's the mailman at the door, don't shoot first and ask questions later, Dirty Harriet."

Andi noticed her red pen at the end of the dining room table, next to her grade book. Looking at it reminded her that everyone in her family thought she couldn't defend herself because she was only a teacher. She snatched it up with one quick move and shoved it into the pocket of her gray shorts.

A broken fan's loud, obnoxious whine told her their father had found the bathroom.

Hoping the fan would prove to be a small fix, Andi sipped her coffee. A gruff male voice at the door caught her by surprise. Turning in her chair, she watched Jessie step aside to allow their visitor inside.

The man looked a lot like Andi's school principal—a balding, short, older gentleman. His chestnut toupee sat askew on top of his natural gray hair. He also had the same tight, pinched expression her father wore whenever his hemorrhoids flared up.

A younger, taller man entered the foyer behind the older one. Recognition sparked deep within her. With his sandy-brown hair and welcoming smile, he

11

resembled . . . Andi's heart stopped. No. It couldn't be. Yet she knew it *was* Luke Ryder. Her mind swirled in a dozen different directions.

Why is he here, in my home, after all these years? I haven't seen him since my freshman year of college.

Their eyes met. His smile faded and his strong jaw tightened. "Andi . . ." Her name hung in the air like a mistake no one wanted to acknowledge. "It's been a long time."

"Luke . . ."

How long had it been since that night? Eight years? No. Nine.

Nine years since he said he couldn't marry her and marched out of her dorm room.

Jessie's gaze traveled between the two of them. "You know each other?"

Long work hours back then had kept Jessie from meeting Luke the half a dozen times he'd been at their family home for Sunday dinner. Since he had never officially proposed, the family knew only that Andi had once been serious about him. They had no clue *how* serious. She had been afraid that telling everyone about their plans before he proposed would bring bad luck. Looking back on things, she realized she might have had better luck carrying a black cat, stepping on cracks, and throwing mirrors while walking under a ladder.

She managed to pull her gaze away from his dark-brown eyes. "We knew each other in college. Luke, this is my sister, Jessie. She lives with me."

A hesitant smile tugged at his lips before he shook Jessie's hand. "It's nice to meet you. I'm the property manager for Euphoria Lane Condominiums." He turned to the older man. "This is Harry Fletcher, the HOA vice president."

"President," Harry interjected in a coarse, nasal tone. "I am now *president* of the homeowners' association."

He acted as if he were the king of a rich, oil-producing country instead of a gated community made up of two hundred condominiums.

Luke studied an envelope on the clipboard he carried.

"Andi, I heard you found Bernice yesterday."

"Bernice?" Andi forced herself to focus on the conversation.

"The dead woman," her sister clarified while eyeing the older man suspiciously. "Have we met before?"

"No." Harry's answer came too fast and too loud.

"I'm sure I've seen you somewhere before." Jessie tapped her lips with her pointer finger as she studied the man.

"You have me mistaken for someone else," he snapped.

Jessie grinned with obvious satisfaction when she remembered. She turned to Andi and twirled her hair the way she did whenever she wore her waitress uniform. Her undercover persona involved playing pretty and dumb.

Andi's gaze traveled between Jessie and Harry. Understanding made its way into her consciousness, past the shock of seeing Luke again. The new board president was clearly a customer at the sleazy diner. A wave of trepidation rolled over her like a premonition.

Not sure what to think, Andi turned back to the man she had once loved. Emotional memories hit her full force. Feeling overwhelmed by the events of her first two days in her new home, Andi aimed for calm and collected. She gestured toward the living room.

"Would you like to sit down?"

"We won't be taking up much of your time," Luke said as he surveyed the condo. "Unpacking is always a huge job."

She tried to see the room as he would. More than a dozen cardboard boxes lined the walls, their lids standing open, half gutted of their contents. Newspaper used for packing littered the carpet and tile. Piles of books and dishes took up room on counters and tabletops. She felt self-conscious and wished she were more organized. Her motto had always been, "Everything has a place—and one day I'll put it there."

This man, with his impeccable hair, tailored tan chinos, and long-sleeved black shirt, had always looked like he just stepped out of the pages of *GQ*. She always looked like she stepped off the cover of *MAD Magazine*.

I would have to see him again, after all these years, wearing a pink, oversize, "I-Love-Chocolate" T-shirt.

Embarrassed, Andi crossed her arms over her chest.

"You the welcome wagon?" Jessie tilted her head as if to get a better look at Luke. "Where's the casserole?"

He glanced down at his clipboard again, but not before his expression gave away his discomfort. "No food today, ladies. Only my assurance Euphoria is a safe community. Since you were the one who found Bernice, I thought I should tell you nothing like this has ever happened here before. There's no need to be alarmed by her unfortunate—"

"Stop pussyfooting around!" The older man snatched the envelope off the clipboard and shoved it at her. "We came over to give you this."

Luke glared at him. "I wanted to handle this *my* way."

Harry scoffed and turned on Andi. "We have rules here, Miss Stevenson. We maintain the value of our homes by adhering to those rules."

She ripped open the envelope as Jessie peered over her shoulder. In large letters, the words WARNING and PARKING VIOLATION jumped out at her. She could feel her face redden.

This can't be.

"Why are you doing this to me?"

Luke jerked back. "It's not personal. It's my job."

Andi sighed. "That is a private street out front. There's no traffic. You honestly expected us to park a moving van a building away and haul everything over? No one does that."

"It's only a warning . . ." Luke insisted.

"A warning I shouldn't be receiving, *Mr. Ryder*. I was told this Bernice woman might have been killed because of her unrelenting enforcement of the rules. She made enemies. I'm sure the rest of the board doesn't want to follow in her footsteps."

Luke creased his brow. "Did you hear a threat made against the board?"

"Not exactly," she admitted. "If I had, I would have called the authorities. You know that."

This time Harry's gaze traveled between them. "Just how well do you two know each other?"

"Boys . . ." Jessie cooed. She looped her arm around Harry's. "Why don't we sit down and relax while you tell us how we can make this thing go away?"

"Let's not!" Harry yanked his arm out of her reach as if she had a contagious disease. He glared at her. "Only respectable people are allowed to live in Euphoria."

Oh, great! He thinks my sister is a drug-dealing hooker because she's playing undercover waitress at the diner.

Jessie glared back at him.

Andi had never seen a standoff before, but she knew she was witnessing one now. Harry obviously wanted them out of his community, but Jessie wasn't going to budge an inch.

Andi stepped between them before Jessie could morph into her lady mud wrestler persona and knock Harry into the next condo.

"Did you know the neighbors referred to Bernice as the Wicked Witch?" Andi asked in her calmest teacher voice. "I'm sure you don't want to be disliked the same way she was."

"I don't care what anyone thinks. The rules are the rules." Harry's voice took on a sinister tone. "The witch may be dead, but the *wizard* isn't. Obey the rules, missy, or you'll wish you never landed here."

She suspected it wouldn't matter if she followed the rules or not for as long as Jessie lived with her. Andi tightened her fists until her nails bit into her palms. Summoning her courage, she strode to the door and swung it open with flourish. The wooden panel brushed against her hip, causing her pen to fall from the pocket of her shorts and clatter against the tile floor. Bright-red ink flowed from the tube like an ominous warning.

At that moment, she once again heard the loud whine of the broken bathroom fan. "Andi!" Her father called out. "Got any matches? It's murder in here."

TWO

Luke pushed open the glass door to the public library located two miles down the street from the Euphoria Condominiums. The large number of disgruntled neighbors attending the monthly meetings made it impossible to gather in the neighborhood clubhouse.

A bright, painted jungle covered the library walls as far as Luke could see. Smirking monkeys swung from one tree to the next over slithering pythons while skulking tigers foraged for prey in the dense underbrush. The mural always reminded him to mentally prepare for the verbal attacks he would endure during the Euphoria Condominiums homeowners' meetings. Angry homeowners, as well as the HOA board, liked to blame him whenever they didn't get what they wanted. A sudden sense of relief flowed over him when he realized Bernice wouldn't be yelling at him that night. And that made him feel guilty. He never wanted to benefit in any way from the death of another.

Luke marched through the lobby. He wished the library would invest in a metal detector. Over a dozen years ago, a man had shot five people at a homeowners' association meeting not more than ten miles from where he stood. One woman died. Now Bernice. He knew he had to get the board to back down from its agenda of sending out one violation letter after another before another life was claimed.

He located the corridor leading to the meeting rooms and instantly recognized the man sipping water from the fountain. "Harry, we need to talk. I'm sure you've heard that the police believe Bernice was murdered because of her work on the board. You might want to rethink your stance on violation letters."

"No one is going to shove me and a dollhouse off a balcony," Harry scoffed.

Luke rubbed the back of his neck. Not once had Harry ever made his job easier. "Just hear me out. It's time for a change. The board doesn't have to be seen as bad guys. You don't have to walk the community daily, looking for violations. It's my job as your property manager to send out violation letters after my weekly visits. Board meetings should become a place where neighbors go for help. Now they see you as the enemy."

"Now *you* hear *me* out," Harry said, pointing his finger like a parent scolding a child. "I am not going to let those whiney neighbors run amok. Bernice's murder does not change anything. The rules are the rules, and I'm here to enforce them."

"Harry, it would be in your best interest to consider lightening up until the murderer is caught."

"It would be in *your* best interest to remember we are your company's biggest account. If you want to take over for the owner when he retires next year, you'd better make me happy," Harry sneered. "You didn't think I knew, did you? Mr. Greer told me all about his plans for you on his last visit to the property."

"My first concern is for the safety of this community—yours included."

"Yeah, right. Keep telling yourself that. One call from me and your fast-track career will shift into reverse." Harry marched off, insuring he had the last word.

Luke knew he shouldn't let the bad-tempered man get to him, but he couldn't help but feel annoyed. Harry, and Bernice before him, got under everyone's skin. That was why the Euphoria account had landed on his desk. Five other managers had refused to work with their board. By staying on, Luke had proved he would be the right man to take over when the company's owner retired. He needed the promotion and the money that would come with it too much to quit now.

He shifted his briefcase into his other hand and turned to find Andi approaching. Her expression turned wary when she spotted him. He always knew there was a chance he might run into her again. He just never dreamed it would be under these circumstances.

He watched as she stepped closer. She hadn't changed much over the years. Her silky auburn hair still reflected the light. And she still had a flawless, heart-shaped face. It was the smile that was missing. She used to beam whenever she saw him. Not tonight. Her grimace could not be confused with a smile by any stretch of the imagination.

"It's nice to see you again, Andi." He meant every word. For years after their breakup, he wondered what had happened to her. *Was she teaching? Was she happy? Did she miss me?*

He had missed her more than he had been willing to admit to anyone, but he didn't regret his decision. Leaving her had been the right choice, no matter how much it hurt.

"*Nice* isn't the word that just popped into my mind," she stated with both hands planted on her rounded hips. "I still can't believe you wrote me those horrible violation letters."

"You mean letter. I wrote one letter."

"I received two. I found another one tucked into the screen door this morning, but then you already knew that."

"No, I didn't." Harry must have given her one without his knowledge. Whenever the man followed his own agenda, he would personally send out violation letters and then send Luke a copy for the files.

"Apparently, my father was supposed to move his car out of guest parking and into the driveway when my sister left for work yesterday. Why should he have to park in the driveway? He *is* a guest. Isn't that what guest parking is for?" Her temper grew with each word.

Luke rubbed his temple, regretting the situation. She had no idea what a mistake she had made by moving to Euphoria. "I understand you're angry, and I truly wish there was more I could do to help, but our company does not make the rules. We mainly handle the finances and paperwork for Euphoria."

"I would think your time would be better spent convincing the board that it is unreasonable to expect residents to play musical cars every time someone leaves their condo."

"As a matter of fact, I did have that discussion with them. As you can see, my advice was ignored." A hint of irritation invaded his tone. He shifted his briefcase again. The weight of both its contents and their conversation had become a burden he wanted to leave behind. It wasn't his fault Euphoria was anything but euphoric. "Andi, I can only give you the same advice I give other homeowners: if you don't like the rules, do something to change them."

"I might just do that." Her brow furrowed with thoughts he wished he could read.

****

Andi watched Luke walk away with long, purposeful strides. *The back view is still almost as good as the front. Too bad. If he had gained three hundred pounds and lost a handful of teeth, maybe then my heart would stop pounding like a jackhammer every time he enters a room.*

"Hi there!" The nurse from the murder scene said as she hurried over. She must have come straight from work. Today's scrubs sported a powder-blue puppy print. "Find any more dead bodies?" Her warm, dimpled smile lightened the mood.

"I'm avoiding dumpsters."

"I don't blame you." The new neighbor smiled and extended her hand. "I never got a chance to welcome you to Euphoria Lane. I'm Meg." Her pastel pink nails matched her lipstick, and her short blonde curls bounced against her shoulders with each move. Either she drank caffeine nonstop, or she was one of those naturally peppy people who brightened your life or drove you crazy. "I've lived here for three years, thirty violation letters, and hundreds of dollars in fines. I've put in a lot of overtime to pay those off."

Andi's jaw dropped. "Thirty? Have you been breaking rules to prove a point?"

"I don't break them on purpose, but there are so many restrictions it's hard to get through the week without breaking at least one rule, especially with a teenage son. Have you seen the twenty-nine pool rules? You can't play music loud enough for anyone else to hear. I guess you're supposed to swim with an iPod."

"You don't look old enough to have a teenager." She had to get the nurse's beauty secret. *I hope it doesn't involve placenta.*

"You and I are going to be great friends." Meg said, squeezing Andi's arm to prove her point. "Chad turned eighteen last fall. You met him when Bernice croaked. He's the good-looking kid with the Mohawk."

"The one walking the wall near the dumpster?"

Meg nodded in response, then her bubbly face grew serious. "I'm glad the witch is dead," she whispered. "That woman had the nerve to film my son and his friends at the pool."

"She *filmed* them?" Andi scowled. "Is that even legal?"

"Bernice wanted to prove a point. At the next homeowners' meeting she played the film and then ranted about teenagers ruining the property." Meg rolled her eyes. "They're not bad boys. There are just too many rules. Stupid ones, too."

Andi gripped her violation letters tighter. "I'm beginning to see your point. What rules did the boys break?"

"Playing Marco Polo," she guffawed. "All chanting games have been banned. Also, one so-called hellion had the audacity to walk too fast before jumping into the deep end. Bernice considered it running." Meg spoke faster and her pitch grew higher. "You'd think they mixed bubble bath with red dye in the hot tub by the way that woman acted."

The more she heard about Bernice, the more Andi wondered why no one had bumped her off years ago. "I guess we should get inside."

Meg smirked. "Don't want to miss tonight's show."

"I'm not so sure. The way my luck's running, I'll sneeze and Harry will write me up for a violation of the noise ordinance."

"Don't give him any ideas." Meg dramatically pushed open the door. "Let's get inside before the good seats are taken."

"Good seats? It sounds more like a circus than a meeting."

A circus Andi could handle. It was a reenactment of the murder she feared. She noticed that both Harry and Luke remained in the corridor, chatting with people she didn't recognize.

Andi stepped into the spacious meeting room filled with rows of metal folding chairs. Dozens of angry faces turned to see who had joined the group. Their narrowed gazes raked over both women and then darted in other directions.

"They're waiting for the board to arrive." Meg gestured toward two empty chairs in the back row. "Let's grab those seats near the door before someone else does. I always sit near an exit. You never know when a fight might break out." Her words sounded serious, but she wore a smile.

"Are you worried?"

"Nope. I'm not on the board. They might as well be wearing big, red shooting targets." The nurse slid onto a metal folding chair. "I just don't want to get caught in the crossfire if there's a gunfight. I can dodge fists, but not bullets."

Andi observed the angry scowls, dramatic gestures, and raised voices of the other homeowners. A long table had been placed in front of the room. It remained empty. She assumed it was for the board, and they apparently were smart enough not to enter the room until the last minute.

Meg grinned and waved to the smoker from the crime scene—the older woman, who thought Bernice's death was ironic. Tonight she wore a zebra-print spandex jumpsuit at least two sizes too small. She waved back with an unlit cigarette gripped between her fingers. Each exaggerated movement threatened to topple the hive teased on top of her head. A huge, ugly, plastic yellow rose had been clipped to the side of hive.

Andi caught herself gawking at the woman's outlandish appearance.

"That's Roxie," Meg announced. "She sold her beauty shop to buy into Euphoria. Now she wishes she had a time machine to go back and right that wrong. Bernice sent her a fine for driving over the seven-and-a-half-mile-per-hour speed limit, so Roxie drove over the speed limit sign. Every time the board sends her a fine, she sends back a notice announcing when she is going to break that rule again."

"Brave. I think." Andi mentally pictured the speed limit sign. "Why seven and a half?"

"Whoever wrote the rules wanted this place safer than a school zone, so he or she took the usual fifteen-mile limit and cut it in half."

"Interesting community. There should be a warning at the front gate: 'Overzealous HOA Board. Enter at Your Own Risk.' " Andi took in the crowd again. "Do you usually have so many people at these meetings?"

"Depends on how many violation letters go out that month. If the board's on a roll, it's standing room only." Meg waved wildly at a middle-aged woman sitting on the other side of the room and then at a couple strolling down the aisle. Her grin never left her face.

Andi realized her new friend was a Chihuahua on speed.

Meg turned back to Andi. "If you came here to complain about those letters you're holding, I should tell you it won't do you any good. Bernice and her flying monkeys never rescinded a violation. Harry won't be any better."

"Then why does anyone bother coming?"

"For the chance to hear someone else give the board a piece of their mind. Most neighbors are too afraid to say anything themselves. But tonight's different." She raised a brow and leaned close. "Word got around that Bernice was murdered. Someone took one of the yellow bricks from her Wizard of Oz collection and hit her over the head."

The dead body flashed in Andi's mind. Goosebumps rose on her arms while the small hairs on her neck stood on end. She scanned the room for anyone who looked like a killer. The air had grown heavy with anger, and her gaze fell on one scowl after another. *Every one* of her new neighbors looked like a killer. "Are they all hoping the murderer will show up?"

Meg nodded. "Roxie is taking bets on when Harry is going to join Bernice in hell." Her face lit up. "I put fifty dollars down on tonight, before the meeting is over. In the heart, with a hunting knife." She touched the middle of her chest. "The location where most people have a heart. If you knock on his chest, though, you'll probably hear an echo."

Andi couldn't keep her eyes off Roxie, the spandex queen turned bookie. She reminded Andi of one of those crazed Wild West townspeople who enjoyed a good lynching. While the rest of the library crowd waited, their eyes full of rage, hers twinkled with excitement.

The metallic click of the doorknob turning caught the crowd's attention. They turned to see who would enter next. So did Andi.

Luke strode in, briefcase in hand. Her stomach lurched. She tore her gaze away, not wanting to make eye contact again. No matter how strong her attraction for him remained, she refused to entertain the thought of rekindling an old flame.

Okay, forest fire.

The man worked for Harry, after all. Not that Luke would ever take her back. He had made that perfectly clear when he dumped her.

He took a seat at the long table up front and popped

open his briefcase, appearing busy and professional. According to the nameplates, the board sat between Luke and the security guard.

If the killer decided to make an appearance, would Luke become a target, too?

She hadn't considered the possibility before. The thought didn't sit well with her now.

The door swung open again and the beady-eyed president entered. He stiffened his spine and held his head high. The only thing missing from his grand entrance was the red carpet.

"Harry," Andi mumbled in disgust.

"See the woman strolling down the aisle behind him?" Meg whispered, glancing at a woman about forty years old with professionally bleached blonde hair clipped a few inches below her shoulders. She wore an attractive floral dress and expertly applied makeup. At her side she carried a wide-brimmed, white straw hat. The kind you would expect Southern women to wear to garden parties. "That's Valerie. She's married to Paul, the computer geek closing the door. Rumor has it she married him because she hoped he would be the next Bill Gates."

Valerie's hips swayed with each move, inviting the men to watch her walk down the aisle. Her double-D cups invited them to drool. Andi caught two women elbowing their husbands in the ribs, forcing them to stop staring.

After closing the door, Valerie's husband turned toward the room. He wore a wrinkled polo shirt over tan knee-length shorts. As he followed his wife, Paul kept his shoulders hunched over and his gaze toward the floor. Either he chose to ignore the attention his wife received, or he kept his mind immersed in his own thoughts.

Meg leaned closer. "Valerie is working her way

toward leaving her husband for Harry." She glanced about as if making sure no one heard. "One night after a board meeting, he started bragging about his millions in stocks. I swear there were dollar signs flashing in that woman's eyes."

"Are they having an affair?"

"Heaven's sake, no. Roxie overhead Valerie talking to a friend. She wants Harry's money. She's not going to give anything away for free. She plans to flirt her way into a proposal and then worry about divorcing Paul."

Andi grimaced. Marrying Harry for money was the Euphoria Lane equivalent of selling your soul to the devil.

****

Like the homeowners in attendance, Luke worried the killer might make an appearance, and he had no intention of dying for his job. Unlike the homeowners, he refused to bet on when the next board member might meet his, or her, maker. He had even taken measures to make sure no one died during the meeting. The two extra security guards he had hired stood behind the crowd, watching over the angry neighbors.

Harry banged the gavel. "Time to sit or leave," he barked. With a glance down at his paperwork, his toupee slid forward. He scowled at the sniggering crowd, adjusted his hairpiece, and called the meeting to order.

Luke ran his hand over his face to conceal his smile.

For the first hour, he watched as Andi's expressions reflected her boredom over listening to tedious decisions regarding landscaping and budget issues. Then came the time for the audience to address the board. She shifted in her chair and her eyes widened with interest. Harry announced that each homeowner wishing to speak to the board would be given three minutes to state their concerns.

Mr. Decker, a retired cowboy of about fifty in worn jeans and a felt Stetson, stood tall and proud. Judging by his deep, leathery tan, he'd spent most of his life working outdoors. His scowl matched Harry's, brow line for brow line and sneer for sneer.

"It's *you* again." Harry regarded his paperwork. "Due to our lengthy agenda tonight and the fact we have the room reserved only until nine, each person will have just one minute to speak."

Luke's gut twisted. That wasn't right. They deserved at least three minutes to vent. Perhaps one of them could get through to the man. "Harry—"

Harry narrowed his eyes into snakelike slits as he directed an intense stare at Luke. "The rules allow for changes when the president sees fit, and tonight I see fit."

The man had memorized every rule and regulation. He knew them better than Luke. "Continue," Luke said, admitting defeat.

The cowboy clenched his fists at his sides. "You fined me because there was a carpet cleaning van parked in the fire lane out front of my condo."

Valerie ran a perfectly polished nail over the condensation collecting on her water bottle. "You should have parked your vehicle elsewhere and made room for the cleaning van in your driveway." She smirked at Harry. "Right?"

The board president winked, then coughed and shuffled his papers, as if the audience wasn't bright enough to notice the exchange. Luke resisted the urge to roll his eyes.

Valerie's husband, Paul, kept his head buried in his own copies of the paperwork throughout the meeting. If he lifted his head even once, Luke reflected, he would probably catch his wife flirting with Harry. Realization dawned on Luke. Paul might know or suspect his wife had her eyes set on Harry. Did he choose to keep his eyes down on purpose?

"I was out of town that week." The cowboy's words grew more pronounced, along with the vein protruding from his temple. "One of the neighbors had their carpets cleaned, *not me*."

Harry's thinning mustache twitched. "You have a history of breaking the rules. You'll need to *prove* you were out of town and that you didn't hire the service."

"*You* prove I *did* hire them! You can't, because I didn't."

Harry lifted a picture. "I have photographic evidence that the van was parked in front of your condo. That's all the proof I need." The timer chirped.

The horror in Andi's eyes reflected Luke's own. This couldn't go on.

Mr. Decker spat an obscenity and stormed down the aisle. The odds of a cowboy in Arizona owning a truck and carrying a shotgun in that truck were quite high.

Luke jumped up to follow him. He rushed down the aisle and caught up with the man at the exit.

"Mr. Decker," Luke pressed his hand against the wooden door to keep the man from opening it. "I'll take care of your violation," he stated, his voice low enough to keep others from overhearing. "I promise it will go away."

The man studied him for a long moment. "Harry might make *you* go away."

"That's a daily threat." Luke offered a wry smile, the only reassurance he could give the man, and then stepped back from the door.

The cowboy's shoulders relaxed, and he nodded before completing his escape.

"Unit 1210," Valerie sang.

Luke recognized Andi's unit number and headed

back to the front table. He strove to keep his expression stoic, not wanting anyone to guess how worried he was over the verbal exchange about to take place.

Andi hesitated, then slowly stood. "That's me."

"The timer started fifteen seconds ago." Harry's stare bore holes through her.

Luke clenched his teeth to keep from interrupting. Interfering would make matters worse for them both.

Andi looked like a timid Dorothy addressing the wizard for the first time. "I'm sure you are all reasonable adults . . ." she murmured.

The crowd snickered. Luke suppressed a groan while returning to his seat. The active members of the board were anything but reasonable. And Valerie's husband was nothing more than a poodle told to sit and not speak. Paul ran for the board because his wife told him to. They needed a yes-man.

Undaunted, Andi continued. "I just moved in and wasn't aware that you held everyone to such a strict interpretation of the rules."

"Not our problem," Harry snapped. "Next."

Luke wanted to knock the man off his chair, but gripped his pen tighter instead. His need to protect Andi took him by surprise. He hadn't known he still harbored such strong feelings for her.

"The timer hasn't gone off. And I'm not finished!" The papers she gripped shook in her hands. "My father didn't know he would be breaking a rule by not moving his car into my driveway after my sister left the complex."

Harry's face contorted into a menacing scowl at the mention of her sister. "Once again, miss, this is not my problem." Harry sneered like a pit bull. "Perhaps you should keep a closer eye on your relatives. They have a tendency to park themselves where they shouldn't."

"Park themselves?"

Ding.

"Time's up!" Harry's gavel hit the striker plate. "Next!"

The security guard standing near the table stepped forward, and Andi quickly sat down.

Meg leaned close to speak to her. Luke found relief in the fact Andi wasn't alone. He had always considered Meg a nice woman, even though he found her boundless energy a drain on his nerves during every conversation they had.

He also felt a twinge of envy. Once upon a time, Andi would have turned to him for emotional support. Back then he could have provided it, too. Not now. Not with his hands tied.

Andi crumpled her papers in one fist. "I can't believe he's getting away with this!"

Her voice rang through the room louder than she probably had intended, and everyone turned to stare.

"The audience will keep their comments to themselves," Harry commanded, "or you'll be removed." He directed every word at Andi.

****

The second the meeting ended, Andi turned to Meg, "Why haven't you all banded together to throw those dictators off the board?"

The cheery pep drained from Meg's face. "It's not as easy as you think. People have tried. No one's been able to get enough signatures to recall the board because they're afraid of retaliation, and rightly so. Bernice and Harry got even with anyone who opposed them." She sighed. "A couple of brave souls were voted on to the board a few years back, but the evil duo chased them off and then appointed their own puppet replacements."

Andi shook her head. "That doesn't sound legal. This

is America. People have rights."

"This is a homeowners' association. No one has rights. There are loopholes, and the board uses every one of them to their advantage. One woman spent her entire savings taking them to court for harassment. She lost and had to pay their legal fees, too."

Andi felt her blood pressure rising. "It's almost impossible not to break a rule. There must be over fifty."

"And many of them are so broad the board can define them as they wish. I received a violation letter for leaving a plastic baggie on my patio table. The board considered it a 'storage container' and there's no storage allowed on the porch. Common sense tells you that rule was written to keep large storage bins off patios, but it wasn't written clearly, so the board gets to define the terms as they please."

"There must be some way to stop them."

The nurse raised a brow. "Short of blowing a hole in them?"

THREE

Andi drove the short distance back to her condo, condemning Harry and his cronies every second of the way. There was no need to check her watch—she knew her sister wouldn't be home from work until well after midnight.

She slowed to ease through the gated entrance to Euphoria. Images of Luke flitted across her mind as if she were watching a movie on the big screen. Since the moment he had stepped into her condo, she had tried not to think of him, but often failed. They used to talk for hours without running out of topics. What they had shared had been special. She would never understand why he threw it away.

After turning onto the private road, her mind wandered back to that night's meeting. She wondered what Luke had said to the cowboy to calm him down. How a mild-mannered, diplomatic man like Luke could work for Harry was beyond her comprehension.

Pressing the remote that triggered the garage door, she heard the initial grinding of gears. The door rose two feet before it stopped.

"No!" She pressed the button again. The door lowered. She pressed it again. The door lifted two feet off the ground, then stopped. "NO!"

She climbed out of her Mustang and began searching for a quick way to force it to lift. Nothing. Not inside the garage, not outside the garage. Fixing the door was beyond her capability.

"Not now!" She screamed as she kicked her tire. "If I don't move my car inside, that jerk is going to fine me for not parking in the garage." She tried again. The door lowered, then rose two feet . . . and stopped.

"No, no, no, no, no!"

Hideous laughter rose behind her. She twisted around and a flash lit the interior of a dark sedan. Camera in hand, Harry leaned out his car window while driving slowly past her garage. "You and that tramp sister of yours don't belong here in Euphoria. You're both leaving; one way or another!"

****

"Can't you get here any sooner?" Andi leaned against the counter, listening to the receptionist for Bob's Fix-It apologize for the third time. "All right, my sister will be waiting here on Thursday between noon and three for your repairman." She dropped the receiver into its cradle, moaned, and returned to work mixing sugar-cookie batter in the stainless steel bowl.

Jessie read the latest violation letter left in the screen door early that morning. "Since we already received two warning notices, the association will now be fining us fifty dollars a day for not parking in the garage. That's outrageous!"

"The repairman can't fix the door until Thursday." As Andi's anger brewed, her movements quickened. Batter threatened to fly out of the bowl.

"That's two days from now." Jessie opened a can of orange soda and cursed when the spray caught the top of her skimpy cheerleader outfit. Tuesday was Sports Night at the diner. She swiped at the soda dots on her top with the back of her hand. "That's what, a hundred and fifty dollars in fines?"

"Two hundred dollars. They'll get me for last night, today, tomorrow, *and* Thursday morning." Andi glanced at the mail on the dining room table. She couldn't afford to pay both the fines and her utility bills. The electric bill had to come first. No electricity meant no oven, no oven meant no baking, and no baking meant her blood pressure would skyrocket. Andi sighed. Paying the utilities on time would mean she would be late paying the association fines and she'd be assessed an extra fee. There was no winning.

While Jessie carried her soda into the dining room, Andi focused on her cookies. She haphazardly tossed flour onto the countertop, dumped the cookie batter on top, and reached for the rolling pin. For a moment, she considered borrowing the money from their father. It took only a second to realize he would just remind her how many times he had told her she wasn't financially secure enough to purchase her own home. Nothing like an "I told you so" to make you feel warm and cheery all over.

She ran the rolling pin rough and fast over the dough, the way a runner might sprint to release pent-up emotions. Her thoughts traveled back to her last conversation with Harry. She still hadn't told her sister about his threat to force them to move. Jessie had enough on her mind between her undercover case and buying the detective agency.

At times like this, Andi wished she had magical powers. Just enough to shrink Harry and trap him in one of her sugar cookies. The house-shaped one. He'd lean out the dough window, squealing for mercy as she shoved the cookie sheet into the oven. She would never do anything that mean, but the thought made her feel better for about ten seconds.

Marching into the kitchen, Jessie aimed and tossed her soda can into the recycling container. "I'll pay the fines."

"No, you won't!" How had their life turned upside down for the worse in such a short period of time?

"I live here, too. It's just as much my responsibility as yours."

"I signed the mortgage papers. I should have carefully read each and every rule before I moved us here."

"It would have taken less time to read *War and Peace*." Jessie pinched off a bite of dough. "At least let me pay half."

"No!" Andi resisted the urge to slam down the rolling pin. "We agreed you were paying for only food and Internet until you had the money to buy Lenny's Detective Agency. I don't want Harry stealing one cent of your savings. Anyone with a conscience would understand the garage is broken and give us time to fix it without fining us."

Jessie and Lenny had worked out a deal where she could pay him directly. Both wanted to keep the banks out of the picture. He preferred a down payment and then monthly installments so he wouldn't spend the money all at once. She would have that down payment in two months.

Andi remembered how excited she had been when she signed the dotted line on her mortgage agreement. "It's bad enough that Harry's destroying *my* dream." All she'd asked for was a quaint place to call her own in a peaceful neighborhood. A place where she could sit on her quiet patio while sipping her coffee and watching the lilies bloom. A place where the handsome, single sheriff and his son waved hello on their way to the fishing hole. She blinked away the reruns of Mayberry.

Jessie didn't seem to notice. "We could move, but interest rates are going up. You'd lose money."

"I'm not moving." Andi pushed the rolling pin hard over the batter. "This is my home. There has to be a way to stop him."

"Just don't break any laws in the process." Jessie adjusted her halter top, making sure she wasn't breaking any indecent-exposure laws.

Andi watched her sister nab another pinch of dough. "You're not supposed to eat raw dough. The uncooked eggs can make you sick."

"I like to live dangerously." Jessie left the room for a moment and returned with the shiny, white go-go boots she'd left by the front door.

"Do you think that good-looking old boyfriend of yours could help?" Jessie had spent over an hour the previous night grilling her about Luke.

"I got the impression his hands are tied," Andi said. *He probably wouldn't want to help me if he could. He turned his back on me years ago.*

"Too bad," Jessie said, slipping on one boot, then the other. "How about that nurse? From what you told me, it sounds like she would be a good ally."

"You're right." A seed of hope sprouted. "She knows everything that goes on around here."

"I hate to leave this mess up to you, but I have to go to work." Jessie patted her on the shoulder the way their father always had when they lived at home.

"I'll be fine. You concentrate on cleaning up the streets." Speaking of cleaning, Andi glanced at the overflowing kitchen garbage can. Guilt ate at her. She should throw it out instead of leaving the chore for Jessie, but she still couldn't shake the memory of

Bernice's dead body in the dumpster.

****

Luke found Meg in her driveway, unpacking groceries from the back end of her hunter-green SUV. The puppies on yesterday's scrubs had been replaced with adorable kittens frolicking with yarn.

"Can I help you with that?"

"Depends on what you're here for." She eyed him suspiciously.

"I'm here checking on the irrigation and thought you might like a hand—nothing nefarious."

"In that case, here you go." Meg dropped a grocery bag into his open arms and scooped up another for herself.

He followed her through her single-car garage, which was lined with bicycles, suitcases, boxes labeled "Christmas," and a step ladder. Holding the bag close, he entered her condo through the bright, orange kitchen. Puppy and kitten magnets decorated the refrigerator. The room fit her personality. "I noticed you've met your new neighbor, Andi."

"I hear you're already fining her. You didn't waste much time."

He was tired of coming up with diplomatic, professional answers that walked the line between defending himself and keeping blame away from Harry. Instead he chose silence. His company wouldn't keep the Euphoria account for long if he went around bashing the board president. Luke placed his haul next to Meg's on the counter and then followed her out to the van for another bag.

Reaching inside the back of the van, he noticed a shadow stretching beside him. His heart skipped a beat. He instinctively knew it was Andi.

"Hey, neighbor!" Meg waved wildly at her new neighbor, who stood on the sidewalk next to the SUV. "What brings you to my end of the prison camp?"

Luke shook his head at her choice of words.

"I'm here to complain." She sneered at him. "Harry is going to fine me two hundred dollars because my garage door won't open. I can't get it fixed until Thursday."

"Wow! Two hundred dollars. You haven't even lived here a week yet." Meg looked Luke over like he was a piece of moldy cheese. "That must be some sort of record."

Luke knew he had been tried, found guilty, and executed for a crime Harry committed. "I have a few minutes. I can take a look at your garage, if you like."

"I would rather you tell us how to make Harry stop over enforcing the rules." She pierced him with her dark-green eyes. "He has no empathy for others. And I know for a fact he has it out for us."

Luke didn't correct her. Judging by Harry's behavior the day they dropped by Andi's condo, he decided she was right. Proving it was another matter. "The best way to stop Harry is for both of you to run for the board at the next election."

Andi threw her arms up. "He's fining me daily. I'll be bankrupt by then."

Luke remembered his promise to the cowboy. That morning, he had called the carpet cleaning company and verified the man had never ordered his carpets cleaned. He closed the case and filed it away because no violation had ever existed. He wished he could do that for Andi and all of her neighbors, but they, unlike the cowboy, *had* technically broken the rules.

"Running for the board has been tried—and everyone has failed," Meg said. "We would need at least five people to run for the board to make a difference, and I don't know five people brave enough to take on Harry."

Suddenly, a mischievous grin played on her face. "But after our conversation last night, I did some research and came up with a way to fight back."

Luke suppressed a groan. "Think long and hard before you poke the grizzly bear with a long stick. Your lives here could get a whole lot worse."

"I doubt that," Andi said, folding her arms over her chest. "Meg, tell us your idea. Or do you want Luke to leave first?"

He tried not to take the question personally, but failed.

"He can stay. He'll find out soon anyway." Meg bounced on her heels. "One second." She reached into the back seat of her van and removed a compact silver camera. "Once we prove Harry is singling people out for fines, we can sue him."

"What?" Luke stared at Meg in disbelief. "I see the fines that go out each and every month. There is no one is this community who is immune."

"I know something you don't know." Meg grinned with delight. "There are a few board members who break the rules on a regular basis and *don't* receive fines."

He shook his head. "I walk the property weekly, and I have never seen a board member breaking the rules."

Meg snorted.

"Let me guess," Andi said, "you walk the property at the same time every week."

He thought for a moment. "Close to the same time."

"Except for today," Meg announced. "You said you were checking on the irrigation."

"I received a complaint regarding the pond."

"And now you are going to receive ours." Meg held up the camera. "Mr. Property Manager, Valerie is breaking the rules as we speak. Follow me."

Luke's gut churned with a feeling of impending doom.

Andi smiled like a Cheshire cat. "This is a no-win situation for Harry. He can't order Luke to take the violation letter out of her file because it will prove he is singling out neighbors. If Harry doesn't make the violation letter go away, Valerie will chew him up and spit him out."

"That's an understatement." Meg quickened her pace over the sidewalk that ran between the buildings leading from the mailboxes to the pool. "She always gets what she wants, even if it means throwing a tantrum. I've heard screech owls make less noise."

Unleashing Hurricane Valerie would upgrade Tornado Harry to a 5.0 storm level. Luke jogged to catch up. Part of him wanted to urge them to reconsider their plan, but they had every right to prove the board was breaking the rules they, too, were required to follow. Luke blew out an exasperated breath. Maybe he could buy a florist shop after his boss fired him.

"Where are we going?" he asked, afraid of the answer. Being a creature of habit, he surveyed the surrounding area. The grass had been mowed that morning, the bushes pruned the previous week. The landscaping company they hired during winter made a point to live up to their promises.

"It's four o'clock," Meg shot over her shoulder. "Valerie's giving water aerobics lessons to the older ladies in the pool. They call themselves the Water Guppies."

"Is she wearing cut-offs or diving into the shallow end?" he asked.

"Even better. Wait till you see this." Meg kept up the quick pace, and Andi followed close behind.

Luke calmly walked in their wake. His wide stride covered more ground than their smaller ones. He could already see the tall wooden fence intended to keep small children and trespassers away from the pool water.

Meg tiptoed as she grew closer, her face lit with excitement.

Andi glanced his way and shrugged.

Refrains from "Love Will Keep Us Together" grew louder with each yard they covered. The aroma of chlorine and freshly cut grass rose and combined in Luke's nostrils.

When they reached the corner of the fence surrounding the pool, Meg sat and handed Andi her camera. "Take a look."

Andi peered through the slits in the fence.

Luke chose an area away from the two junior detectives. While he didn't approve of their plan, he had no intention of outing them either. Following Andi's lead, he peered through the slits as well. A group of women with their backs to him jumped up and down in the water. Many wore neon pink bathing suits that drew attention to their aging bodies. The purple flowers on their bathing caps swayed to the music and waves of water splashed over the sides onto the cool decking. The music slowed, and the women bobbed.

Valerie stood in the shallow end, facing them. The string bikini she wore barely contained her figure. "Great job, ladies! It's time to cool down, but keep moving. Right foot, kick. Take a sip." With great flare, she brought a crystal glass filled with a red concoction to her lips. She swallowed and continued. "Left foot, kick. Take a sip."

The other women scrambled for the plastic margarita glasses lining the pool's edge, just out of reach of the splashing water. They held their drinks high while bouncing back to their exercise area in the center.

They chanted together, "Right foot, kick. Take a sip. Left foot, kick. Take a sip."

Luke's jaw dropped.

Since when had water aerobics become a drinking

game?

"You have got to be kidding," Andi whispered.

He found, to his dismay, that Meg and Andi had moved to his side. If Valerie spotted them, Harry would fire him.

"The Water Guppies are drinking strawberry margaritas," Meg said. "Notice Valerie's drinking out of crystal, NOT plastic like the rules dictate. Hurry, take a picture before she sees us."

Andi positioned the camera and pushed the button. After handing the camera back to Meg, she shot Luke a look of satisfaction. She must have felt like she was finally taking back control of her life. He was happy for her, although the ridiculous nature of the scene lingered in his mind.

"Right foot, kick. Take a sip. Left foot, kick. Take a sip." The entire group lifted their drinks and Meg snapped off two more pictures before anyone noticed they hadn't turned off the flash.

Luke grabbed for the camera, but missed when Meg dodged his efforts and hid the camera in her pants. He peered back through the fence, hoping no one had noticed.

Valerie squinted in their direction. "Hey, you! What are you doing? Are you spying on us?"

"Run!" Luke ordered as softly as he could manage under the circumstances. "She's coming after you."

As they raced over the grass, Luke waved over the fence. "It's just me, Valerie. No need to be alarmed. I'm checking on the property as usual."

"Oh, okay. I'm conducting my water aerobics class," she said, sliding the margarita glass behind her. "We'd like some privacy, please."

"No problem." He waved his good-bye and strolled back to his car.

No problem? Who am I kidding? The problems here

are going from bad to worse. And we still have a murderer on the loose.

He glanced over his shoulder to make sure he was still alone.

****

On the way back from the pool, Andi spotted a small, wire-haired terrier. He darted across Meg's driveway, dragging a string of sausages behind him.

"That's Bernice's dog." Meg whistled. "Toto! Come here, boy." She crept closer when he stopped to consider her, the sausages still hanging from his mouth. "Come here, boy. I'll take you home to Reverend Nichols."

"Reverend Nichols?"

Didn't Jessie say Bernice's last name was Nichols?

The dog backed away on his tiny paws. His ears pointed upward, ready to detect any movement in his direction.

Meg glanced in her direction. "Bernice's son is a minister. Sort of. He left his position after a minor 'situation'." She held her palm out for the dog. "You poor thing," she cooed, edging closer. "I bet you miss your mommy, even if no one else does."

She took another step closer and the terrier took off like a tiny greyhound. Meg raced after him.

Andi raced after Meg. "Wait a minute!" This conversation was too interesting to let it drop. "The witch gave birth to a religious man?"

"Stranger things have happened . . . and usually do around here." Meg followed the dog onto the grass, between two bushes, then back onto the street. They passed one building after another.

Toto dodged every attempt they made to capture him. Just when Andi decided to give up, the dog ran under a garage door that had been left open a few inches.

Meg gasped for air, then bent at the waist to whistle under the door. "Come here, Toto. I'll take you home, boy."

Both women crawled over the cement to spy under the garage door. An overhead bulb illuminated the inside. Professionally finished garage cabinets lined the wall. A work area and sink in the back appeared neat and tidy. The aroma of a strong cleanser penetrated Andi's nostrils and stung her eyes. She blinked repeatedly while searching for the dog. She spotted Toto sitting beside a freezer, chomping down on his stolen goods. A dozen or more sausages littered the surrounding cement. At least they knew where he'd found the meat.

"Looks like a doggie buffet," Meg said.

"He has no reason to leave anytime soon, and I can't squeeze under that door." Andi stood and dusted off her jeans. "So tell me about Reverend Nichols. Why did he leave the church?"

Meg sat on the driveway, as if hoping the dog would change his mind and crawl out to her. "One of his parishioners caught him kissing a woman in their congregation and turned it into a scandal."

"Interesting." Andi had never known any religious men who left their church.

"The reverend is an okay guy. He's the only sensible person on the HOA board. Unfortunately, he's outnumbered by lunatics."

Andi heard the metallic grinding of the gate opening, followed by the purr of a car's engine. A black BMW entered through the main gate.

Meg jumped to her feet. "That's Chris Owens. This is his condo."

Both women stepped aside to make room for the vehicle.

"Chris is a veterinarian. His wife, Tess, is also on the

board. She missed last night's meeting," Meg whispered. "If he wasn't married, I'd book myself an appointment at his office and pretend to be a poodle in heat." She smiled and waved at the man who stared through the window in obvious confusion.

The dark-haired, clean-cut doggie doctor killed the engine and climbed out of his car. Andi was surprised to discover that the tall, broadly built man wore gray slacks and a crisp white shirt. She would have thought a veterinarian's patients would cover him with pet dander and dog drool while resisting long needles and objects stuck up galaxies better left unexplored.

Perhaps he showered and changed clothes at the office, she mused.

"Meg, what's up?" The apple cheeks brightening his round face made him appear ten years younger than the lines fanning from his eyes revealed him to be.

"Hi, Doc. This is Andi, our new neighbor."

He took in her dust-covered jeans and pastel-yellow T-shirt and managed a smile despite the hint of disapproval in his expression.

Andi gestured toward the garage. "We were trying to capture Bernice's dog."

"He ran inside, but we couldn't squeeze under the door. Not that we *would*," Meg added quickly.

Doctor Owens lifted his keychain, pressed a button, and the garage closed, trapping the dog inside. "He's been running around here for the past couple of days. Thanks for cornering him. I'll take a look at him and make sure he's in good health before I call Reverend Nichols. It's the least I can do after . . . what happened to Bernice."

"That's nice of you." Meg nudged Andi forward. "We'll get out of your hair. Say hello to the missus for me."

He offered a simple nod. "I will when she calls. She's

visiting her mother."

The front gate squealed as the arms opened again. A Prius entered and drove past them.

Why would anyone choose to live close to the main entrance to the complex?

The sound of the gate opening and closing throughout the day would drive Andi nuts.

Perhaps it was the only unit available at the time the doggie doctor bought his condo.

Before the gate could close, a sedan barreled through the opening.

It headed straight for them.

"Run!" Andi screamed, pushing Meg out of the way.

The sedan swerved, rammed the fire hydrant five feet from where they stood, rolled on its side, and came to rest against a "No Parking" sign. Water shot up like a geyser, pounding down on the grass, the road, and the smashed car.

Andi peered through the car's front window. Her jaw fell open.

Harry, sitting in the driver's seat, pressed his hand to his forehead. He gaped at her as if he'd never seen her before, then passed out.

****

Luke had just finished checking in with the company secretary when he heard a squeal of tires followed by a loud thud and female shrieks. He ran full speed across the property, toward the front gate. Curious neighbors followed in his wake. The first sign he was closing in on the source of the trouble was the gusher shooting into the sky. As he ran closer, he watched it rain down on the passenger side of Harry's wrecked car before flowing onto the grass and asphalt.

He found Andi huddled in conversation with Meg—

away from the splash zone. The wind feathered her hair while concern revealed its presence with lines furrowed in her brow.

She reached out to grab his arm. "It's Harry. He mumbled something about his brakes."

"We already called for help." Meg hugged herself tight. "Doctor Owens is looking for a blanket. We both decided it was best not to drag him out of the car. He's safe until the paramedics arrive."

Luke peered into the driver's side of the car and found Harry passed out over the steering wheel. His chest lifted and fell. At least he was still breathing. There also weren't any signs of blood or broken limbs. Before Luke could decide what action to take, the high-pitched sound of a siren pierced the sky. He jogged over to open the gate for the ambulance and fire engine.

The paramedics filed out of the ambulance as he returned to Andi's side. "What happened?"

"It was quite a sight." Meg pointed to the front of the complex. "Harry raced through the gate and rammed right into the hydrant." She slammed her hands together with dramatic flair.

"The firefighters will cap the hydrant," he said, for lack of anything better to say. There wasn't much he could do other than to keep the growing crowd of onlookers from interfering with rescue efforts. He watched the paramedics take Harry's vitals. The fact he hadn't yet opened his eyes worried Luke.

Doctor Owens stood silently in front of his condo, still clutching the blanket he had retrieved, but was no longer needed. Being a veterinarian, his skills weren't required.

Luke rolled up the cuffs of his white, long-sleeved shirt and went to work inspecting the sedan's metal underbelly—now exposed by the accident. He couldn't find any obvious signs of brake tampering, but he wasn't a mechanic. He hated to think that Bernice's killer had gone after another board member, but anything was possible.

A police cruiser rolled through the open gate and Andi headed to the location where the officer parked. Luke trusted her to mention the brakes.

"Wait! Wait!" Valerie, wearing a flimsy black bathing suit cover and gold-beaded sandals, handed her empty crystal glass to one of her friends who had come to watch the show. "Tell my husband I went to the hospital with Harry. Tell him I had to go. I was the only board member here."

Luke joined Meg, who was waiting for Andi to return. He overheard the younger paramedic telling Valerie that she would have to follow them in her own car. She gripped his shirt and lied about being Harry's only living relative. He reluctantly relented, and she climbed inside the ambulance with his assistance. The glint in her eye revealed her pride. Once again, she had manipulated a situation to get her way.

"Valerie doesn't know we took the pictures," Meg whispered when Andi reached her side.

"You're right," Andi agreed. "She totally ignored us."

"Unbelievable." Luke shook his head. "You are still going to carry out your plan?"

Andi tilted her head. "We haven't had a chance to discuss it yet, but let me ask you a question: Do you think Harry is going to leave us alone now that he's had a brush with death?"

Meg lifted her chin defiantly. "Did you see him sprout a halo in the last ten seconds?"

"I didn't see horns and a tail either." Luke knew they had every right to dislike Harry intensely, but he also knew car accidents could change a person. "All I'm asking is that you wait and see how Harry acts when he returns home. If he's up to his old tricks, I'll send the violation letter to Valerie."

Andi used the toe of her tennis shoes to tap the water running down the street before answering. "You promise that the first time he acts like a complete heel, you'll send the letter?"

Luke promised, hoping it wouldn't be necessary. Sending a violation letter to Valerie would unleash the storm of the millennium.

Meg chuckled. "And send a violation letter to Harry as well." She pointed to the car. "He parked in a fire lane, vandalized the property when he destroyed the hydrant, and flooded the common area. If Andi has to receive violation letters for circumstances beyond her control, then so does Harry."

FOUR

Andi listened to the joyful sound of grinding gears as her garage door lifted above two feet. She exhaled in relief. Luke had fixed it. Where was Mr. Handy-with-a-Wrench when she'd needed her margarita machine fixed in college?

Luke stepped back inside her condo, wiping his hands on the now-greasy rag. He strode through the kitchen as if he owned it. "A wheel came off the track."

Andi tossed him a clean hand towel. "Thanks," she offered in a noncommittal tone.

Although she was grateful for his help, she hated to be in his debt. The opposite had been true back in college. They'd helped each other quite often back then. She taught him how to organize his life and he cooked for her. His signature dish, Pasta Hamburger Surprise, quickly became a staple. The "surprise" was an extra ingredient or two he would throw in, which was anything left over in the refrigerator. Emeril Lagasse had nothing to worry about, but she enjoyed every bite because it had been made with love. At least she had thought so—before he left her.

"You're welcome." He shot her a warm smile, then downed half the lemonade she'd made for him when he first started the job.

She studied his strong jaw and each slight movement of his neck as he drank the cold liquid. Years ago, she would have run her hand through his thick hair, gripped the back of his neck, and pulled him close.

Shutting the door on those memories, she asked, "How much do I owe you?"

He leaned against the counter and appeared to read her serious expression. "A smile now and then."

"Why do you care if I smile?" The man had given her a warning letter the first time he stepped foot into her condo. Now he wanted her to like him?

"I'll always care about you, Andi." His jaw tightened. "I'm sorry you hate me. I thought you would have gotten over our breakup by now."

Breakup? The word trivialized the way she felt when he had ripped her heart out nine years ago.

"I did get over you," she lied.

Memories of him holding her in his arms revisited once or twice a year. She found it hard to believe anyone completely got over their first love. In her case, there hadn't been a second. She sipped the lemonade, finding its tartness hard to swallow, just as she had found his parting words hard to swallow. He claimed to have broken up with her because he couldn't understand her family loyalty. He was an only child. He didn't know what it was like to be part of a tight family unit. She, on the other hand, had three older sisters, and they were close. The Stevenson sisters were there for one another.

Gripping the glass between both hands, she turned away from the past and faced the present. "I'm angry with you for becoming Harry's yes-man. I expected more from you."

"Like I said before, I'm just doing my job. Your

neighbors understand that. They don't hate me. Sure, sometimes they get upset over a fine, but they calm down after we talk." He tossed back the towel.

She caught it midair. "The man I knew would have stopped Harry. If you do that, then you won't need to keep calming the neighbors down."

"In college we were idealistic. I'm sure there are circumstances in your job you wish *you* could change, but can't." He lifted his hand in a simple gesture. "For example, I hear you became a teacher. When are you going to increase teacher salaries?"

Her jaw tightened. "Point taken."

To his credit, he didn't grin over his victory. "Besides," he continued. "I know Harry's strict, but he truly believes he's maintaining the value of this property. You have to admit, one of the reasons you bought here is because the neighborhood is well kept."

"It doesn't matter how manicured the lawns are if word gets out that the board is harassing people. No one will want to buy here."

His brow furrowed. "I wouldn't let him hear you claim he's harassing people. He might take you to court for slander."

"Were we at the same board meeting? Harry harassed every neighbor who voiced a concern." She threw the soiled towel that Luke had used into the trash can. Her way of saying what she thought of that meeting, Harry, and Euphoria Lane Condominiums.

His gaze followed her throw. "I admit Harry's behavior has been growing progressively worse. I'll keep trying to get through to him. Who knows? Maybe the car wreck was a miracle in disguise and Harry will become a kinder, gentler president. Close calls with death have been known to change people."

"Yeah, right." Her sarcasm hung in the air. "That won't happen unless we discover the murderer cut

Harry's brakes today, and he's scared nice."

Their gazes met, the implications of that possibility traveled wordlessly between them.

"Can we finish this conversation at the pond?" His voice sounded upbeat, as if he were speaking with a friend instead of an upset former girlfriend. He set the glass on the counter and headed for the door.

She rinsed the glasses and placed them in the dishwasher. "Why the pond?"

"I received a complaint about dead fish. I need to check it out."

She stared at him, not sure what to say.

He opened the door and hesitated. "You're not going to make me walk all the way over there by myself, are you? I hear this place is filled with runaway cars and out-of-control geysers." His impish grin lit up his eyes. "Besides, it will give me a chance to find out what you've been up to since college, and you can finish listing off all the reasons why you hate me."

"How can I turn down such an irresistible offer?"

What is he really up to?

****

Luke had actually invited Andi to join him on his inspection of the pond in hopes of persuading her to change her mind. He wanted her to give up the idea of antagonizing Harry. That was a no-win situation. She would be better off following the rules and avoiding the man altogether. Luke also wanted to make peace. His gut twisted with guilt whenever their paths met. He felt bad about the warning letter. More than that, he felt horrible about breaking up with her back in college. No matter what she said, he could see the pain that lingered in her eyes. Not that he could have done anything different in either situation. Both had been unavoidable.

Andi kept a more-than-respectable distance between them as they strolled to the pond. Whenever the distance closed by even a foot, uneasiness flickered over her features.

"I won't take up too much of your time," he promised.

"I'm warning you now, if the ducks attack because you've sent them a violation letter, you're on your own, pal."

He chuckled. "I'll take my chances."

Walking side by side across the property, he sneaked glances at her. The breeze played with the auburn wisps of hair surrounding her face. Once upon a time, he would wrap the silky strands around his fingers while he kissed her cheek, then her mouth.

Those sweet-tasting lips . . .

"How is your mother doing?" Andi scanned their surroundings as they walked.

"She's well. I'm trying to get her to retire, but she can't afford to yet." His mother had been working in an elementary school cafeteria since Luke started kindergarten. All his life, she set aside every extra penny to put him through college. His father left them when he was young and never kept in touch, other than to send child-support payments.

"I always liked your mother. She was a nice lady."

"Still is. Once I get this promotion I've been promised, I'm going to buy one of those houses with a mother's cottage. It's about time she relaxed and enjoyed life instead of working so hard."

"She'll probably still find projects to keep her busy."

"True, but that will be her choice and she can do as little or as much as she likes." He causally glanced in her direction. She had been cute in college—now she was beautiful. "What grade do you teach?"

"Second."

"I bet you're good at it. You always were good with kids."

"Thanks," she mumbled, as though a compliment from him made her uncomfortable. Their excursion was taking them by the edge of the golf course. "Do you think Bernice's killer cut Harry's brakes?"

"It's a possibility." He hated to admit the truth. For the most part, the residents of Euphoria were good people. He couldn't imagine any one of them resorting to murder.

"Who would want to kill them both?" She shook her head. "Let me rephrase that. Who *wouldn't* want to kill them both? That list would be much smaller."

"Tell me this," he said, stopping several yards from the water, "if you hate following rules, why did you buy a condo with a homeowners' association?"

"I didn't receive those rules until closing, so I only had time to skim them. They appeared reasonable on paper, and of course no one warned me about Harry. There should be a law requiring sellers to disclose the presence of any annoying nuisances like demonic hauntings or HOA presidents with Napoleon complexes."

Each step brought them closer to the pond's edge. A fountain in the center sprinkled water drops across the pond's surface, sending ripples toward the outer banks. Ducks gathered on the grass on the opposite side.

Luke strolled along the water's edge, annoyed by the facts and his inability to resolve the chaos born from the board's decisions. "I admit Harry needs to get a hobby, but now that your garage door is fixed, everything should settle down."

"Not from what I hear." She planted both hands on her hips and turned on him. "I can't believe you chose this career."

"The other homeowners' associations I work with are

not as bad as Euphoria's."

"I don't care about the other associations right now. I care about *my* community, my sister, my new neighbors, and my new friend. Are you going to do the right thing and toss out the fines I owe? Toss out everyone's fines?"

How can I make her understand?

"My hands are tied."

"No one tells you when you sign on to live in a community with an HOA that you are about to be ruled by dictators. I have never seen a small group given so much power over others. How is this allowed in a country based on a system of checks and balances?"

"HOAs do have their good points. They keep the roads and buildings in good repair."

"Do you live in a community with a homeowners' association?"

"No. Does that make me a hypocrite?"

"Until someone has spied on you on your own property, turned you in repeatedly for their interpretation of the rules, and sent you violation letters with fines attached, you can't possibly understand how the people in this community feel. It's like having a police officer following you around with a radar gun all day long." Her gaze followed a duckling waddling across the grass to catch up to his mother and siblings. Her voice softened as though the innocence of nature had touched her heart. "Put yourself in my place, Luke—and then stop Harry."

"Andi, I'll do what I can, but I can't make any promises. My job is more of an advisory position. I can't make the board listen to me. My advice to you is to make sure you follow any interpretation of the rules and run for the board. Make more friends and persuade them to run for the board, too. Nothing will change until Harry is outnumbered."

"These people are either too busy or afraid of retaliation if their fight against him is unsuccessful.

Many would rather pay the fines than fight back. I, on the other hand, am a Stevenson. I'm going to beat that man at his own game."

He couldn't blame her for being angry.

She crossed her arms over her chest. "Harry parked on a fire hydrant and Valerie drank from crystal glasses at the pool. They broke the rules. So you have to send them violation letters. It's your job."

"Are you sure you want to antagonize Harry? Once you start this war there is no going back."

"Someone has to stop him. At the very least, he needs a taste of his own medicine. Maybe he'll see the light, but I doubt it. Regardless, by proving the board is breaking the rules, I will be able to prove he is singling people out. Homeowners will be able to sue the board. I will win one way or another—even if it costs me everything I own."

"Why are you willing to risk so much?"

"He told me he was going to force us to move. He believes my sister is an 'undesirable'." Before he could speak, she held up her hand. "I can't prove anything."

Harry could be singling out Andi and her sister, Luke realized. He had made a strange comment about people being worthy of living in the community. He would have to find a way to help the sisters. A way that wouldn't involve losing the account—or his promotion.

Andi turned toward the pond, shielded her eyes with the side of her hand, and then pointed to a dozen dead carp near a clump of reeds. "What's up with the fish?"

"I'm not sure." He was hoping the answer would be obvious, like the Exxon Valdez oil spill. He had no clue what might cause fish to turn belly up. "I'll have the water tested."

Andi's gaze traveled from the pond up to the first hint of color peeking up from the horizon. Night was approaching.

Watching her took him back to a sunset of long ago. They had spread out a blanket beside Lake Pleasant and watched the sky burst with waves of pink, orange, and red. He had held her in his arms for hours, wishing the evening would never end. Holding her then came as easy as breathing. The realization of all they had lost physically hurt.

"I never fully understood why you dumped me when you did," the words blurted out of her. "Why couldn't you accept that family is important to me? Why didn't you even try to understand?"

His jaw fell open. "I *did* try to understand. I do believe family is important, but you took it to the extreme, Andi. You repeatedly cancelled dates with me to talk to one of your sisters."

"They needed me."

"How would I know that? You never shared why they called you, yet every single time you dropped everything to run home. Whenever I asked questions, you said it was a 'family matter.' And in case you've forgotten, I was about to become family at that time. We talked about getting married, yet still you treated me like an outsider."

"I'm sorry," she mumbled.

His jaw tightened. Those words didn't help back then, and they didn't help now.

"Their secrets weren't mine to share," she said blandly, as if knowing her excuse wouldn't matter.

"Your sisters have more secrets than most politicians. Besides, couples are supposed to be able to confide in each other and even share family secrets." Agitated, he ran his hand through his hair. "I couldn't spend the rest of my life being treated like an outsider." He angled his head and caught her pained expression. "Andi, all I had back then were my dreams, my pride, and you. Then I found out I didn't really even have *you*."

****

Wednesday afternoon, Andi turned off the oven and then mixed food coloring into white icing until she created the perfect ghastly black. Meanwhile, the aroma of freshly baked sugar cookies cooling on small wire racks wafted through the small kitchen.

She placed several bat-shaped cookies on a spin plate to decorate. Since receiving her first violation letter from the HOA, she had been more angry than at any other time in her life. Thinking of Harry had prompted her to sort through her box of Halloween cookie cutters even though it was only March.

Spreading black icing over a blood-sucking creature seemed appropriate for her mood. She made a mental note to drip red icing near the bat's mouth.

The doorbell rang, interrupting her work and her thoughts.

"Coming!" She licked icing off her finger on the way to the door and then peered through the peephole. Not that she expected the murderer to come calling like a salesman in disguise, but you could never be too sure. She spotted a head full of bouncing blonde curls.

"Meg!" Andi said, turning the knob.

"Come on, time's a-wasting." Meg pulled her out through the open door. "I just e-mailed Luke the pictures of Valerie and Harry breaking the rules. We need to get to work—before the other members of the board hear we've declared war."

"Where are we going?"

"To take more pictures, of course. Helen's washing her car." The perky nurse held up a digital camera, then skirted off, gesturing for her to follow.

Andi rushed to keep up. "How do you know these things?"

"I followed the water trail." Meg took two steps, then stopped in her tracks. "Down!"

She yanked on Andi's arm, causing them both to fall on their knees behind a bush.

Meg held an index finger to her lips. "Shh."

Andi lifted her head to peek through an opening in the fuchsia-colored petals of a bougainvillea. Harry and Valerie stood in front of a condo down the street. Those two together meant trouble. Andi hunkered down. The petals that had fallen to the ground felt like silk touching her hand. Carelessly, she pushed aside a branch to get a better look at the diabolical duo. The thorns from the branch bit into her skin.

"I see he lived through the accident," Andi stated as she rubbed at the reddish marks on her wrist.

"According to the Water Guppies, he was released from the hospital this morning." Meg sounded as irritated as she felt.

Harry carried a camera with a telephoto lens, and Valerie followed him with her clipboard.

"Meg, his camera is bigger than yours."

"He's compensating for his—"

"Lack of hair."

"Okay." Meg giggled. "His hair."

"Are they documenting violations?"

"That's what they call it, but I know better," Meg whispered. "They're taking advantage of the opportunity to flirt and talk dirty."

Harry aimed his camera at a sedan parked an inch off a driveway, on a border of gravel. The rules stipulated parking on paved surfaces, not on the grass or gravel in the common areas. While Valerie wrote on her clipboard, he glanced about, as if making sure they were alone. He then looked down at whatever she'd written and rubbed her arm.

"Y-u-ck," Andi moaned. "I wouldn't want that man

touching me."

"Even thinking about it creates a nausea no antacid could ever cure." The nurse shifted her weight onto her other knee. "I wonder if Valerie's husband would be interested in how dedicated she is to her volunteer work."

"Volunteer work? You make it sound like she's saving the planet."

"She's saving herself from a middle-class lifestyle," Meg announced. "They say charity begins at home."

The two board members strolled casually around the corner.

Andi dashed to the safety of the closest building, keeping them in sight. Her heart pounded with excitement. "I think I'm getting the hang of this spy stuff," she whispered, then hummed the theme music to *Mission: Impossible*. "Da, daaa da da . . ."

"Da da da . . ." Meg joined in, flattening herself against the wall.

Andi sneaked a peek around the corner.

Meg dropped and rolled to the next bush.

Unwilling to drop and injure herself, Andi quickly walked to the bush. "We already have pictures of both of them breaking the rules," Andi whispered. "Why are we following them now?"

"Because it's fun." Meg bent low and ran to the next building with Andi close behind. "Besides," Meg continued, "sending Luke the pictures felt great, but he's not going to send Harry a violation letter for running over the fire hydrant."

"But we sent him evidence," Andi protested. "He *has* to."

"When a violation is iffy, like parking on a hydrant because someone cut your brakes, it's his job to take the case to the board to decide."

A feeling of defeat settled in her gut. "The board will

defend Harry. Luke failed to mention that particular loophole." Andi leaned away from the wall to see what Harry was doing now. "Come *on*! He's busy taking a picture of a potted plant."

They ran and hid behind a truck.

"You're not allowed to have a potted plant near your front door," Meg shared. "Only on your back porch."

"That must be rule number two hundred fifty-three," Andi said sarcastically.

Pressed flat on the cement driveway, both women peered underneath the truck's running board to watch the board president snap a picture of Roxie walking her Chihuahua without a leash.

The aging woman wore leopard-print spandex pants and a matching shirt. Her dog, wearing a rhinestone-studded collar, barked incessantly at Harry.

Roxie flipped the man off between puffs of her filtered cigarette. "Get a life, prune face!"

Harry snarled and snapped more pictures.

Roxie turned, yanked the back of her pants down, bent over, and mooned the two board members. Valerie screeched, Harry yelled obscenities, and Andi's jaw dropped.

"It's fake." Meg elbowed Andi and chuckled. "Her tush is fake."

The older woman shot a devilish grin at the spies before pulling her pants back up. The barking grew louder as the miniature pet followed its owner down the path leading to the pool. Harry must have been in shock; he hadn't snapped a single photo.

"Oh, my!" Andi shifted away from the truck, hoping Harry and Valerie couldn't see them.

Meg snorted between giggles.

"How can Roxie's tush be fake?" Andi whispered.

"She ordered a plastic, strap-on derriere online to fill out her spandex pants. Her real bum is as flat as a pancake." Meg's grin lit up her eyes. "Harry only saw plastic, but he doesn't know that."

"He'll never recover." Andi snuck a peek at Roxie and her dog, ambling along in the opposite direction. "Roxie saw us," she whispered. "Do you think Harry figured out we're here, too?"

"Nah," Meg answered. "When Valerie's around, he thinks with his—"

"Toupee," Andi finished, sneaking another peek in his direction.

Harry leaned toward Valerie for a kiss. The gold digger glanced about for witnesses, then apparently, satisfied there were none, planted a kiss on his cheek.

Andi slapped her hands over her eyes and moaned. "How can she kiss him? I don't care how much money he has."

"Does the word *gross* come to mind?" Meg stepped away from the side of the truck. "Come on. They're going into Harry's condo. The coast is clear."

Andi breathed a sigh of relief. "I never want to see anything that revolting ever again."

"Too bad. You will as long as we keep spying on Harry. Let's check on Helen. She'll break at least one rule now that they've finished their rounds. I'm betting on two or three."

"So all of these board members break the rules they push on the rest of us?"

"Behind Harry's back," Meg stated flatly.

Disgusted, Andi shook her head and then followed her new friend down the street. "Does the reverend break the rules, too?"

"Not usually. He's too busy feeling sorry for himself and regretting what happened when he fell in love with Helen."

"Helen? The board member we're about to spy on?"

"Yep. She was the member of the congregation he

was caught kissing. Ministers are allowed to date and marry, but it becomes a scandal if the woman just broke up with the wealthiest member of the church. The gossips accused the reverend of coming between the couple and causing their separation, which placed their church in financial jeopardy. Helen claims she never let on to Reverend Nichols that she was in love with him until after she broke up with Mr. Millionaire. I believe her."

"What happened?"

"Bernice convinced Helen to leave him."

"Why?"

"Too many theories to discuss now. We have a job to do." Meg quickened her pace.

"Bernice sure knew how to make enemies." The number of murder suspects continued to grow. Andi glanced around her, wondering which condo hid the neighbor who had killed the former board president. An involuntary shudder traveled across her shoulders and upper back.

She realized she had fallen behind and rushed to catch up with Meg as she rounded another condo building. Out in the open, they strolled nonchalantly, side by side across the grass in the neighborhood's common area.

One moment Meg was walking beside her, then the next she was gone. Andi twisted and found her friend hiding behind another bush and pointing toward a woman washing her cheery yellow Smart Car in her driveway.

Afraid to be caught, Andi bent her knees and waddled like a duck behind the bushes to Meg's side. Spying was giving her quads a workout.

"That's Helen," Meg mouthed.

The rail-thin woman, most likely in her mid-thirties, squeezed a sopping wet sponge over the roof of her car, then stepped back out of the way as water cascaded over the side. She wore orange Capri pants with a matching floral, sleeveless top and flip-flop sandals. The outfit said, "Going on a spring picnic."

Meg lifted her camera. "Washing your car on the property is against the rules."

An earth-tone, midsize sedan drove down the street, approaching the condo. With a hesitant smile, Helen lifted her open palm in a weak wave. The driver ignored her. She lowered her gaze, rejection written all over her sullen face.

"She was waving at the reverend," Meg said. "He drives by her condo on the way home from his new job and she *just happens* to be out front so she can wave hello, but he pretends not to see her. He rejects her day after day after day."

"How sad." Andi's heart ached for the woman, even though she had never met her.

Helen slowly turned off the water, tossed the sponge into a plastic, gray bucket and carried it away by the handle. Before she reached her door, Meg began clicking pictures of the car wash scene.

After Helen disappeared behind her front door, they both left their hiding place.

Andi couldn't forget the look on Helen's face when the reverend drove off without acknowledging her. She knew how it felt to lose the man you love. "Maybe we should leave this poor woman alone. She's been through enough already."

Meg leaned close to the wet car and snapped a picture. "Helen hands her proxy over to Harry whenever he asks for it. She's not lifting a finger to stop him or help her neighbors. That makes her guilty in my book. Besides, all she'll get is a warning. She'll stop washing her car on the property and the daily rejections will stop. We are actually doing her a favor."

"I guess you're right," Andi said, hoping Helen would stop torturing herself.

Meg zoomed in on an oil drop the size of a nickel. "I can blow this up to look like the inside of a mechanic's garage."

"Let's get out of here," Andi encouraged, still not comfortable recording evidence against Helen.

Meg hid the camera in her pocket and the two of them power-walked down the street, following the trail of water leading away from Helen's driveway.

"Once I e-mail these pictures to Luke, the entire board will know we are out to stop them." Meg slowed her pace after they turned the corner. "I can't wait to see the look on Harry's face. He's going to explode, and I'm going to catch it all on film."

Andi pictured Harry throwing a fit. "A temper tantrum would break the excessive noise rule."

"I have to admit, at first the idea of this whole war scared the nail color off my toes, but now it feels good to be doing something to fight back." Meg grabbed Andi's arm. "Stop." She pointed to a squad car up ahead. "They have Bernice's son."

Two officers were escorting a tall, lanky man to their police cruiser.

Andi watched them fold his thin body into the backseat. *Bernice's son?*

"They're arresting the reverend?"

FIVE

Andi adjusted her eyes to the dim lighting of the bar down the street from the diner where her sister worked undercover. They couldn't talk at the diner and Jessie didn't have time to go home, so they met at a bar owned by their uncle Max, the black sheep of the family. The heavy aroma of stale beer made Andi gag. Nearby a leather-clad biker with a scraggly beard leaned back to follow her movements.

Max's longtime girlfriend tended bar during the less-crowded hours of the day. Clad all in black and sporting more tattoos than most men, Agnes could put the fear of God into any man with just a look. She set her evil snake eyes on Scraggily Beard and he took his sights off Andi.

"Your sister's in the back, sweet thing," Agnes said. She pointed the way with a whiskey bottle.

"Thanks," Andi mumbled with a half smile. Clutching her purse to her chest like a shield, Andi rushed past the empty bar stools in search of her sister. Not that anyone would mistake her for a single woman on the prowl for a one-night stand—after Jessie called and pleaded for her to come right away, Andi had pulled an oversize, gray sweatshirt on over her clothes.

A man occupying the last stool leaned toward her, then passed out cold on the peanut-shell-littered floor. Andi gasped. A drunk stumbled over him on his way to the john. She spotted a bulky bouncer and pointed to the man on the floor. He nodded and sauntered over.

"You came!" Jessie slid out of a dark booth. Her undercover outfit of the day, a tie-dye top, a peace-sign-print miniskirt, and white go-go boots caught the attention of every man in the bar.

Andi shook her head with a smirk. "Nancy Sinatra called. She wants her boots back."

Jessie turned in a circle to model her ensemble. "You like? Sixties night. Of course, I hear if you remember the sixties, you didn't experience the decade."

Impatient and wanting to escape, Andi changed the subject. "So what was so important it couldn't wait until you got home?"

Her sister's expression turned serious. "Bathroom. We need to hurry. I have to be back at the diner in ten minutes." She pulled Andi by the hand.

"Here we go again." Lately she'd been dragged from one bizarre situation to another. As far as restrooms go, this was one of the worst. It smelled like someone had dropped a case of cheap perfume on top of a mixture of hair products and citrus room freshener. Andi chose her steps carefully, doing her best to avoid the trail of toilet paper that had unrolled from the stall without a door. Her sister marched over the stained, scuffed, gray linoleum that bubbled beneath a scum-coated, leaking sink.

Jessie checked to make sure they were alone before locking them inside the bathroom. "I have good news. Lenny lowered the price on his agency."

"That's wonderful!"

"We're meeting tomorrow morning to sign papers."

Her smile finally reached her eyes. "I own a detective agency!"

They screamed with joy while jumping up and down like teenagers.

A knock sounded on the door.

"Occupied!" Jessie yelled.

"Open up!" a woman's shrill voice pierced the door. "Stop making out with your girlfriend and let me in. I have to go bad."

Jessie kicked the wall. "Stop whining! I'll be out in a minute."

"Why didn't you tell me over the phone?" Andi asked.

"I'm in a bind." She lowered her voice. "Lenny just took on a new client, and he's already cashed the man's check."

Understanding dawned on her. "You can't work the case, can you?"

Jessie shook her head. "It would jeopardize my undercover assignment at the diner."

"What do you need me to do? Play *Charlie's Angels* for you?" She laughed, but her sister didn't. "Jess, I'm joking. I can't play detective. I wouldn't know what to do."

"Relax. I just need you to ask a few questions for me. No big deal." Jessie retrieved a piece of paper from her cleavage. "The client is Reverend Nichols. He lives in our complex."

"Bernice's son?"

Jessie nodded. "He was taken in and questioned. He wasn't booked, but he's afraid he'll be pegged for the crime. He hired the agency, but Lenny is leaving for Hawaii tomorrow, and I can't talk to the reverend without jeopardizing my undercover assignment."

"So, what do you want me to do?"

Jessie took Andi's discount-priced black purse,

unzipped the opening, and placed the slip of paper inside. "This is Reverend Nichols's number. Call him tonight and set up an interview for tomorrow."

"You want *me* to interview him?" Andi shook her head. "I'll mess it up."

"No. You won't." Jessie dropped the purse back into Andi's waiting hands. "Just tell him you're Lenny's assistant. Think of it as being my secretary. You can do that."

"I don't know . . ."

"It's not as crazy as it sounds. You tape the conversation, and I'll do the behind-the-scenes work on my time off."

"You mean during the three minutes a night you sleep?"

Pounding at the door interrupted them again.

"Use the little boys' room!" Jessie yelled, then calmly placed both of her hands on Andi's shoulders and pleaded with sad eyes. "Please. I need you."

She hated it when Jessie resorted to the puppy face. Andi could never resist, but she wondered if she should this time.

Could I play PI and not make a fool of myself?

Her sense of adventure knew this was an opportunity of a lifetime.

The pounding at the door grew louder, more insistent. Jessie responded with a swift kick to the side of a stall.

Their father's voice sounded in Andi's head, *"You should let someone else do it. It's too dangerous."* She balled her hands into fists. All her life she had been coddled, protected, and treated like an invalid. This was the first time her sister needed her and trusted her to help. She would prove she wasn't the baby of the family any longer.

"Okay, Jessie, I'll do your interview." Andi shoved the paper into the pocket of her jeans. "So, you're going to prove the reverend is innocent?"

"I'll try. It's not going to be easy. The circumstantial evidence is pointing to him." The door and wall reverberated from what had to be a full body slam from the other side. "Okay! I'm coming!" Jessie patted Andi's shoulder. "Just don't do anything without my approval. And make sure you meet with this guy in a public place, like the food court in the mall. And ask Dad to sit at a nearby table, just in case. My gut says the reverend is harmless, but you never know."

****

The next afternoon, Luke discovered that a mattress had been discarded next to the dumpster where Bernice's body had been found. He jotted down a reminder in his electronic notepad to have it removed.

He rounded the corner and spotted Andi standing next to her front door, clutching a manila envelope. She wore an attractive gray pencil skirt along with a long-sleeve black blouse, leather belt, and matching pumps. She looked more like a lawyer than a teacher. Knowing he was glutton for punishment, he walked toward her.

She juggled a tape recorder and spiral notebook in her hands while she attempted to rip open the envelope and read the contents. "Harry! That horrible, despicable, low-life, bottom-feeding . . ."

Even from four feet away, the large type that read VIOLATION couldn't be missed. A lesser man would have hidden before she spotted him.

Andi skimmed the condemning message. "I do *not* have oil on my driveway." She glanced up and was taken aback by his presence. "I do *not* have oil on my driveway!" she repeated.

Since Luke hadn't written the violation letter, he didn't know what to say. The wiser option was to silently follow her, he decided. She marched to her driveway and poked at the dime-size circle with her toe. The once-gooey substance was so old and dry it wouldn't stick to her shoe.

"That is gum, not oil!" she barked at him.

She had every right to be angry. Harry wasn't backing down, despite the attempt made on his life.

Luke studied the dirty spot on the driveway. Tire tread had turned the once-light-colored gum dark. "You're right." Harry wouldn't win this battle. Luke's gut instinct was to make all of her troubles fade away. Without thinking, he reached out to touch her arm. "I'll destroy the violation when he sends me the copy."

She stepped away, her scowl letting him know what she thought of him. He dropped his hand, feeling like a fool. He had broken up with her because she emotionally kept him at arm's length.

Why risk opening myself up to heartbreak again?

Andi ripped up the letter. He took the remains from her grasp. The last thing he wanted was for Harry to catch her littering.

"Let me deal with this," he offered.

She tapped her toes. "I assume you sent a copy of Meg's pictures to Harry. It's no coincidence that Helen had an oil stain on her driveway and now he is accusing *me* of having an oil stain."

He nodded. "You're probably right. I doubt he got close enough to your driveway to realize it was gum."

"Because then I would have received a 'No Gum on the Driveway' violation letter."

"Don't say that too loud, or it will be on next year's version of the rules." He wished Andi and other like-minded neighbors would run for the board. It would make his life easier. Then he considered the ramifications of seeing her every week to review business matters. Spending time near her made him wish

73

their relationship could have been different. He had dated several women over the years, but none of them captivated him the way Andi had.

A rush of exasperated breath escaped her lungs. "If I argue against the oil spill violation at the next meeting, Harry will probably hold up the picture Meg took of Helen's driveway and use it against me, claiming it is a picture of *my* driveway. Valerie will demand a lynching and Harry will conveniently pull a rope out of his briefcase."

He tried not to laugh, but a smirk made its way to his lips.

She took in a deep breath. "What are you doing here, anyway?"

"I'm just making sure everything is in order."

"I don't see why. Harry walks the property hourly and if there isn't a problem, he makes one up." She kicked at the gum.

Chaos suddenly marched around the corner. Meg and Roxie, wearing bright-red T-shirts that read "Anti-Board," held up their cameras and grinned.

"Is he bothering you?" Roxie coughed on the smoke ring she'd blown a moment before. Luke could swear her neon-pink spandex pants were glowing. The long, flowing, gray wig was new. The crotchety woman could start her own clothing line: Freaka of Hollywood Blvd.: Sexy Apparel for Aging Hookers.

Luke rubbed his jaw with his thumb. "Ms. Blackwell, those cigarettes are going to kill you one day."

She pointed the lit end at him. "Sonny, I've crammed two lifetimes into this one. I'm not planning to stick around for a third."

Beaming, Meg tossed a red shirt to Andi. "We've been waiting for you to get home from school." The nurse bounced with excitement. "Word got out that we're retaliating, and two more neighbors want to join our Anti-Board."

"We've started a petition to have Harry removed from the board." Roxie waved the paper with a flourish. "They said they'd sign it."

"Now that there is an official fight against Harry, neighbors are willing to stand up and help. Well, at least two are." Meg eyed Luke as if expecting a response. "They're waiting for us at the pool." She grabbed Andi's arm. "Let's go."

Andi resisted. "I'll catch up with you later. I have an appointment."

"Ladies," Luke began, aiming for his usual calm, professional tone, "we need to talk about this group of yours."

Roxie poked his chest with one of her brightly striped acrylic nails. "We are exercising our rights as Americans, Mr. Hot Stuff. We have the right to wear Anti-Board shirts, the right to start petitions, and the right to prove that board is full of hypocrites."

"True," Luke said, stepping back, away from Roxie's lethal nails. He hoped one day she would stop calling him "sonny" and "hot stuff." "The petition sounds like a step in the right direction. I'm not so sure about the Anti-Board shirts."

Meg toyed with his tie. "Sorry you don't approve, but we're not about to stop now. We're just getting started."

Luke turned to Andi, imploring with his eyes to help. Roxie would take this anti-board to uncontrollable levels. "Please talk some sense into your friends before someone gets hurt."

"Too late," Andi answered. "What do you think Harry's been doing? Making friends? He's been hurting this community for a long time."

Meg planted her hands on her hips. "Prove Harry's finished, and then we'll stop."

"That's right!" Roxie said, cheering them on. She

turned on her high-heeled sandals, revealing the back of the Anti-Board T-shirt. In big block letters were the words, "BEWARE OF HOAs."

Luke sighed. *Harry will stop at nothing to destroy them.*

****

The reverend opened the door. "Yes?"

The sight of jeans and a blue polo shirt knocked Andi off guard. She didn't know why, she hadn't expected him to wear a clerical collar around his own home.

She straightened her posture. "I'm Andi Stevenson with Lenny's Detective Agency."

"I was expecting Lenny." His brow furrowed with confusion.

"About that . . ." She glanced back over her shoulder at two elderly women huddled over a clump of bushes. "Can we talk inside? The neighbors are watching, and I know you want to keep this discreet."

"Of course."

She slipped into the living room and wondered if she was supposed to genuflect when she spotted the four-foot-tall wooden cross. Paintings of the Last Supper and martyred saints decorated the remaining walls. Scanning the rest of the living room, she noticed religious candles and statues perched on every flat surface. She felt the need to confess her sins—and she wasn't even very religious.

"Who's your decorator?" Andi mumbled.

"What?"

"Nothing."

Sarcastic personalities should come with an "Off" switch.

"Can we sit?"

He pointed to a brown leather couch.

"I'm going to ask you a list of questions and tape your responses." She eased onto the leather. It didn't seem right to record an interview with a former reverend with so many religious symbols staring at them, somehow.

"Where's Lenny?" he asked.

"My employer prefers to send me first." She caught a glimmer of disbelief in his eyes. "In this case, the owner feels it gives us an advantage. Keeping the agency's involvement a secret will allow our detectives to work incognito. People are more likely to open up if they think they are speaking to me, just another neighbor," the well-rehearsed speech, provided by her sister, flowed from her lips without a single pause for breath. It wasn't exactly a lie, but it wasn't the total truth either. Silently, she asked for forgiveness, promising she would go to church again soon.

"That makes sense."

She inhaled, rather than breathing a sigh of relief, then turned toward the cross with a silent nod of thanks. *This really is for everyone's good,* she rationalized.

He sat on the wing-back chair facing her. "What did you want to ask me, Miss Stevenson?"

She pushed the "Record" button. "Why were you taken to the police station?"

It didn't make sense to take a man of the cloth to the station if you weren't planning to arrest him. "Were you uncooperative?"

"Not at all. One of the officers said he was uncomfortable questioning me here and asked if I wouldn't mind joining them at the station."

She looked about the room again. "I can see how they might have been . . . distracted." She redirected her attention to the questions written in her notebook. "What exactly do you want Lenny's Detective Agency to do for you?"

He picked up a Bible-study guide from an end table and placed it in his lap. Absently, he played with the silver cross hanging from a burgundy silk bookmark. "Find my mother's killer. I'm offering a ten-thousand-dollar reward for information that leads to the arrest of her murderer. You could earn that reward, Miss Stevenson. I heard you're a teacher. Teachers can always use more money. Isn't that why you're working for Lenny in your spare time? To earn extra money?"

Andi nodded. She could do a lot with ten grand—perhaps even invest in her sister's agency. As the business grew, so would her share of the profits.

"I hear the police think you killed your mother," she said flatly.

"Harry told them I should be their number-one suspect. He's telling anyone who will listen."

Is the board president guilty and trying to divert the attention of the police?

"Harry's also claiming I cut his brake line. He gave the police a photograph of me looking beneath his car."

Talk about damning evidence.

"What were you doing near his car?"

"I was searching for my mother's dog."

"The vet didn't contact you? He has Toto," she said. "He was going to check him over and then call you."

Was the doggie doctor keeping the dog for a reason?

"I'm glad Toto's not lost." A stress line or two relaxed on his face.

According to Jessie's background check, Reverend Nichols was forty-five, but he looked sixty. Andi felt sorry for him. She also felt sorry for Helen. It was too bad they broke up. They needed each other, from what she could tell. "Toto appeared happy and healthy when I last saw him," she said.

"I haven't been home much lately. I had to plan the funeral," he explained without emotion. "Doctor Owens probably called, but I turned my answering machine off. Too many reporters requesting interviews. I'll fetch Toto after we conclude our business." He dragged in a deep breath as he rubbed the cross he held between his fingers. "My mother's world centered on Toto and the homeowners' association."

Was that concern in his tone?

"How would you describe your relationship with your mother?" she asked.

"I'm afraid my answer won't help my case." Reverend Nichols continued to play with the burgundy bookmark. "Despite my religious indoctrination, I couldn't stand my mother. She was a woman who insisted on controlling every aspect of her life. That included me."

Okay. He liked the dog, not his mother.

"In what way was she controlling?"

"From the time I was born, she scheduled every moment of my day. The number of hours I studied, which sports I was allowed to play, the friends I could spend time with, even the girls I was allowed to date."

Norman Bates had a nicer mother. Her mind wandered down a dark path. *What if he was guilty? His mother had come between him and Helen. Did that push him over the edge?*

"It was your mother's choice for you to become a minister?" Andi concluded.

"No, it was mine. It was the first time I stood up to her. We argued for months. She wanted me to become a high-priced attorney." He paused and gazed up at the cross. "I wanted to serve the Lord—not her."

"I see." She glanced down at her questions. "While we are on the subject of your career choice, I need to ask you about—"

"Helen." Pain filled his tired eyes. "I made a mistake, Miss Stevenson. I knew her former boyfriend was upset over their breakup and might retaliate if I entered into a relationship with her. I chose to ignore that fact. As a result, he turned my own church against me. I should have put them first, and they reminded me of that every chance they got. I fell into a depression and decided it would be best if I left the church. A friend of mine offered me a job counseling teens."

He sounded like a sad, intelligent, reasonable man, but when she scanned the room, she couldn't help but wonder. She had never been inside the home of a spiritual leader before, but she doubted their personal surroundings usually contained more religious artifacts than most cathedrals.

Is he a zealot? Did he step off the sanity bus a long time ago? Am I sitting alone with a killer? Maybe I should have brought Dad along. Why do I always think I can do things by myself?

Bernice had been killed with a yellow brick. She scanned the room for heavy objects. Statues stood in every corner, staring at her and making her feel uneasy.

Glancing down at her notebook, she tried to contain her overactive imagination. "I heard your mother broke up your relationship with Helen."

His head jerked up. "How do you know that?"

"Rumor mill. Could Helen have killed Bernice?"

"She would never harm anyone. My mother was the monster, not her. Bernice yelled at Helen during one of the board meetings, accused her of ruining my reputation and soiling our family name. Even though my mother publicly humiliated her, Helen only walked away. She never said a mean word."

Andi wanted to ask why he wouldn't look at Helen when he drove by her condo every night, but decided it didn't pertain to the case. She checked Jessie's notes again. "When was the last time you saw your mother?"

"At the board meeting the night she died."

"Was anyone upset with her that night?" She already knew the answer, but the question was on the list.

"Everyone who received a violation letter or fine that month."

"So most of the people living in the complex?" she concluded.

"Correct." His pressed his lips into a flat line.

That didn't help narrow down the list of suspects. "Who was at this meeting?"

"I can get you a copy of the minutes from the board secretary. It won't have every name, but it will list all the board members in attendance and anyone who pleaded their case. I remember that cowboy lost his temper. That's nothing new."

"It would save me time if you could try to remember which board members were there."

He glanced about the room as if trying to jog his memory. "I believe Helen and Tess, the vet's wife, were the only absent board members."

"Do you know where they were that night?"

"Helen rarely attends meetings nowadays. She originally joined because I've been on the board for years."

The woman stands outside her condo every day, waiting for him to drive by on his way home. Why would she stop attending the meetings? Andi eyed him suspiciously.

"I asked her not to come," he explained. "She agreed, as long as she could give me her proxies."

"The neighbors think she gives her proxies to Harry."

"The rumor mill isn't always right." He glanced at her notebook. "The other board member who didn't show was Tess Owens, the vet's wife. She wasn't feeling well. Mother planned to check in on her after the meeting."

"Did she?"

"According to Tess's husband, Mother was there for about two minutes, but never actually went inside. She was afraid of catching her cold." He shrugged as if it were common for his mother to avoid anyone who might be sick. "Harry saw Mother leaving the Owens's place, but no one heard from her after she reached her own condo."

"Where did you go after the meeting?"

"Here, to pray for the community. There's so much anger."

"You're telling me." Andi lifted her brows. "Did you see or speak to anyone else after the meeting?"

"I'm afraid not." His words rang true, but they wouldn't give him an alibi.

Andi glanced down at the last question on her notebook. She didn't want to ask it, but Jessie had insisted. She faced the reverend, ready to read his body language. "Did you kill your mother?"

He didn't even blink. "No. But I won't miss her."

"Thank you for your time." She stood to leave.

He stood to walk her out. "When will you be speaking to Lenny?"

"Lenny? Oh yeah, Lenny." She had to remind herself that as far as the reverend was concerned, she was working for the former owner. "Well, it's hard to say. Could be today, tomorrow . . . He has his hands full right now. Not that he has too many clients. I mean, he has a lot of clients, but not so many that he can't help you. Every client is important to Lenny." If she wanted to help her sister, she was going to have to get better at bending the truth without rambling on and on.

"I understand," the reverend answered. "When you do speak to him, please tell him I'm innocent. I didn't like my mother, but I didn't hate her either. Her death could very well have been retaliation for her work with the HOA. The real killer is out there, and Lenny needs to find him before he strikes again."

****

"Do you spend your life looking for trouble, or does it just follow you around?" Luke asked Andi. He had spent the last ten minutes waiting outside of Reverend Nichols's condo, hoping to prove the rumors that she was inside were not true.

Andi arched a brow as she shuffled down the path toward him. "I beg your pardon?"

"Is it true? Are you working for the detective agency looking into Bernice's murder?"

"Not your business," she stated as she looked both ways before crossing the street that wound through their private community.

He caught up to her and stopped her escape with a hand on her shoulder. "As someone who cares about you, I beg to differ. If you aren't careful, you are going to have both Harry *and* a murderer chasing after you."

She lifted his hand with one finger and dropped it off her shoulder like it was a smelly rag. "I already forgave you for dumping me in college. You don't have to feel guilty anymore, so you can you stop acting like my father by trying to control my life choices. I'm a big girl."

Am I acting like her father? Could I be protecting her now because I know I hurt her and am trying to make up for it somehow? A pang of truth resonated from that last thought.

"Besides," she continued. "I'm beginning to think Harry is the murderer. Once the police find the evidence, all our problems will be solved."

He continued to follow her as she walked across the street and over the grass between two buildings. "What possible motive would Harry have for killing Bernice?

They were of like mind. They both committed their lives to making sure everyone follows the rules."

"Did you ever think Harry might be embezzling money from the association?" she tossed her accusation over her shoulder as she marched away. "He could have sent violation letters with directions to send the payment to a private PO Box. Greed has been a strong motive for murder since the beginning of time."

"Someone would have caught him by now."

"Bernice caught him. That's why she's dead." She adjusted her grip on her tape recorder. "It's just a theory. Don't quote me, but you should keep your ears open." She reached the pool fence and peeked through the gaps between the wooden slats.

He leaned close to the fence, too. The fountain sprayed water over a quiet, deserted pool. Each drop hit the glassy surface and created a tiny wave that spread away from the point of impact, then quickly died away. No Valerie. "Harry's girlfriend must have canceled her aerobics class after receiving the violation letter."

"I'm not surprised. She's probably too angry to 'right foot kick, take a sip.' "

"Getting back to Harry," he said, pulling back from the fence. "I don't think he killed Bernice."

"I think you're wrong." Her deep eyes reflected both the light and her stubbornness.

"It's more likely an angry resident killed her. She fined almost every unit at least once."

"Or, Harry was embezzling money. Bernice found out, confronted him, and *whack!*" She pretended to hit herself on the head with an imaginary brick.

"Highly doubtful."

"From your point of view."

Harry couldn't embezzle money without my discovering his subterfuge, could he?

Continuing down the path leading away from the

pool, Luke followed Andi through the common area. From where they walked, he could see the back porches of over a half-dozen condos. They passed one gas grill and patio furniture set after another. Nearing the opposite end of the complex, he detected movement behind Harry's condo and Barry Manilow music blaring through an open window.

Meg stood next to a tree, standing clear of the scene, watching Roxie aim a cell phone camera at Harry's bedroom window. Two new recruits to the anti-board stood next to the adjacent building, keeping their distance. One was Dinah, a middle-aged caterer who considered herself the next Martha Stewart. She wore her red "Anti-Board" T-shirt over a pink dress spotted with black polka dots. The other recruit was her friend Carla, who was clearly more down to earth. She wore jeans with her tee. When Luke and Andi approached, they waved and ambled away. The only person brave— or foolish—enough to spy into Harry's bedroom in front of the property manager was Roxie.

Meg waved Andi over. She pointed at Luke and then used her fingers to motion for him to walk away. He frowned, not willing to retreat and unleash mayhem on the community.

From inside the condo a woman squealed, "Harry, you behave yourself! You know I sleep only with my husband."

"What's going on?" Andi squinted to see what had captured everyone's attention.

Meg grabbed hold of Andi's arm and pulled her close. "Roxie has flipped. She is *so* mad."

Luke was afraid to ask, but had to know. "What did Harry do now?"

"He rigged the irrigation system so that water hits our bedroom windows every hour on the hour throughout the night. I didn't get more than two hours' sleep. I doubt

Roxie slept at all. She's furious." Meg gestured toward the window. "She's recording them. Either Harry backs off or she'll send pictures of him playing kissy-face with Valerie to her husband."

Luke noticed the distance between Meg and Roxie. "I gather you don't approve."

"Oh, I approve," Meg snorted. "Roxie doesn't care if Harry catches her and calls the police. If I'm arrested, though, I'll lose my job, so I'm staying back here."

"Smart move," Andi said. "I'm not going any closer either."

Meg sent Luke an easy smile. "Harry's breaking the excessive noise rule. Go get 'em, Mr. Property Manager."

"Shh," Roxie warned. "Don't give us away."

Luke watched Roxie snap another picture. He groaned.

Why didn't I become a florist?

Determined to break up the scene, he strode across the grass to Roxie's side. He couldn't help but glance into Harry's condo. The blinds were tilted, but not closed. From their close proximity, they could easily see into his bedroom. *Copacabana* provided the background music for the antics going on inside.

Harry pulled Valerie into his arms and kissed her full on the mouth. "Stop being a tease."

Luke's stomach churned with disgust. "Go home, Roxie."

He felt like he was standing in the middle of a circus sideshow.

"*You* go home," Roxie retorted. "I'm on a mission. It's called getting revenge."

Enough was enough. Luke marched up to Harry's window and was about to knock on the glass pane when he spotted Paul, Valerie's husband, leaning over Roxie's shoulder.

"What's going on?" the unsuspecting man asked. He had no clue his life was about to change dramatically.

Roxie shrugged as if apologizing and pointed toward Harry's condo. "You might as well know the ugly truth, sonny."

Luke followed the man's gaze into the bedroom. Harry and Valerie were entwined in a passionate embrace and completely oblivious to the outside world.

Understanding flickered across Paul's face, followed by shock. "Valerie?" His cheeks and neck grew red, then scarlet. "Val-er-ie!"

The world shifted into slow motion.

At the sound of Valerie's husband screaming his wife's name for the third time, Harry leaned away from her and stared out the window. His gaze locked on Andi first, then, recognizing Paul, his eyes grew wide with fear.

Valerie's husband dove through the window, destroying the screen in the process. After recovering from the tumble, he grabbed Harry by the neck and shook him violently.

Valerie screamed.

Andi screamed.

Meg and Roxie screamed.

Luke sighed.

Harry's head flopped back and forth as he tried to pry Paul's hands off his neck.

"This is what I get for accepting the Euphoria account." Luke held on to the windowsill as he lifted one leg inside. If Paul had paid more attention to his wife, she might not have reached out to Harry. If Harry had closed the window and blinds, Roxie wouldn't have caught them. And if no one had screamed, the whole neighborhood wouldn't be gathering in the common area. They were probably expecting to see another dead board member. Luke hoped not.

"Super hunk to the rescue!" Roxie announced.

"Knock it off!" Luke grabbed Paul's upper arm, effectively breaking the hold on Harry's neck.

Harry gasped for air, coughed, and rubbed at the red fingerprints left on his pale skin. The music ended abruptly and an eerie silence filled the air. They all exchanged angry glares, then Valerie's husband pulled back his fist and punched the board president square in the nose.

Valerie screeched.

Andi, Meg, and Roxie stood outside the window with mouths agape.

Harry fell back against the mirrored closet door. It shook from the impact and the vibration caused his toupee to slide off his head and land on his shoulder. Harry reached for his nose just as crimson liquid began to ooze from his nostrils.

The scene exploded with one obscenity after another. Not only could Valerie's husband cuss like a sailor, he could probably spell every one of the names he called his wife as well.

"I knew I shouldn't have married you." He pointed his skinny finger at her. "I want a divorce!"

"I . . ." Valerie bit her lip while tears slid down her cheeks. "I never slept with him," she proclaimed to everyone—the group looked at her as if she had risen from the bowels of hell.

Keeping a safe distance from the outraged man, Harry followed Valerie out of the room, holding his nose while blood seeped between his fingers.

Valerie's husband crawled back out the window a hopeless, dejected version of his former self.

Everyone waited for what would happen next. Still standing in the bedroom, Luke stuck his head out the window and stared at Roxie, Meg, and then Andi. "Are you happy now?"

Roxie propped her hands on her hips. "Don't go getting your knickers in a knot, young man. No one here told those two to play kissy-face with the window wide open for all to see and hear. If you want to blame someone, blame *me*. I'm the one who spied on them, no one else. And I don't care what you think of me. You don't live here."

Meg crossed her arms over her chest. "We also didn't tell Valerie's husband she was here. You know it was only a matter of time until he found out his wife is a . . . what her husband called her."

He couldn't believe they were rationalizing the situation.

"Paul would've killed Harry if we hadn't been standing here to witness the murder," Roxie added. "Not that I would have testified against him if he *did* kill him."

"See, our being here was a good thing!" Meg said. "We kept Paul from killing Harry."

"Good Samaritans, huh?" Luke shook his head. They all knew things had gotten out of hand, even if they didn't want to admit it. He pointed to Andi. "Like I said—trouble."

SIX

Andi had no sooner placed her belongings on the dining room table than there was a loud knock on the door.

Peering through the peephole, she saw Luke standing on her welcome mat. Embarrassment over the scene at Harry's flooded over her. "What could he possibly want now?"

Taking a moment to gain her composure, she stood with her fingers on the knob, simply breathing. Finally ready to face him, she stiffened her spine and tugged the door open.

"We need to talk." His stoic face revealed nothing congenial. Long strides took him through her dining area and into the living room, which was more presentable than the last time he'd been inside her home. Between interviewing the reverend and spying on the board, she'd still managed to find time to unpack a few boxes and toss them into the corners.

Luke sat on the new red accent chair next to the white linen sofa. He leaned forward, his elbow resting on his thighs, his hands clasped together. She remembered that look. He was contemplating his next words. She lowered herself onto the sofa and waited. This could take a while.

"Andi . . ."

"If you came over here to lecture me about the anti-board spying and how somehow this is all my fault—"

"No lecture."

She waited for him to continue, certain whatever he had to say would turn into a lecture despite his assurances. In her defense, she hadn't intended to spy. Meg called her over to the tree before she knew what Roxie was doing.

Okay, I had some clue what Roxie was doing, but still . . .

"I'm not one to gossip." He stood and walked over to the sliding-glass door where she had left the blinds pulled back. Agitated, he faced her back porch while running a hand through his thick hair. "But I think you deserve to know why Harry tries to control the property as strictly as he does. I'm not asking you to feel sorry for him, just to understand."

Oh, great! A lecture in disguise.

"I grant you he has gone off the deep end," Luke said as he glanced in her direction. "But when I first met him he had a soft side. I saw it only a few times, but it was there. I'm hoping he might find it again now that Valerie is free to be with him."

Andi stifled a string of sarcastic comments.

"Harry's wife died of cancer a few years ago. That was when I first met him. I wasn't the property manager back then, but I was helping an associate at the board meetings. Six months after that, the company he worked for merged with another, and he was forced into early retirement to make room for younger, less expensive employees. He became an angry man struggling to maintain some degree of control over his life. His biggest mistake was running for the board. Bernice was president when he joined, and unfortunately, a role model for those who don't want to win friends and influence people in a positive way."

Andi felt a twinge of guilt. Then her line of vision fell on the violation letters piling up on her table, and she snubbed out that guilt like an ugly cigarette butt. "I'm sorry he lost his wife, but he has no right to make the rest of the world miserable in an attempt to lighten his own pain."

"True. I bring this up only because I'm thinking there's a good chance he might soften up now."

"Not in this lifetime."

"I just saw Harry hauling Valerie's clothes into his condo."

"That was fast, don't you think?"

"Not when you consider her husband was throwing them out of their bedroom window. Harry promised to buy her a ring in the morning. Between the attempt on his life and now having someone to share his second chance with, he might change."

Andi grabbed the throw pillow beside her and held it close to her chest. It served as a barrier between her and Luke's insistence that she soften her heart where Harry was concerned. "And how's that going to turn our board president into a marshmallow?"

"He's getting what he needs—a full-time companion."

"Don't bet my bank account on him becoming a changed man. I can't afford any more fines." She stood and walked to the sliding-glass door, where she peered out to the barren porch. She should be planting pansies in pots and baking cookies in the shape of tulips, not fighting Harry. "I'm not the only one he's harming. These fines are placing a financial burden on this entire community."

Luke placed his hand on her forearm. "I understand

how you feel and why you started the anti-board."

His touch sent a shiver down her spine that she tried to ignore. "*I* didn't start the anti-board."

"I stand corrected." He withdrew his hand, letting it drop to his side. "Regardless, this has gone far enough. A marriage has ended. Can you please try to rein in Roxie until we see how Harry reacts to Valerie moving in with him?"

"No one can control Roxie. And you should probably know that Meg's started a petition to have Harry removed from the board. I won't discourage her." Remembering the look on Paul's face ate at her conscience. She had to take some responsibility for the fallout since she participated in the war. "I promise I won't wave the petition under Harry's nose."

"That's fair." He glanced about the room. "I guess I should leave you to your unpacking."

She nodded, even though the part of her who remembered how good they had been together wanted him to stay. Forcing her mind to switch tracks, she closed the blinds and turned to follow him to the foyer.

A forced smile appeared on his handsome face. "Despite everything, I'm glad our paths have crossed again. I hope one day soon we'll get a chance to talk about something besides the homeowners' association." He paused, his gaze fixed on hers. "If it's okay with you, I'd like to get to know you again. You were an important part of my life. I miss our friendship."

Her breath caught in her throat.

One cost of breaking up is losing your best friend. He should have thought about their long evenings watching old movies together, holding hands on long walks, and debates covering everything from politics to religion before he threw it all away.

She wanted to tell him all of that and more, but all she could say was, "You hurt me."

"I know." He reached up to sweep a stray strand of hair away from her face. "I'm hoping we can find a way to at least be friends again. I've thought about it a lot. I know it wouldn't be easy at first, but I think that friendship is worth finding again. It was special. Maybe our mistake was taking our relationship to a level where it became serious and complicated."

"Friends . . ."

Could my heart handle seeing him, getting closer to him, knowing we could be only friends?

She shrugged, but she knew better. Traveling that path would only break her heart.

****

Friday morning, Andi hit the snooze alarm and rolled back onto the bed. Remembering that the first day of spring break had finally arrived, she smiled and contemplated falling back to sleep. Instead, she stared up at the ceiling fan, allowing her thoughts to wander.

She planned to bake up a storm. The events of the previous day flickered through her mind, and she decided to leave a gift bag of chocolate chip cookies on Paul's doorstep. If he threw it in the trash, she wouldn't blame him, but she felt the need to do something. A sugar fix might make him feel better, even if for only a moment.

"That creep!" Jessie stormed into Andi's bedroom, holding a cream-colored paper high in the air. "Harry taped another violation letter to the door last night."

"For what?"

"He's claiming there's litter on the back porch."

"No there's not!" Andi threw back the covers and charged into the living room. "I looked outside last night. The porch was spotless. Luke is my witness."

When Andi pushed back the blinds, she found an

empty milk jug, juice carton, cookie and candy wrappers, tuna cans, and a mayonnaise jar strewn across the cement, along with used napkins, crumpled tissue, cereal bits, and coffee grounds. An empty white trash bag hung over the floral-print patio chair cushion, flapping in the breeze.

A typed note, taped to the trash bag, caught her attention. She slid the door open, stepped outside, and kicked the cereal box across the patio. The aroma of decaying food wafted to her nose. "Gross!"

She peeled the note away from the bag and read, "Here's your housewarming gift. Since you live with trash, you should feel right at home." She folded the note and palmed it before her sister joined her.

"Didn't you say Luke thought Harry would be a better man now that he has Valerie?" Jessie stepped out onto the porch. "This doesn't look like a happy man to me."

"Valerie is the one who isn't happy, and I'm willing to bet it has everything to do with her soiled reputation and nothing to do with her sunken marriage."

"*She* acted like trash so her boyfriend is throwing it on *our* porch?" Jessie scowled. "That doesn't even make sense."

Andi squeezed the note tighter, making sure Jessie could never read the message. She didn't want her sister worrying about Harry and what he might do next because he thought Jessie was a drug-dealing hooker. Her life could depend on her mind remaining focused on her undercover assignment. "Don't expect that man to make sense."

"I'm tempted to pistol-whip him and make him clean it up himself." Jessie held up an empty cracker box with two fingers, then tossed it on top of a margarine tub.

Luke was wrong when he thought Harry might lighten up on the fines now that Valerie had moved in with him—not to mention because of his brush with death. Andi shook her head. Harry wasn't about to lighten up on the fines for any reason. He wanted her to move out and take her sister with her. He wanted the anti-board, and anyone associated with it, to go away. "I can't believe I felt sorry for him for two whole seconds last night. That baloney brain."

"What did you call him?"

"Baloney brain." She shrugged. "I heard one of the kids at school say it. It's a lot better than what I want to call him."

"Okay. Let's find a way to make that baloney brain pay for his crimes."

"Wait!" Andi ran to the garage to collect one of the smaller empty packing boxes. While standing beside her sister's SUV, she scanned the wall until she found the metal fuse box. She hid the note inside, making a mental note to destroy it after Jessie left for work that night. She seized a cardboard box and closed the door to the garage behind her.

"I bet he left fingerprints on the trash bag," Andi yelled from the kitchen where she stopped to grab a pair of tongs. By the time she reached the back door, she had the box assembled. "You have a fingerprint kit, don't you?"

"At the agency." Jessie, the new legal owner of Lenny's Detective Agency, shifted her weight uncomfortably. "Even if there are prints, it wouldn't stand up in court. We can't prove someone else didn't steal his trash bag out of the dumpster."

"We don't have to take him to court. We just need to scare him into thinking we can," Andi explained, realizing she sounded a lot like their father.

"Just don't—"

"I know. Don't cross any legal lines." Like playing Peeping Tom. Remembering the events of the former evening made her cringe. Andi held her nose with one hand while she snatched the trash bag between the tongs with the other. Keeping her distance, she dropped the bag inside the open box, careful not to touch it and contaminate the fingerprints.

Andi hadn't been excited about the idea of spending half of her first day of spring break helping her sister sort through the old files Lenny left behind in his office, but now she couldn't wait to get to the detective agency. A fingerprint kit from Lenny's Detective Agency might actually get Harry kicked off the board. At the next board meeting, she would stick around to prove to Luke that the fingerprints on the bag matched the one on Harry's water glass.

The sisters had dressed and spent twenty minutes cleaning up the grime off the porch when Jessie's phone chirped. She emptied the dustpan filled with eggshells into one of their own garbage bags and checked the number. "Back in a minute. I have to take this," she said, retreating back inside the condo.

Andi scanned the porch for any remnants of debris, then looked down at the stuffed bag. "I have to throw you in the dumpster, don't I?" She couldn't ask Jessie to do it. Her sister would tease her endlessly for being afraid of a big metal box.

With the stench of garbage still lingering in the air, she resisted dragging in a deep breath for courage. She grabbed the bag with a fist, then stepped lightly through the condo and out the front door. Nearing the dumpster, she glanced back over her shoulder. None of the neighbors were watching. None that she could see, anyway.

"I can do this," she mumbled beneath her breath. "I can do this." Fear crept over her shoulders and down her spine as she lifted the latch and opened the gate in the fence surrounding the trash bin. "I can do this." She stood, facing the dumpster, determined to carry out her mission "There's no dead body in there."

She took one hesitant step forward, lifted her free hand, reached for the lid, and . . . "I can do this. I can do this. *I can't* do this!" She threw the bag on top of the metal lid. It landed with a resounding thump. The echo inside mocked her. Shuddering, she slammed the gate shut and turned to find a police cruiser entering the complex.

After following the cruiser, Andi found Luke standing in the grass, near an ambulance in front of Helen's building. The second police cruiser came to a stop across the street behind the first one on the scene. Half a dozen neighbors stood on the sidewalk or in the grassy common area, including Roxie and Meg. Word traveled fast on Euphoria Lane.

"What's going on?" Andi quickened her steps.

****

The scent of Andi's strawberry shampoo enticed Luke's senses as she drew close. Taking in the sight of her shorts and floral blouse, he was reminded of picnics they had once shared in the park. He missed those lazy, carefree days. Their only worry then was passing the next college exam. The past faded, however, when Roxie and Meg rushed to join them.

"Something happened to another board member," he said, watching the EMTs roll Helen's body out of her condo on a gurney.

"Is she alive?" Concern furrowed Andi's brow.

Helen lifted her hand to her forehead, answering her question.

"If she's not alive, she's a zombie," Meg said, waving to Helen.

"I vote for zombie." Roxie chuckled, then coughed

on her cigarette smoke.

Andi gazed up at him quizzically. "What are you doing here so early? I thought you walked the property only once a week."

"I called him." Roxie tapped her cigarette, causing a chunk of ash to separate and float through the crisp morning air. "How else are we going to find out what the police know?"

"Sorry, ladies." He crossed his arms. "The officers asked me questions, but didn't answer any of mine. Although they did call it a crime scene."

"Then we know more than you do." Roxie puffed her zebra-print-clad chest out with pride. "See those medical students?" She pointed to two young men speaking with one of the officers. "Helen stumbled out of her condo carrying one of those shots for people who are allergic to stuff. She couldn't breathe and was too out of it to treat herself. Those med students said she would have died if they hadn't found her."

"EpiPen," Meg said in a quiet voice. "Helen carries an EpiPen. She must have been too disoriented from the lack of oxygen to give herself the shot."

Andi watched the EMTs loading Helen into the ambulance. "What is she allergic to?"

"Peanuts," Luke, Roxie, and Meg answered together.

"You would have to be new to Euphoria—or deaf— not to know." Roxie guffawed. "She broadcasted loud and clear at every pot luck that she couldn't eat any cookies containing peanuts."

Meg kicked at a stone with the toe of her tennis shoe. "Helen is always careful about what she eats. I bet someone slipped peanuts into something in her kitchen. She wouldn't have suspected she was having an allergic reaction until it was almost too late."

Andi's gaze traveled the crowd. "That's one murder and two attempted murders. No one can argue the fact now that someone is trying to kill off the board."

On the other side of the street, the angry cowboy spit on the asphalt, then strode off. His scowl warned, "Stay out of my way." Not that you would want to stand too close. He spit chewing tobacco like an automatic sprinkler.

Luke had heard that murderers often returned to the scene of the crime, especially when the police were investigating. Sort of a twisted version of an artist watching his work being admired in a gallery. "What do you ladies know about Mr. Decker?"

"Keeps to himself," Meg said, waving to Dinah and Carla, the new members of the anti-board standing on the corner. "Unless he's received a violation letter, then he's threatening to kill the board. You already know that." Her eyes twinkled. "You don't think *he* tried to kill Helen, do you?"

Luke lost sight of the cowboy when he slipped between two buildings. "Of course not. I was just wondering."

Andi's expression said she didn't believe him. Once upon a time, he swore she could read his every thought—at least those not concerning her sisters. She tuned him out when the conversation turned to family.

"I can tell you one thing," Andi said. "I'm glad I'm not on the board."

"I'm glad Tess is out of town," Meg added. "She's the only board member I like, aside from the reverend."

Luke had to agree. Tess had a kind heart. He had never once had a problem with her.

"She's the only board member who doesn't deserve to be whacked." Roxie patted the curls of her long, blonde wig. "Tess is a sweetie. Even Bernice liked her."

Meg nodded. "Bernice called her Dorothy because she's from Kansas."

"Did I hear my wife's name?" Doctor Owens ambled

their way, wearing a black, long-sleeved shirt and gray slacks. "I heard Helen was murdered." He leaned around Meg to check out the crime scene.

Meg peered up at him with admiration in her eyes. "Only an attempted murder. She—"

"Doc," Roxie interjected, "you had better keep that wife of yours out of town until this is all over. Someone's trying to take out the board."

"It looks that way, doesn't it?" Doctor Owens eyed Luke as if asking for his opinion.

"Staying out of town might be a good idea," Luke conceded.

The vet nodded, and his dark eyes filled with concern. "Tess is going to be devastated when she hears about Bernice."

"She doesn't know Bernice was killed?" Meg asked.

The crease in his brow deepened. "I didn't think that was the type of news to deliver over the phone, but I don't have any choice now. I have to tell her so she'll change her flight plans and stay with her mother until the murderer is behind bars."

Doctor Owens pushed a button on his iPhone and then lifted it to his ear.

"Hello, Mother Rose. This is Chris. How's the weather there?" He paused. "That's great. May I speak to Tess, please?" Another pause. "Oh, can you have her call me when she returns?" He stood quietly. His face paled, then turned stark white. "What do you mean, she's not there? She left here to visit you last Thursday." Another pause. "When was the last time you spoke to her?" His breathing grew quick and shallow. "Please tell her to call me when you hear from her."

Meg grabbed the doctor's shoulders and led him to an air-conditioning unit positioned on the ground next to the building. "Sit down before you fall," she instructed, then whistled and motioned toward the crime scene for help.

A young officer with dark hair and a mustache approached them. "Yes?"

"It sounds like the doc's wife's gone missing." Roxie shook her head. "Poor thing."

The rough edge to the woman's voice made it difficult to detect sincerity in her tone, although she did say she liked Tess.

"We're concerned because she's also a member of our board," Andi added.

Luke and the officer had already discussed the possibility of someone targeting the board, so he clearly understood the gravity of the situation.

The officer removed a spiral notebook from his breast pocket. "Your name, sir?"

Doctor Owens spent five minutes answering questions. Meg stood over him, watching him with concern. Roxie watched him with interest.

Luke rubbed his chin. *If there is a serial killer targeting the board, the odds were against finding Tess alive. Andi had interviewed Reverend Nichols. What if the police were right in suspecting him? He had the strongest ties to Bernice and Helen. He also spent time on the board with Harry and Tess.*

Meg patted the vet's shoulder. "They'll find her, Doc. She probably decided to spend time with a friend before heading to her mother's."

"She wouldn't have felt the need to if I hadn't been so stupid." Tears welled in the man's eyes. "We had a horrible argument over golf. Can you believe it? Golf."

That caught everyone's interest, including Luke's. They stood still, quietly waiting for him to explain.

Doctor Owens pressed his thumb and finger beneath his eyes as if trying to push back the tears. "I renewed my membership at the country club," he continued, "and she found the paperwork. Tess is normally a soft-spoken woman, but not that night. She threw a fit, said I spent too much time and money at the golf course." He turned to Meg, the person showing the most empathy. "She'd already planned this trip to visit her mother. I figured she'd spend time with family, calm down, and everything would go back to normal once she returned."

"You didn't think to call to make sure she made it to her mother's house?" The officer asked.

The vet hung his head low. "I know I should have, but she was so angry." He turned his attention back to the officer before continuing. "She wouldn't let me drive her to the airport, said she'd take the shuttle. She didn't want me doing anything for her." He wiped away the tears that managed to escape. "She said she never wanted to see me again. It seemed like no matter what I said, I made things worse. I thought it best to give her time to cool off."

The officer studied him. "Did you see her get into the shuttle?"

"No," Doctor Owens reluctantly admitted. "I couldn't get our argument out of my head and I had to perform surgery on a Great Dane the next day, so I took a sleeping pill and went to bed. When I woke, she wasn't in our home and her suitcase was gone. I assumed she'd left for the airport as planned." He turned to Meg with tears glazing his eyes. "I should have called. If anything's happened to her, I don't know what I will do. She's my life."

Roxie patted his knee. "Don't worry, sweetie. I'm sure she's alive and well. She just left you, that's all."

The color drained from his face again. That option didn't sit well either.

SEVEN

Luke looked good standing in her doorway. Correction, he looked great! He filled out a polo shirt and faded jeans better than any man she'd ever met before. The fact he'd brought pizza from her favorite Italian restaurant didn't hurt his case.

"Is that an I'm-sorry-I-sent-you-violation-letters pizza?" Andi took a whiff of what she hoped was a decadent, thick crust, stick-to-your-thighs supreme pie.

"No. It's an I-thought-you-might-be-hungry pizza." He stepped around her to enter the condo, then stood in the foyer as if waiting for her next move. "Packing is a huge job. I'm here to lend a hand."

"Lend a hand? Of course, moving means packing and since I just unpacked, sort of, I guess I would be *repacking*."

It'd been barely three hours since Meg told her she had fired up the rumor mill. Her new friends knew her bank account couldn't afford any more fines, so after Harry dumped trash on her porch, Meg and Roxie came up with the bright idea of telling everyone Andi was moving. They hoped Harry would back off with the violation letters long enough for them to prove he was the murderer. Not that any of them had any real evidence pointing in his direction. They just *wanted* him to be guilty.

It was kind of Roxie and Meg to want to help her, but she hated being less than honest. She should have told them no, but the plan had already been set into motion. Watching Luke carry the pizza to the dining room table, she realized no one had considered Luke's possible reaction to hearing the news.

I should have, but I didn't. Now what?

Luke set the pizza down on the dining room table and the enticing aroma beckoned. "I told Harry you were moving. Hopefully, now he'll stop sending violation letters."

"*You* told him?" She wanted Harry to find out, but certainly hadn't expected Luke to be the one to tell him. She wondered how often they got together to discuss the community—and just how much information Luke chose to share.

"Of course I told him. You want him off your back, don't you?" Luke waited for her answer.

"Yeah . . . I want him off my back." She pictured the two men talking, and it didn't sit well with her. For now it would probably be best if she kept the truth to herself. Telling him would place him in an uncomfortable position as the property manager. And she was a bit afraid he might let it slip to Harry that she wasn't really moving.

Andi glanced about the room. Two boxes, left unpacked in the kitchen, gave the story she was moving a touch of validity. But since her stomach clenched with the thought of lying, it would be best to change the conversation. She reached for the pizza and pulled back the lid. "A supreme. You remembered what I like."

"Sugar cookies. You remembered what *I* like." He

reached across the table to remove the clear plastic from the plate of frosted bats. "The Halloween spirit still gotcha?"

"I call them Bloodsucking Harries."

He chuckled and bit off a wing. "Funny, yet tasty."

At least he hadn't lost his sense of humor. "I added extra vanilla," she revealed.

He gave her an appreciative look, then bit off the other wing. A mischievous twinkle lit his eyes. The chemistry between them begged her to forgive all, be his friend, and hope that one day he would want more.

Self-preservation made her turn to the pizza. She snatched a slice and then plopped onto a dining room chair. "I thought about what you said before. I'm surprised you want to be friends. It's not like I've made your life easy since I moved to Euphoria."

"Harry's enough to get anyone riled up."

She sunk her teeth into the pizza's thick, chewy crust and enjoyed a huge bite. For two seconds it took her mind off her troubles.

"I hope you noticed that isn't just any old pizza. It's a Double Meat Lover's Supreme with *extra* pepperoni." He slid onto the chair next to her.

Andi nodded her approval as she chewed.

"I'm hoping I earned extra points for remembering what you like?" He lifted a brow.

She shrugged and swallowed. "I guess I can spare a few points, but don't be in a hurry to cash them in. I still don't like the idea that you work for the enemy."

"Once you move, it won't matter who I work for."

"Right . . ."

He selected a slice of pizza and, just like old times, his awkward smile touched her heart. The last time they had eaten together, they had been stretched out on the carpet in front of the television. Back then, life was simpler. They watched horror flicks or talked for hours and knew everything about each other. He even knew that Jessie was a police officer—a fact he still hadn't mentioned, and she was too afraid to bring up, hoping he'd forgotten.

"Roxie confirmed that you're working for a detective," Luke said, as if reading her mind—and ignoring the fact she had told him it was none of his business.

"Part-time. You know what it's like on a teacher's salary."

"Does your boss think he can clear Bernice's son?" Luke said it more like an accusation than a question.

Andi placed her slice on the edge of the closed box. "You don't think Reverend Nichols is innocent?"

"I'm not sure. On the one hand, reverends rarely turn into serial killers. It sounds more like a plot in a B-rated horror flick. On the other hand, he started acting strange after Helen left him."

"Strange?"

He looked at her as if she had to be joking. "You saw his condo. He turned a bachelor pad with minimal furnishings into a thirteen-hundred-square-foot monastery."

His condo *had* made her feel guilty for not attending church in a long time. "Maybe he's hoping the biblical statues will fill his heart with God's love where Helen left a gaping hole."

"Or . . . he could be seeking God's forgiveness."

"Perhaps. We haven't found any proof to exonerate him." Deciding napkins and plates would be a good idea, she scooted the chair back and headed to the kitchen. "Harry has photos of Nichols snooping around his car about the same time someone cut his brakes." She spoke louder so Luke could hear. "We know this because the picture had a date and time stamp. At least that is what I was told."

"It's strange that Harry would accuse the reverend. They've known each other for years, even shared holiday meals. Harry and Bernice were thick as thieves."

Thieves. They were thieves, all right. They stole from their neighbors by manufacturing violations.

Andi removed two paper plates from the stack in the cupboard, grabbed a handful of napkins from a kitchen drawer, and a couple of orange sodas from the fridge. "What if Harry is trying to misdirect the police investigation?"

"You still think Harry killed Bernice?"

"I'm asking *you*." Returning to the dining room, she handed him a plate and soda, then tossed the napkins onto the table between them.

"Thanks." He finished his slice of pizza and then pulled the tab on the can. "Harry may be stubborn and vindictive, but he's not a murderer."

"Anyone can commit murder under the right circumstances." At least that was what her sister kept telling her. "To tell you the truth, I think I just want Harry to be guilty. Anyone in this complex could have killed her. Most of them had motive and opportunity."

His facial expression tightened, growing as serious as she felt. "I hardly think a violation letter is motive for murder."

"Not just letters—fines." She tried to explain it so he would understand. "All I know is how angry I felt every time I received a violation letter. This is my new home. It should be a safe haven, but Harry keeps eating away at my sense of security."

"But you signed—"

Andi lifted her hand like a stop sign. "You don't get it. It doesn't matter that I signed a piece of paper agreeing to follow some rules. In fact, it makes the situation worse. I went through a lot of trouble to make sure I followed the rules, and I *still* received violation letters."

"Trouble?"

"The rules state that we have to park the first car in the garage, the second in the driveway, and only then can we park a car in guest parking. Since my sister comes home late and sleeps in, she has to call me at three in the morning and wake me up so I can pull my car out of the garage and she can pull in. My car needs to be in the driveway since I go to work before her."

"Why don't you just switch them yourself in the morning when you go to work?"

"Where can I park her car while I pull mine out?"

He leaned back in his chair, contemplating her question. "I see your point. If you park *her* car in guest parking or the fire lane while you drive *yours* out of the garage, you're breaking a rule."

She nodded, glad he was finally listening to her. "And I don't want to wake her when she's been asleep for only a couple of hours, so I crawl out of bed in the middle of the night to rearrange cars."

"I can see how that would upset you," he conceded, his voice low. "But you wouldn't kill someone over it."

"That's not all. Throughout the day, I constantly have to stop and ask myself if I'm breaking a rule. I can't just toss the box the soda cans come in. I have to put it in a bag first. If a bird targets the hood of my car, I can't whip out the hose for a quick cleaning. Those blasted birds drop their bombs on my hood every single day, but I can't put a wind chime in the tree to scare them off. When friends or relatives come to visit, I have to make sure they park in the driveway if Jessie isn't home, and then I have to check for oil stains when they leave. If anyone visits for more than three days, I have to notify the board or they'll tow their car. My life revolves around making sure all the rules are followed, and to top it off, I'm always looking over my shoulder for a board member with a camera. This is no way to live."

"Then Harry lies about the oil stain on your driveway anyway."

"Correct. But even before that, I knew he was watching my every move. I've lived here only a week. I can only imagine how some of the other residents feel. Over time, these fines could drive anyone into a state of rage. Look at the cowboy."

Luke nodded. "And Harry's gotten worse since he became president. I can throw out fines that are not legitimate, but if the residents break the rules he has every right to send them letters and eventually fine them if they refuse to stop. And there isn't anything that says he can't check every hour for violations." He shook his head with regret. "I keep hoping he'll go back to being a decent guy now that Valerie's moving in with him, or at least have more to do with his time than walk the property checking for violations."

"Forgive me if I don't hold my breath. Did the Euphoria Lane rumor mill tell you Harry threw trash on my porch this morning?"

Luke's brow furrowed. He didn't know. "Are you sure it was him?"

"Yes, and I'm going to prove it. I was going to try and match his fingerprints to those on the bag, but he was smart enough not to leave any." She retrieved a tiny surveillance camera she found when she helped her sister clean at Lenny's Detective Agency earlier that day. "Then I found this. I'm going to install it out back tonight."

"You know that's—"

"Don't you dare tell me it's against the rules, Luke Ryder. Harry is behind this. I'm going to prove it, and nothing is going to get in my way."

"I was going to say it's difficult to install." He examined the box. "I can put it up for you. I'll hide it where Harry will never look."

"You'd do that for me? Why?"

"Like I said, I want to be friends again. I'm hoping this . . . gesture will prove I'm serious."

"What if you get caught?"

"I won't." He slid the chair back as he stood. "Got a tool kit?"

Guilt ate at her again. He had offered to install a camera for her without knowing she was keeping the truth from him. "Luke, you've done enough bringing the pizza. I'll take care of this myself."

"I want to help." Conviction backed his words. He made quick work of opening the box and removing the directions.

"There's something you need to know before you decide to help."

"You're not really moving." His smiled turned devious.

She jumped to her feet. "How did you know?"

"The Andi Stevenson I know would never run from a fight. It's not your style. On the other hand, that rumor is definitely Meg and Roxie's style." He lifted the soda to his lips and drank, the grin never quite leaving his face. "I knew you would tell me the truth before the evening was over."

She wasn't sure if she should be angry or relieved. "Meg and Roxie are trying to help. They feel bad about Harry trashing my place after they started the anti-board."

"They spied on him in the privacy of his bedroom," Luke added.

"We are all guilty of that." She lifted her brow to punctuate the comment. "Even you."

"True, but I was doing my job. Now, where's your tool kit?"

Luke really was that good guy she knew back in

college. "Wait here."

Inside the garage, Andi gripped the toolbox, struggling to accept being friends with the man she still loved . . . deep down inside. Lifting the heavy box, she gathered her wits about her. When she returned to the dining room, she found Luke hauling her kitchen two-step ladder out to the back porch. She set her toolbox down on the cement, then eased onto a patio chair where she could watch him play handyman. It had been a long time since she'd enjoyed watching any man work. The fact the man on her porch was Luke Ryder felt surreal.

Luke turned to position the ladder, and she noticed the way his jeans hugged his muscular thighs and backside. Her pulse quickened. She tried to turn away. Really, she did, but her head only tilted to the side so she could get a better view.

He glanced over his shoulder. "Can you hand me that screwdriver?"

Afraid he had caught her staring, she jumped up, grabbed the tool, and handed it over. She berated herself for staring at him instead of doing something more productive. A thought occurred to her. "Why would anyone want to kill Helen? It's not like she's an active member of the board from what I hear."

"The murderer might not care how active or inactive the board members are."

"True."

"Unless the murderer is Reverend Nichols," he said softly, as if not wanting any of the neighbors to overhear. "Helen left him after he gave up his church."

"True." Her heart weighed down like a boulder planted in her chest. She felt sorry for the both of them and hated to think a man of the cloth would turn to murder to even the score.

"Done." Luke admired his work and stepped down from the ladder. "Follow me and I'll show you how the system works." He led Andi back into the living room with his hand placed gently on her lower back.

It had been a long time since he'd guided her into a room with a gentle touch. She missed the feeling, the sense of protectiveness.

Luke, seemingly unaware of the power he had over her, bent over the laptop she'd left on her coffee table. A few quick strokes of the keypad and her porch appeared on her monitor. "You need to stop using the same password."

"I don't have anything for anyone to steal—it all belongs to the board now."

His deep brown eyes darkened. "Why don't I hang around awhile—in case Harry shows up? I don't want you confronting him by yourself."

Is he hoping to spend the entire evening together?

If they were going to establish a friendship and nothing more, she could take Luke only in short increments of time. Deep down she wanted him back, but she knew it was impossible. The reasons they broke up hadn't changed. She still kept her sisters' secrets—like the fact Jessie owned Lenny's Detective Agency. "Thanks for the offer, but I can handle things myself."

"If you're sure . . ." He looked at her with obvious doubt.

"I am. What I'm not certain about is your change of heart. I have trouble accepting that you suddenly want to be friends. When you left me, you said you never wanted to see me again. That it would be too painful."

"I know." Regret flickered in his eyes. "I let my pride get in the way. I thought I had done the right thing, but seeing you again . . ." He shook his head. "I realize I was too unyielding."

"I never thought I'd hear those words."

"I'm simply admitting I shouldn't have said I never wanted to see you again. I took it too far. I admit that.

There's no reason we can't spend time together."

"*If* I ignore the fact you work for Harry."

"I just put up a spy camera. That should be worth at least a thousand brownie points, don't you think?"

She angled her head and smirked. "999."

"I'm going to take that and run before you change your mind." He patted her shoulder like an older brother might.

His touch was light and comforting, but her heart yearned for more.

How had this happened? One moment I'm moving into a new community, dreaming of making cookies in my new oven, and the next minute I'm fighting the HOA president and solving a murder while trying to figure out how my old flame fits into my new life.

Luke was even trying to help her. For now. Until he discovered she was keeping family secrets again. This was getting too complicated. She knew herself well enough to know she was already falling for him again. She should put a halt to the whole friendship idea, but she knew she wasn't strong enough.

What was that definition of insanity again? Oh, yeah. Doing the same thing over and over while expecting a different result.

Following Luke to his car, Andi spotted a cream-colored envelope tucked under his windshield wiper. Her name showed in big, block letters.

"It's for you," he said, yanking the envelope free and handing it to her.

"An envelope for *me* on *your* windshield?" The words VIOLATION LETTER caught her eye. "It's from Harry," she said, handing it back to him. "So much for thinking he'd lighten up when he heard I was moving."

Luke read, "Photographic evidence of litter on the porch."

She gritted her teeth and then swallowed a string of

expletives before daring to speak. "He set me up. He dumped the trash and took a picture." Taking a deep breath, she remembered the camera out back. "*I'll* have the photographic evidence next time."

Luke ripped the letter in half, proving he was taking her side. "I hope you catch him in the act."

"He left it on your car on purpose." She scanned the shrubbery and trees for any sign of Harry. "He's telling us he knows you're spending time with me."

Luke followed her gaze out into the darkness. "Let me worry about Harry."

****

Fifteen minutes later, Luke found himself standing in the center of Helen's spotless living room with Andi, Meg, and Roxie. Black leather sofas sat perpendicular on the plush white carpet with a gleaming glass coffee table nestled near both.

He dropped several of Andi's empty, flattened packing boxes near an oak bookcase, thinking it was as good a place to start packing as any. Roxie had volunteered their services when Helen refused to return to her home until after the murderer was caught. The two happened to be good friends. Luke never could see what the flamboyant, retired hairdresser and conservative college professor had in common.

According to Helen, the police found peanut bits at the bottom of her liquid coffee creamer bottle. The killer was someone who knew she was highly allergic to peanuts. That eliminated the possibility that he or she was a stranger. No wonder the woman didn't want to come back to Euphoria.

Luke took in his surroundings. Several silver-framed photos scattered throughout the living room displayed Helen and the reverend holding each other at holiday gatherings. It was hard for him to believe that man, who appeared to be so happy, was the same man who had turned his home into his own monastery. Luke had tried not to gawk when he entered the reverend's home a few months ago to check on a report of water damage. The previous year it had resembled any other single man's home. It basically contained a sofa, coffee table, and big-screen television set.

"They looked very happy together." Andi pointed to a photograph of Helen kissing the reverend's cheek.

Meg sighed. "They were. I used to pass them on their evening stroll down to the lake. They were always holding hands. He would watch her toss bread crumbs to the ducks, and I could swear he was so much in love he glowed."

Roxie moved to the bar and poured herself a glass of bourbon. "Once his congregation found out they were going to lose donations from Helen's former boyfriend, everything went to hell and Bernice stepped in to make it worse."

Luke began assembling packing boxes, ready to hear the parts of the story he didn't already know. "How did Bernice make it worse?"

Meg accepted the box Luke handed to her, her expression grim. "Bernice convinced Helen to leave Reverend Nichols at the altar. She told Helen that her son loved his church and, with time, would grow to resent and hate her for taking that life away from him. Bernice went on to tell her that his new job—counseling teens—would never fill the void left by losing his flock."

Luke knew what it was like to have a void you could never fill. His gaze fell on Andi. She listened intently as she helped Meg pack books. Her expression reflected the melancholy mood the story elicited. There were nights when he missed her so much he questioned his decision to break up.

Did I try hard enough to get her to open up back then? He wasn't so sure anymore.

Roxie swallowed a swig of bourbon. "To send her point home, Bernice showed Helen pictures of the reverend smiling while he worked church events, followed by a picture taken the day he left his church. I can tell you he wasn't smiling. The before-and-after pictures were too much for Helen to take. She decided right then to break up." Roxie shook her head in disgust. "Bernice was a piece of work, I tell you. I bet she's giving the devil lessons on how to be mean and spiteful."

"I knew Helen taught religious studies—I never knew that included voodoo." Meg lifted a book on the practice in New Orleans. "Hey, Andi, do you think this might help us fight Harry?"

Andi shrugged. "If you're into that sort of thing. Let me know if you find a Get-Harry-to-Move-Away curse."

Roxie rolled her eyes. "I vote for some old fashioned butt whippin'."

"Speaking of Harry, Paul put their condo up for sale." Meg set the book on the coffee table next to her can of soda. "I also heard he made an appointment with a divorce lawyer."

"Bet he's wishing it wasn't a community property state," Andi answered. "Valerie will get fifty percent of their assets."

Roxie snorted. "She doesn't deserve a penny. That boy should have opened his eyes and divorced her years ago."

Luke had always suspected that Paul knew deep down that his wife was bound to leave him, but didn't want to face the fact.

Did Andi suspect I was going to break up with her back in college? Or did it come as a shock? He hated to think about how much he had hurt her.

"So who do you think killed Bernice and attempted to kill Helen?" Meg placed another book in the box and then closed the flaps.

"Don't forget Harry," Andi said. "Someone cut his brakes."

"No one cares about Harry," Meg and Roxie answered in unison.

"I'll bet you fifty dollars the cowboy did it," Roxie said, tossing Meg a roll of packing tape.

"My money's on Harry," Meg answered. "He's wanted to be the association president for years. Right, Luke? I bet he killed Bernice and Tess saw the whole thing. Now that poor woman is out there running for her life, too afraid to call her husband to let him know where she is hiding."

Wait a minute.

Luke tossed books on Eastern religions into a box. "What makes you think Tess witnessed Bernice's murder?"

"It's a theory," Andi explained.

"All right. What about motive?" Luke dared to point out. "Why would either man try to kill Helen?"

Meg sealed her box shut. "Maybe Helen found evidence linking Harry to Bernice's death. I bet he cut his own brakes to throw suspicion off himself."

"Could be." Andi took the roll of tape from her friend and placed it gently on the glass table, next to the voodoo book.

Luke hauled the filled boxes to the door. A few minutes later, they started work on the kitchen. Roxie sat at the table to finish her drink. Luke chose the cupboard containing the plates and saucers. He separated a sheet of newspaper from the piles he found in the recycling bin and wrapped it around a navy-blue plate.

Meg sat on her knees in front of the cupboard beneath the sink. "We should put the cleansers in a plastic bin. They are bound to fall over and spill." She held silver polish in one hand and liquid car cleaner in the other.

Roxie leaned forward as she squinted. "Is that soap biodegradable?"

Luke realized he must have reacted to the statement, because the older woman glared at him while wagging her finger.

"You think I don't care about the environment?" Roxie asked.

"I hadn't thought about it before," he confessed. He never thought Roxie cared about anything other than her friends and family.

She removed a cigarette from the left side of her bra and a lighter from the right side. "I care about the fish in the pond," the woman insisted while lighting up. "Fish don't send fines or violation letters."

Andi turned to Luke. "Does the drain in the street lead to the pond?"

"As a matter of fact, it does." Luke glanced at the car cleaner Meg held. "There's nothing wrong with the aerator, so it must be some sort of chemical killing off the fish. Car wash products contain chemicals, but I wouldn't place the blame on Helen. She isn't the only one who washes her car around here, even if it is against the rules."

Meg studied the detergent in her hand. "Nope. Helen did not kill Nemo. My nephew could safely drink this stuff and only burp bubbles."

Roxie chuckled, which forced bourbon out her nose. She slapped her hand over her face and ashes from her cigarette flew across the table.

That woman ought to consider giving up at least one of her vices.

Luke couldn't get the dead fish out of his mind. It couldn't be a coincidence that Bernice was murdered and suddenly there were also dead fish floating in the pond. He didn't believe in coincidences.

Andi glanced up at him. "You mean to tell me if someone cleaned their driveway with bleach and hosed it off, those chemicals would work their way down the street, into the drain, then into the lake, where they would kill the fish?"

"The chemicals would kill only the fish they first came into direct contact with, before diluting," Luke explained. "There's a lot of water in the lake, or pond, or whatever you want to call it."

Roxie grinned. "You want to clean Harry's car with bleach?"

"Ladies . . ." Luke warned.

"I'd probably end up burning my eyes with it, anyway." Andi glanced at the cover of the book on voodoo. She obviously found it intriguing. "I was just thinking out loud."

"I know what's on your mind." Meg placed the cleanser in a wash tub she pulled out from under the sink. "The murderer may have killed Bernice somewhere on the property and cleaned up the blood with bleach, right?"

"It's a possibility," Andi agreed. "All I know for sure is there are dead fish in the pond." She opened the pantry door, ready to fill another box.

Luke selected another plate to wrap. "I'll tell the police about the fish, just in case the killer did clean up the crime scene."

EIGHT

Saturday morning Andi awoke on the living room sofa. Her last memory was of watching the computer monitor and listening intently for noise outside. She jumped up and rushed to the sliding-glass door, ignoring the multiple kinks in her neck, back, and side from sleeping on cushions instead of a mattress. A feeling of panic overtook her. A fluttering sound signaled trouble even before she pushed aside the blinds.

She felt her eyes widen involuntarily. Pigeons and birdseed blanketed the patio from one end to the other. The pesky flock cooed between pecking at the seeds littering the cement floor. One larger bird pushed aside the smaller ones. They fluttered their wings and flew to perch on the decorative railings built into the three-foot-tall wall surrounding her porch. That was when she noticed the droppings covering every exposed surface.

"No!" Rushing back to the computer, she cursed under her breath. It took just seconds to rewind the footage captured by the camera to the spot where the birdseed fell out of a large, plastic baggie. She let the recording rewind for another second or two and then pushed "Play" again.

A hooded figure in black, hiding behind a dark umbrella, emptied five quart-size baggies on her porch and then ran. He must have known about the camera. Why else would he hide behind an umbrella? It was a smart move—she had to give him that. With the umbrella there, she couldn't see much. She couldn't even tell if the person who threw the trash was a man or woman, young or old, thin or fat. But she knew it was Harry. It had to be. Anger grew in her gut.

How had he found out about the camera? Did he have his own camera hidden out back?

She marched to the back porch and scanned the trees, bushes, and brick wall that surrounded the complex. She saw nothing. That didn't mean there wasn't one out there.

Not ready to tackle the mess on the porch, she scooped coffee grinds into the coffee maker. While the machine huffed and puffed, she scanned her pantry shelves. She had never baked this early in the morning before, but there was always a first time.

Andi picked up but then set back the cardboard cylinder containing oatmeal on her pantry shelf. "I'm not in the mood for oatmeal cookies." She shoved the olive oil aside and found a bottle of light corn syrup. "Something sweet might keep me from murdering Harry." Since she'd moved into Euphoria Lane, the need to bake to settle her nerves grew daily. Unfortunately, leisurely activities had taken a backseat to the war with Harry and her work for Lenny's Detective Agency. "What should I bake?"

"Talking to yourself again?" Jessie's tired voice sounded from the kitchen, just around the corner from the pantry.

"If I talk to myself I am always assured of an intelligent conversation," Andi answered, then joined her sister in the kitchen.

"If you say so." Jessie smirked and went about pouring herself a glass of milk. She wore her favorite sleeping attire: a Cardinals jersey and shorts. "Baking again?"

"Once I figure out what I want to make." She glanced down at the plastic box marked "Christmas Cookie Cutters." "I know. I'll make little, ugly gingerbread men that look like Harry and then bite off their heads."

"Ah, you found Harry's present on the porch." Jessie gulped the milk from the glass. "Save some of those Harry cookies for me. I'd like to bite off a limb or two." Jessie rinsed her glass and placed it in the dishwasher. "I gather Harry's trying to get us to move because you started the anti-board."

"*I* didn't start the anti-board," Andi said, her agitation growing with each passing minute.

"You inspired it by having the audacity to fight back. I bet no one ever fought back before."

"Only once or twice, and they paid the price. Harry's giving me a lot more credit than I deserve. I barely helped fight back. Meg took off running with the ball and then passed it to Roxie." The idea of that eccentric old woman, who apparently had no boundaries, being in charge of the anti-board was probably scaring Harry to death. It frightened Andi because she paid for everything they did.

"Harry probably thinks he can regain control of the community if he can get you to move, you instigator."

"Yeah, that's me—a horrible instigator." Andi pulled the sugar and flour canisters to the center of the kitchen counter. She was still determined not to tell Jessie that Harry also wanted them to move because he thought Jessie was a drug-dealing hooker.

"I'm going back to bed," Jessie announced. "But first, I need to ask a favor."

Andi resisted the urge to sigh. She really needed some downtime. "Can I make my cookies first?"

"Sure. I need you to question a few of the parishioners from the reverend's former church. I received an anonymous message at the detective agency from a woman who thinks the reverend's former girlfriend, Helen, is the real killer. Whoever left the message used a church phone. It came up on my Caller ID."

"What about the porch?"

"I'll take care of the porch later." Jessie yawned loud and long. "I made you a list of questions and left them on the kitchen table. It'll be easier than making those cookies look creepy enough to resemble Harry. You'll see. Now, don't forget to save me a few of those gingerbread men," she said on her way to the living room.

"I'll save you a whole plateful." Andi inspected the gingerbread man cookie cutter. "I bet I could turn you into a HOA president voodoo doll." She snickered at the thought before prying open the flour canister.

****

Luke hopped into the passenger side of Andi's Mustang before she could protest. "I'm glad I caught you before you left. I was just out back, checking on your porch."

"Then you saw the pigeons and the birdseed." Her expression twisted from one of surprise at seeing him to one of disgust.

"And the bird droppings." She had to be ready to shoot Harry. Roxie would gladly draw a target on his chest for her. "I hope the camera caught a great picture of him creating that mess." Luke wanted that man off the HOA board almost as much as Andi did.

"No such luck. He hid behind an umbrella. I swear he had to have known about the camera."

They should have known Harry would cover his tracks. "He might have just been cautious. We'll figure out a way to catch him, you'll see." He buckled up the passenger side seatbelt. "So, where are we off to?"

"We?"

"Yes, we. There's a murderer running around here. Consider me your bodyguard."

"I hardly need a bodyguard to question parishioners at Nichols's former church."

"Sure you do." He patted the dashboard. "Let's go." He resisted chuckling at her annoyed expression.

How can I explain that I just want to spend time with her?

The reverend's former church turned out to be a quaint wood-and-lattice building in need of a coat of fresh paint. Folding tables covered the lawn and women of all ages were decorating them with linens and trays. A sign leaning against the bushes read "Bake Sale. Support the Church Renovation Fund."

Luke stuck to Andi's side as she strolled over to a young woman covering a long table with an enormous cloth.

"Here, let me help you with that." Andi took a corner of the freshly washed, white linen from the blonde wearing a lilac sundress with a dark-purple ribbon tied in a bow at her waist. She handed Luke the other corner.

"Thanks." The woman stepped around the corner of the table. They stood at opposite ends. "I haven't seen you before. If you are here for the bake sale, you're early."

"Early bird gets the worm," Andi said with a bright smile that quickly turned into a cringe that said she just remembered the mess on her patio. "Or in this case, homemade brownies."

Luke remained silent, wondering how Andi would work Reverend Nichols and Helen into the conversation. On the way over, Andi told Luke she needed to know what the congregation was saying about their former members now that they were gone. Did they have information that would make them think Nichols or Helen killed Bernice? He heard about Helen's former boyfriend. Could the millionaire have arranged for Bernice's death and framed the reverend for the ultimate revenge?

Perhaps I should ask a question or two of my own.

The pleasant young woman smoothed the wrinkles out of the cloth. "You've come to the right place. Mrs. Cox makes walnut brownies that are to die for." She gestured toward a table near a large paloverde tree. "She's the woman in the apron with the bun in her hair."

If this woman didn't know Reverend Nichols, the gray-haired, brownie lady might. "How long have you been attending church here?" he asked, unable to stay out of the conversation.

Andi shot him a warning look.

"About . . ." the woman's lifted her gaze upward to the sky, as if asking God for help remembering. "Four months."

"So you heard about Reverend Nichols and why he had to leave?" Andi sighed, as if the reverend's plight was so sad.

The young woman shook her head. "Not the details."

"Did you ever meet Helen?" Andi leaned closer to the parishioner. "I heard it was all her fault."

Nervous, she glanced over her shoulder at the other women preparing for the sale, as if she didn't want them to overhear. "I don't know whose fault it was. The first week I was here, someone said the whole ordeal was scandalous, but someone else said he left to get married. The women who run the church haven't taken me into their confidence. Whenever his name comes up, they form the sign of the cross and pray."

"The women here are cliquish, huh?" Andi nodded her head knowingly.

The woman rolled her eyes. "Worse than high school. I help with every fund-raiser and they still treat me like an outsider."

Andi nodded again, smoothed out a wrinkle in the tablecloth, and glanced across the lawn. "Those brownies over there are calling my name."

Luke followed, impressed by her ability to get the woman to tell what she knew, even if it wasn't much.

"You're not going to tell me what really happened either," the woman complained as they walked away. Her voice revealed her frustration at once again being left out of the loop.

Feeling sorry for the young woman, Luke noticed how Andi acted as if she hadn't heard the plea and strolled across the lawn. It wasn't like her to ignore anyone. Detective work couldn't be easy for her. Ready to assist in a new approach, he pulled a twenty-dollar bill out of his jeans pocket and handed it to Andi. By the time they reached the brownie lady, the woman had her table set up and was ready for business.

Andi pointed to the plate of brownies with her twenty. "I'll take those."

The woman with the bun in her hair removed the plastic wrap from the brownies. "How many would you like?"

"The whole plate." Andi lifted a brow. "Do you have a bag? I want a little of everything." She placed her arm around Luke's shoulder. "I have a hungry man here."

The feel of her arm on his back left Luke wanting to pull her close, but he managed to resist. Instead, he pointed to the chocolate-chip cookies. "Don't forgot those, sweetie."

"Of course." She patted his shoulder. "They're your favorites."

And they were.

The brownie lady's smile turned warm and genuine. "I have enough bags to hold the entire table."

The not-so-subtle hint wasn't lost on Luke, but he wasn't going to give in so easily, not unless the woman planned to talk like a parrot. He pointed to the lemon tarts. "We'll take three of those."

The woman reached under the table and brought up a brown paper sack with a grocery store imprint on the side. First she placed the plate of brownies on the bottom, then she added the lemon tarts.

Andi pointed to the chocolate-chip cookies. "Half dozen of those." She appeared nonchalant as the woman worked. "I'm going to miss Reverend Nichols. I can't get over the fact he left."

The woman's smile faded. She eyed Andi over her wire-framed glasses. "Reverend Morris is nice. You'll like him in due time." She placed the decadent desserts in the bag. "What else?"

"Half a dozen peanut butter cookies." She pointed to a plastic plate nestled against a pecan pie. They appeared to be a bit on the dry side. A great peanut butter cookie needed to be moist and chewy.

"Half a dozen coming up."

"I ran into Helen recently," Andi said, scanning the contents of the table. "She looked tired."

Tired was an understatement. Helen looked like a zombie.

"She should take a vacation." The woman stiffened her posture, her dislike for Helen more than evident. "Is there anything else you'd like?"

Not if you're not going to talk. Luke hoisted the bag into his arms.

"I was just wondering if you know how Helen's old

boyfriend is doing," Andi said. "Is he still raging mad over the breakup?"

"No, he's not. He's found a lovely new fiancée. Not that it is any of your business," the woman snapped.

Luke was quickly getting used to sticking his nose in other people's business. In this case, it paid off. The millionaire was most likely not their murderer.

Andi glared at him while handing the woman his twenty. She held out her palm until the woman reluctantly handed over her change. After leaving the table, Andi scanned the sale. "Who looks like they have a loose tongue? We need someone to spill their guts about Helen and Reverend Nichols."

"Let's take a cookie break." Luke found a cement bench on the side of the building. He dug eagerly into the bag while Andi reluctantly joined him. "You need a new game plan," he said.

"I know. I'm new at all of this." She reached for the lemon tart he handed to her.

They had just settled into quietly eating the sugary confections when he heard two women speaking around the corner of the building.

"I bet that girl was another one of those nosy reporters," the brownie lady said in a disgusted tone.

Luke lifted his fingers to his lips, suggesting they both remain quiet.

The voice that answered sounded high-pitched. "Did you tell her anything?"

"Of course not, Agnes. You can't trust the press and the police already think Reverend Nichols killed his mother."

"We both know he would never hurt a fly. He helped my Joey turn his back on a life of crime. You know he shoplifted those candy bars. Who knows what he would have done next if Reverend Nichols hadn't talked to him? He also paid for Gracie's wheelchair when she couldn't afford it."

"Who could forget?" the brownie lady said, "but the police don't know him the way we do. We have to protect him."

Protect him? I thought his church had turned on him?

"This is all Helen's fault," Agnes replied. "She turned him away from his good work."

"You may be right, Agnes. I think she killed the reverend's mother. I heard his mother convinced Helen to break up with him, and then when she changed her mind, he was too hurt to take her back." After a pregnant silence the brownie woman added, "My husband told me that the reverend hired a detective agency. I called the owner and told him to look into Helen. I'm not going to let the reverend pay for a crime she committed."

If the brownie lady's theory was correct, then Helen put peanuts into her own coffee creamer to keep the police from suspecting her. Since she carried an EpiPen with her, she wasn't really putting her own life in danger. She could have seen the medical students out front through her window and timed it perfectly.

"Do you have proof Helen killed his mother?" Agnes asked.

"No, but the detective will find proof. Helen has to be guilty. There is no way Reverend Nichols killed his mother. It's not possible."

"I tried to convince the reverend not to leave the church, but he wouldn't listen." Sadness laced Agnes's words. "He knew too many people blamed him for losing the money needed for the renovation project."

"I believe Mr. Money Bucks would have left the church anyway, to avoid seeing Helen," the brownie lady replied in a matter-of-fact tone. "In any case, we owe it to the reverend to steer nosy reporters away from the church. Without their interference, the police will eventually catch the real killer."

"True, and once Helen is behind bars, we can all relax."

****

Back home, Andi strolled down the street toward the pond. Their trip to the church uncovered only another theory, no real facts. The women there wanted Helen to be guilty because they liked the reverend. Not unlike the fact that she wanted Harry to be guilty because she couldn't stand him.

She hated to admit it, but she missed Luke. He had promised his mother he would take her shopping for a new dining room set. A smile tugged at her lips. He was such a good son. His mother probably had no idea that Luke put up with the likes of Harry just so he could buy a house with a mother's cottage. The other men she had dated would never want their mother to live near them, let alone out back nestled in a cottage.

Her thoughts returned to her mission. She had no idea what she expected to find at the pond. She knew only that her gut kept telling her the dead fish held the key to the mystery. According to Jessie, the police were convinced Bernice was killed in her condo. If the murderer did not kill her elsewhere, move the body, then clean the crime scene with bleach, why were the fish dying? Luke said there was nothing wrong with the aerator located in the center of the pond.

"Miss Stevenson?"

She turned to find Doctor Owens, the veterinarian, standing behind her.

"I'm sorry to bother you, but I need your help." He stood before her, tall and not so proud, unlike the first time they'd met. She also noticed his eyes were bloodshot and his gray suit was wrinkled, as if he'd slept in it.

"My help?"

What could I possibly do for him?

"More precisely, that of your employer."

Now she was even more confused. "You know my principal?"

"Your principal owns a detective agency?"

"Oh, you mean Lenny." She shouldn't have been surprised that word of her investigation to help Reverend Nichols had spread so fast.

"I want to hire your boss to find my wife. The police are doing their best, but they don't have enough to go on, and I can't wait around here doing nothing."

"Your wife is Tess, right?"

"I can afford to pay Lenny twice his normal fee. The police found peanuts in Helen's coffee creamer. Someone put them there because she's on the board. My wife is on the board, too. I'm worried, Miss Stevenson."

"Twice the normal fee, huh?" Jessie didn't have time to work another case, but her new agency could use the money. Andi, on the other hand, did have free time now that she was on spring break. She'd already baked a few dozen cookies to calm her nerves, and her fight against Harry was on hold until she could come up with an idea that did not involve any illegal activities.

How difficult could it be to find a missing person?

She'd watched hundreds of detective shows on television. And Jessie wouldn't mind once she cashed the check, but Andi knew better than to ask. Her sister would say no. For the sake of the new agency, she would keep this under wraps for now. Besides, her sister had always said it was easier to ask for forgiveness than permission.

"It looks like you've hired yourself a detective agency," she said. "Provided you understand that the owner keeps a low profile. All of your questions will have to go through me."

Doctor Owens scowled. "I don't work through intermediaries. I'm talking to you now because I need Lenny's phone number."

"Sorry. My employer doesn't work that way." She sidestepped him and continued her walk toward the pond.

"You win. I accept Lenny's conditions."

Andi paused before she turned to face him. She didn't want to appear too eager. "Are you sure?"

"Positive. I have to find my wife. She's my life." His voice broke on the last word.

Emotion overwhelmed her as she watched the man stare up at the sky and blink the tears away. Perhaps he should get a professional. A real detective. A trained one. Andi coughed to clear her throat. "There are agencies that are more hands-on, who are willing to meet with you as often as you wish."

"I made some calls. Lenny is good."

Lenny *was* good. Lenny was also in Hawaii.

Andi swallowed a sigh. She could always call her sister if she needed help. Jessie would tell her what to do after she yelled at her for half an hour.

"Okay. If you're sure. Let me go get my notebook and tape recorder so I can conduct your interview." She didn't want the man inside her condo—Jessie had tossed her badge onto the dining room table before going to bed. "I can meet you at your place in five minutes, if you like."

"That would be perfect. After you ask your questions, you can go through my wife's belongings. Maybe you'll find a clue the police and I overlooked."

They walked silently together until they parted ways in front of her condo. As she entered the path leading to her front door, she spotted the flames on her welcome mat. Fear spurred her into action. She raced forward and found a paper bag untwisting as fire danced over its surface. The unmistakable odor of doggie dung saturated the air.

The vet ran up the path. "You would think Harry could come up with something more original."

The birdseed was original enough.

Andi rushed inside her condo and grabbed a vase filled with daisies. Making haste, she pulled out the flowers and then dumped the water onto the burning bag.

The vet managed to jump out of the splash zone just as the water hit the sack and pavement. "You're awfully calm for someone whose home could have gone up in flames."

"I refuse to get upset." She watched the water spread over the welcome mat as the now-open bag exposed its gift. "That's what Harry wants—for me to get mad and make a scene."

"I heard he has it out for you."

"Now you know it isn't just a rumor. Just a minute." She dripped the daisies back inside the vase and added water from the kitchen sink. After grabbing her notebook off the kitchen counter, along with her tape recorder, she locked her front door.

The vet pointed to the wet dog mess. "Try bleach. I had to use it on my garage floor after Toto paid a visit. Those pet cleaners don't get rid of the odor. Bleach was the only thing that worked."

"The strange odor I smelled in your garage the day we met—"

"Was dog feces mixed with bleach and floral fabric softener. My wife hates the smell of bleach, so I poured fabric softener on top to mask the odor. It helped a little."

So much for thinking the killer used the bleach to clean a crime scene. The only crime covered up was Toto's dump and run.

"Tell me about your wife." Andi pressed the "Record" button on her mini tape recorder, officially beginning her interview as they headed toward Doctor Owen's condo.

"Tess." A gentle smile touched his lips. "We met three years ago. She lived next door to me in an apartment complex. One day she had a flat tire, and I helped her out. The rest is history."

"Until now."

"Correct." He suddenly stopped walking. "I'm worried. And not just because there's a psycho killer after the board." Tension and fear filled the air. "My wife suffers from depression. I've tried to persuade her to get help, but so far she's refused."

"How do you know it's depression?" Andi stepped closer, hoping the recorder caught every word. "Was this confirmed by a doctor?"

He eyed the device and hesitated. Resigned to continue, he spoke as he walked. "There were signs. Before we got married, she seemed carefree and happy, but there were other moments when she remained quiet. I didn't think anything of it at first. After the wedding, those quiet moments grew longer and more frequent. Our relationship changed. I couldn't get through to her."

"Did she go out? See friends?" Andi asked, feeling like an intruder into his life.

"Tess never went anywhere, except to those insufferable board meetings," he said, his footsteps growing louder, as if each step grew heavier. "She quit her job. Stopped seeing her college friends. Whenever I came home for lunch, I'd find her back in bed. She had other . . . issues, too."

Andi walked faster to catch up with him. "Issues?"

"She said she hated her life and blamed me for her problems. The delightful, beautiful lady I married changed into an angry, spiteful woman whenever we were alone together."

Andi stepped onto the sidewalk on the opposite side of the street, glad to see his condo up ahead. She wanted to set the recorder down where she could be sure she was getting every word of the conversation. "I heard Tess and Bernice were close."

"Bernice adored Tess. But then Bernice was an angry, controlling woman. She fed my wife's new, slanted view of the world. I guess you could say they were friends, but they only spent time together working for the HOA."

"How well did Tess get along with the other board members?"

"Fine. Bernice appointed Tess to the board position. I think they're all kindred spirits, except for Reverend Nichols. He's a good man. He tries to persuade the others to 'love thy neighbor,' but has gotten few results for his efforts." The vet's pace slowed as they stepped onto the cement path leading to his condo. "Tess is quiet when she's at board meetings, so most people think she's shy. They have no idea how sick she truly is. They have no idea how much hate is raging beneath that calm exterior."

He reached into his pocket for the keys.

She could see the tears building in his eyes. "Doctor Owens, what do you think happened to your wife?"

"I think my wife got angry and left me."

Andi remembered him telling the policeman they had an argument over him playing golf at the country club. She watched him open the door, then followed him inside.

He closed the door behind her and let his hand linger on the knob. "For the past few months, I have been concerned that she might be suffering from more than depression. I've heard her talking to herself."

"I talk to myself."

"Excessively?"

"I don't think so."

Did Tess suffer from a split personality? Or was this the rambling of a man who wanted to think his wife had to be sick to leave him?

Andi turned to face the spotless living room. The vet's expensive taste wasn't restricted to his clothing. She could swear she'd seen this same room, with its rich mahogany wood, in an Ethan Allen furniture catalog. The Waterford crystal arranged on the bar and the books of Impressionist painters conspicuously displayed on the glass coffee table completed the picture of wealth and sophistication. She wondered if it was all for show. If she were wealthy, she would own a spacious house—not a condo in Euphoria.

"I need you to find her—fast. I'm afraid of what she might do if she doesn't get help. I should have forced her to go to a doctor. I know that, but I kept hoping she'd turn back into the old Tess."

"I understand. Mind if I take a quick look around while we talk?"

"Not at all. Where do you want to start?"

"The bedroom."

He flinched as if the memory of their most intimate moments was too much to bear.

"Her dresser."

Stiffening his spine, and most likely his resolve to be strong, he led the way.

A moment later, Andi ran her hands beneath the empty underwear drawers, searching for anything that might be secured there with tape. She'd seen that particular hiding place in a movie.

"Doctor Owens, does your wife usually take all of her undergarments when she visits her mother?"

"No. That's why I think she left me for good this time."

Andi checked the jewelry box. Empty. She ran her hands beneath and behind the drawers, dresser, mattress, and the portraits on the wall. Nothing. She tried not to look at the sadness in the doctor's eyes.

What if I find his wife and the woman refuses to come home? What does he expect me to do? Call the police and have her committed? Was that even possible?

"Have you talked to the police about your wife's condition?"

He lowered his eyes. "No. I don't have any proof. She's never been diagnosed."

Andi could only nod. Finding nothing useful in the closet or under the bed, she entered the bathroom. "Was Tess taking any medications?"

"Birth control."

Andi opened the medicine cabinet and discovered her pills. Flipping open the container, she found over a dozen pastel-colored tablets. Women didn't usually take off without their medication. "Did you know she left these behind?"

The vet took the package and stared at its contents for a long, silent moment. Finally, he spoke. "This is her way of stabbing me in the heart."

"I don't understand."

He sat on the edge of the tub, still staring at the pills. "I want kids. She wanted to wait." He gestured with the package. "Leaving the pills means she's going off them, but not to have children with *me*."

Andi sat next to him. "Sounds like she has a flair for the dramatic."

He nodded, then placed his head in his hands.

She forced herself not to pat his back to comfort him. He was a client. She was a detective. Well, sort of. "Let's keep looking. Maybe we'll find another clue."

He lifted his head, stared straight ahead, and then stood. "Where next?"

"Does she have a desk?"

An hour later they had gone through every inch of the condo. She didn't find anything the police might have overlooked. Not that she'd expected to, but she had hoped she would. If she was going to help her sister, she wanted to be useful.

"Do you have a picture of your wife I can use for the investigation?"

He opened his wallet and slid out a photo of the two of them on a beach. "It was taken on our honeymoon in the Bahamas."

The woman smiling for the camera wore a black, one-piece bathing suit. Her blonde locks flowed over her shoulders. Her pale-blue eyes reflected the ocean. She looked happy. Too bad she had so many problems. Andi followed the vet into the kitchen and then stopped beside a closed door.

"May I see the garage?"

He appeared startled. "Uh, sure."

She opened the door and the strong stench of floral bleach almost knocked her off her feet.

"Sorry," he said. "I had to clean up after Toto again this morning. He paid me another visit." The vet pushed the button to open the garage door. "I should air this room out."

"Where's the dog now?"

"Home with Reverend Nichols."

Andi eyed the chest-style freezer. In horror films, freezers always held a dead body. She pictured the killer surprising Tess while she stood in the open garage. He would have knocked her out and then shoved her limp remains into the freezer.

Was Tess hidden inside this very freezer?

She had to know. Needing to be alone, she turned to the vet. "Can I trouble you for a glass of water?"

"Sure." He eyed her suspiciously, but didn't say

139

anything else.

As soon as he shut the door, she summoned the courage to touch the lid of the white, oversize appliance. "You can do this." She had to work fast. He wouldn't be gone long, and she had to know. "You can do this. You know you can. One, two, three—pull."

Prepared to scream and run out of the garage as fast as her feet would carry her, Andi yanked the lid open. She peeked with one open eye, then the other and found . . . dead . . . fish. Breaded, deep-fried, store-bought fish, along with an assortment of TV dinners and sausage links.

"Why are you looking in there?" Doctor Owens's deep voice resonated from the door.

She jumped and almost wet her pants. "I . . . I wondered what you kept in a freezer this big. You don't have a large family."

"Once a month we shop at one of those discount stores where you buy in bulk. One minute I'm eating samples, and the next I'm buying sausage by the ton. Tess says I'm a discount addict."

Andi remembered Toto dragging sausage links down the street. Doctor Owens must have dropped them onto the cement and not realized it. She couldn't picture a vet giving a dog that much sausage, if any.

"I can relate." She eased the lid down. "I won't have to shop for paper towels again until I'm sixty."

He handed her the glass of water. "Are you going to the board meeting tonight?"

"It hasn't been a month."

"The board called an emergency meeting. They're going to appoint me to the board to fill Bernice's slot."

"You're going to be *one of them*?"

He nodded with a grim expression. "It's temporary. I have no desire to do this on a full-time basis. I'm hoping they'll pass along any information about the killer they discover. I'll do anything to locate my wife."

The rules required the board to give twenty-four-hour notice of any meetings. She intended to add this to the list of violations committed by Harry.

She caught the look of unbearable pain in the vet's eyes. Her heart ached for him.

"We'll do everything possible to find your wife."

NINE

Luke entered the library, shook off the creepy feeling the jungle mural gave him, and marched down the hall to the meeting room. He dreaded every one of the meetings he attended on behalf of the Euphoria Homeowners' Association.

He pushed the door open and, at first glance, was taken aback. Andi stood in the center aisle with Meg. A dozen of her neighbors, clad in red "Anti-Board" T-shirts, greeted her with smiles, thumbs-up signs, and pats on the back. The heat of a blush rushed up her neck and over her cheeks. Obviously embarrassed by the attention, she eased down to the front row, where Roxie waited.

The anti-board was growing—and so would the trouble. Luke located his usual seat at the table up front and turned when he heard the heavy click of male shoes. Harry and Valerie approached, both with smug expressions. The association president scowled at Andi and the anti-board before handing her two envelopes. The trouble came faster than Luke had expected.

He ambled over and Andi held up both envelopes for

him to read. VIOLATION had been typed on one and FINE had been typed on the other.

"Harry, you're a weasel!" She ripped up both envelopes and threw the pieces into the air. "*You* pay your own blasted fine! *You* dumped that trash and birdseed on my porch!"

Harry stepped closer. "Prove it, sweetheart."

Luke stepped between them and the pungent odor of Harry's onion-bacon-cheeseburger breath struck him like a weapon. "Harry . . ."

The president of the association narrowed his eyes into snakelike slits. "Don't 'Harry' me. You are one call away from losing this account—and probably your job."

"Luke," Andi said, "This isn't your problem." She narrowed her eyes to mimic Harry. "The rules say there have to be two violation letters and a third offense before a fine can be assessed. You've littered my porch only twice."

Valerie slapped a French-manicured hand to her lips. "Whoops. I forgot to give you this." She handed Andi a picture of her messy porch dated Friday morning, another dated Saturday morning, and finally, a picture of a clean porch, except for two leaves, dated an hour ago. She pointed to the last picture. "That there is the third offense needed to fine you."

"You're fining me for two leaves on the porch?"

Harry smirked victoriously. "The rules say you have to keep your porch clean. They don't *define* clean, that's my job. Leaves don't belong on your porch, therefore—"

"Your porch is *not* clean," Valerie finished for him. She lifted her snooty nose as if Andi's presence soiled the air.

"Enough." Luke rubbed his chin, forcing himself to remain calm and professional. "Harry, this war is only going to escalate. Nobody will win in the end, especially the community."

"I'll win. You can count on it," Harry snapped. His stare bore into Andi. "I don't care what your anti-board throws my way, sweet cakes, because I'm not going to back off. Just the opposite. You won't be able to get out of here fast enough."

Harry placed his arm around Valerie's waist and escorted her to the table up front. There was no sign of Paul, her soon-to-be ex-husband. So much for thinking a brush with death and a life with Valerie would put Harry in a better, more forgiving mood. They didn't.

"I'm sorry." Luke knew Andi couldn't care less if he was sorry. She wanted—no, needed—results. "With your permission, I'll take the picture with the leaves to our company lawyer. I sincerely doubt Harry can get away with declaring a porch dirty because of two leaves."

Uncertainty flickered through her expression. "Why didn't you do that for Meg? She told me Harry sent her a violation for a porch 'dirtied' by one leaf."

"This is the first I'm hearing about it. He might have sent the letter before I took over the account."

What else had Harry gotten away with over the years?

Luke was sure Harry would send creative violation letters only to neighbors who didn't have the resources to take him to court. He preyed on the weak.

"Perhaps you didn't receive a copy of the violation letter because it was part of his effort to embezzle money." Andi looked at Harry as though he was the slime clinging to an algae-infested pool. "We can both agree he has stepped up his efforts to get rid of me. You're assuming it's because of the anti-board. What if the real reason is he heard I'm investigating the murder?"

If Harry was the killer, Andi had a lot more to worry about than violation letters.

Luke leaned in close. "If it's all right with you, I'll drop by your place after the meeting. I would like to talk to you." He needed to impress upon her the importance of never being alone. "In the meantime, *try* to stay out of trouble."

"Who? Me?" She feigned innocence.

"Yeah, you." Grinning, Luke strode off to the front table for the start of the meeting. From his vantage point, he scanned his surroundings. Mr. Decker, the cowboy, sat in the third row, looking as malcontent as ever.

He could be the killer.

Roxie cackled in the front row. He had always considered her eccentric.

What if she's crazy? She could be the killer.

His line of vision fell on Doctor Owens.

What if the anti-board was right about Tess? What if she witnessed Bernice's murder and ran off to hide? What if her husband killed Bernice because of her influence over Tess?

Next, he slanted a glance Valerie's way.

What if Bernice had tried to stop the budding romance between Valerie and Harry? Everyone knew Valerie had her sights set on Harry's money. Could she be the killer? Then there was Reverend Nichols. The police suspected him.

Luke ran a finger over his brow. Everyone had a motive to kill Bernice, but no one, other than Reverend Nichols, had a motive to kill Helen. She had lured him away from his beloved church and then dumped him.

Harry banged the gavel, calling the meeting to order. "Valerie, please note in the minutes that Helen and your soon-to-be-ex have resigned their positions and Tess Owens is not here tonight. Either she ran away or she's dead, so she won't be considered a board member for long."

He did not just say that!

Luke shot Harry a warning look that he knew would be ignored.

Doctor Owens's face turned red, then stark white. Several female neighbors patted him reassuringly on the shoulder and back.

Roxie loudly proclaimed, "Don't worry, doc. I'm sure she's alive. She probably just wanted a real doctor—like a surgeon."

His jaw fell open at the insult and Luke cringed. He was working in a loony bin. He had to find a way out.

Since this was an emergency session, violation letters and homeowner concerns would not be addressed.

"I called this meeting to appoint a new member to the board," Harry stated.

"Don't we get a vote on who gets on that sorry excuse for a board?" the cowboy asked in his usual gruff voice.

Harry shook his head. "Voting by the community takes place only at the annual meeting. When a member of the board vacates their seat, or in Bernice's case, is knocked off, then the remaining board members appoint the new member to fill the vacancy until the next annual meeting."

"And we have no say?" the cowboy seethed.

Harry glared at him. "That's correct. You have NO say." He gestured toward Valerie. "*We* have decided to appoint Doctor Owens to fill the vacated seat left by Bernice."

The crowd murmured, not sure if this was good news or bad. Luke wasn't sure himself. He never got the impression that the veterinarian was another one of Harry's yes-men, but then again, they never discussed rules and violations.

With a solemn expression, Doctor Owens took an empty seat at the table. Luke wondered why he would willingly make himself a target for the killer.

Was it worth it to him if it meant having access to information about the community? Did he think Tess was hiding in one of the condos, or was he hoping the board could tell him something that would help him find his wife?

Luke rubbed his face. He was tired of second-guessing everyone in Euphoria and dealing with Harry.

Meg surprised the room by standing. "I nominate Roxie to fill the other vacant seat."

The room exploded in applause.

Harry glared at Meg as she sat. He pounded his judge's gavel to quiet the room. "I make a motion we lower the number of board members from seven to six," he stated smugly.

Luke groaned under his breath. Meg munched loudly on her cheese puffs in either a stress- or anger-induced frenzy.

"I second the motion to lower the number of board members from seven to six." Valerie sent Andi a Cheshire-cat grin.

"All those in favor . . ." Harry continued with the vote.

In a show of solidarity, the board, including Doctor Owens, agreed to limit the number of seats on the board. The vet was off to an inauspicious start.

The meeting ended and the cowboy marched out with red in his eyes and a wad of chewing tobacco bulging one cheek. Luke hoped he didn't have a six-shooter hidden in his glove compartment.

Once the rest of the homeowners left the building, the board entered the library lobby, preparing to exit. Luke followed, anticipating doom and gloom around every corner. He found Andi standing between Meg and Roxie at the library doors. She glared at Harry as if he was the devil himself, and then she gave his girlfriend an assessing once-over.

"You know, Valerie," Andi said, matching the gold digger's smug and arrogant attitude, "I may have to sell *way below* market value in order to get out of here as fast as possible. I hope that won't have any effect on the sale of *your* condo. I would hate for you to lose money."

Harry came up behind his pillow partner. "You can't afford to dump your place. You're a teacher."

"Never underestimate an angry woman, Harry, especially one that can move back in with her parents. I'd rather 'dump' my place than pay your fines."

"I'll believe it when I see it," he guffawed.

Andi watched them leave the building. "We'll see who has the last laugh, you tyrant."

Luke placed his hand on the small of Andi's back and led her outside. "You only have to scare Valerie to make his life miserable, and I think you accomplished that."

The cool evening breeze ruffled Luke's hair as he took in the surrounding parking lot. He had expected to see a heated discussion of that night's events going on, not a gathering of residents reading yellow sheets of paper. Harry snatched one from under a sedan's windshield wiper and bellowed with laughter.

One woman leaned into her husband and then pointed in their direction. Not a good sign. Andi marched to her car, where a yellow paper waited for her. Meg and Roxie rushed to her side. Luke angrily tugged one out from under the windshield wiper of a van. The picture on the flyer featured Andi's sister Jessie. She wore a skimpy outfit and was accepting money from a man. At the bottom of the page, someone had scrawled CALL ME along with Andi's home telephone number.

"That horndog is behind this." Roxie's features twisted into a scowl.

Meg rushed to Luke's side. "I saw Harry hand a shaggy-haired teenager an envelope before the meeting. I think he paid that kid to put these on our cars." She pulled a handful of jelly beans out of her jeans pocket and popped them into her mouth.

He had noticed she was stress eating more often since forming the anti-board.

Andi held out her hand. "Got any more of those?"

Meg reached into her other pocket and handed over an assortment. Andi shoved over a dozen into her mouth. Luke watched her chomp down on her hatred before it boiled over into rage.

Roxie held the flyer with Jessie's picture up to the circle of light provided by a streetlamp. "I didn't know your sister was a hooker." She tilted her head and examined it from another angle. "I have boots just like those."

"My sister is *not* a hooker. She's a cocktail waitress."

Roxie handed Andi the flyer. "We believe you, dear." Her tone didn't match her words. "What do you want to do about Harry? I can hold his head under the water spout over there until he confesses. It's some sort of torture they do to terrorists."

Meg swallowed her candy. "Terrorist, President of the Euphoria Homeowners' Association—all the same to me."

****

Andi heard a knock on her door an hour after she had slammed her purse on her dining room table and screamed obscenities at the ceiling. Luke had said he would be over after the meeting. If he told her to run for the board again, she couldn't be held responsible for her actions. Yanking the door open, she shot him a warning glare.

"Harry is evil. Pure evil!"

"Okay . . ." he answered, obviously wondering if it was safe to enter the premises with her temper flaring.

Stepping cautiously into the foyer, he carried a video camera in one hand and a bottle of her favorite white zinfandel in the other. He had changed into jeans and a white polo shirt that showed off his tan. "Sorry about the flyers with the picture of your sister. I would have never guessed Harry could sink that low."

"She's *not* a hooker."

"I didn't say she was."

"She's *not* a hooker," Andi repeated, tears welling in her eyes. "Take my word for it." His opinion of her and her family mattered to her more than she cared to admit, even to herself.

The house phone rang for the fourth time since she had arrived home. Reading Unknown Number in the caller ID box, she picked up the receiver and dropped it back down onto its cradle.

"At this hour, it has to be another prank caller wanting to book a 'date' with Jessie." She unplugged the cord and let it hang against the wall.

He set the camera and bottle of wine down on the dining room table before placing a strong hand on her shoulder. "I believe you. The last time I saw you in college, Jessie had joined the police force."

Andi's breath caught in her throat. He remembered.

"Don't worry. I haven't told anyone." He wiped away the tears born of anger that were sliding down her cheeks. "I figured she might be working undercover, so I kept my mouth shut."

"You've known all along and never said anything?"

"The truth is, it came back to me about an hour ago. When I saw the picture of Jessie on the flyer, my first thought was that James Stevenson would never allow one of his daughters to become a hooker. He'd lock her in a closet first."

Andi nodded her agreement.

"Although I never believed she was a hooker," he

continued, "looking at the picture, I did notice she was in good shape. That's when I remembered you once told me Jessie was running every morning to prepare for the police academy."

"You can't say anything to anyone, Luke. Promise me."

He pressed a kiss to her forehead. "I promise."

"No matter what?"

"No matter what. If there's one thing I learned dating you all those years ago, it is *don't mess with the Stevenson women.*" The twinkle in his eye told her he was half-joking.

"True." She felt a smile tug at her lips while she studied his warm expression. He was a good man and would do the right thing to protect Jessie. She should have trusted him back in college to keep his sisters' secrets. They were never life-or-death issues—usually overspending at the mall or a love gone bad. Andi never told because of the oath she shared with them. The sisters once swore to never tell anyone what they said in confidence. They should have made an exception to the oath for fiancés and husbands.

Feeling the warmth of his hand on her shoulder brought on a yearning for better times between them. The temptation to relax into the feeling was overwhelming, but the need to avoid emotional pain remained strong.

"Luke?" Andi stepped away from his touch. "I kept the fact Jessie was working undercover a secret, but you're not upset."

Realization reached his eyes. "In this case, I understood because I knew the importance of your secret. Back in college, I was kept totally in the dark."

"I see."

He had a point. How could he gauge the importance of the secret unless he knew the subject matter?

She realized she should have at least told him what her sister's secrets were about, even if she left out the details.

Maybe then he would have understood. I might have saved our relationship.

Her gaze landed on the flyer she had left on the dining room table. Anger turned to rage. "Harry! He has to be stopped!"

Over the last hour, she had plotted Harry's pretend death a hundred different ways. Her sister was her role model, her hero. No one was going to turn her into the joke of the neighborhood and get away with it.

"I have an idea." Luke joined her at the table and held up the video camera. "This is going to nail Harry for you."

So this was the real reason he had wanted to come over tonight. "Why is this camera going to be any more effective than the one we already installed on the porch?"

"Location, location, location. I'm going to plant this one out back, in the bushes, at the corner of the building. If Harry tries to dump anything on your porch again, we'll catch him with this camera before he gets to your patio. I'm betting he won't hide behind the umbrella until he gets near your condo."

Andi eyed the camera in his grip. "Aren't you afraid Harry will fire your company for siding with the enemy?"

"If we catch him, he won't be in a position to fire anyone."

He sent her a warm smile and her heart ached. If he lost his job because of her, she could never forgive herself. He ought to remain neutral in this war. His mother's retirement depended on it.

"You don't have to do this for me."

"Yes, I do." He tapped her chin with his finger. "I'll

have this up and running in no time." He strode over to the sliding glass door with the camera in his hand and a screwdriver sticking out of his back pocket.

She grabbed a flashlight from under the kitchen sink, then followed him outside to act as lookout in case Harry showed up. The cool air sent goose bumps over her arms. Scanning the sky, she spotted an isolated star flickering in the night sky.

Luke held her hand to keep her from falling when she crawled over the porch's half wall and into the grassy common area. When they reached the bush, she held the flashlight as he set to work on installing the camera. The circle of light illuminated his biceps, which flexed with each move. She swallowed the lump forming in the back of her throat.

He glanced her way, and she felt her cheeks blush.

When he finished, he worked on her computer. "I set the monitor to a split screen so you can see the view from both cameras." He swiveled the laptop for her to see. "Harry is as good as caught."

"Thanks. That was nice of you." She held out a glass of wine for him.

A guilty expression flickered over his face. "Nice has nothing to do with it. Harry has gone too far. I promise you, I'll stop him."

Luke cupped her cheek with his palm. His eyes grew dark with unspoken thoughts. His intensity drew her in, capturing her like a spell. She felt her body lean toward him. He closed the distance and his lips touched hers. Her heart skipped a beat. Memories of kisses just like this one flooded over her. She kept her eyes closed long after the kiss ended, allowing the sensation to linger.

When she finally opened her lids, she found herself confronting doubt. His doubt.

"I'm sorry," Luke whispered.

"No. Don't." She turned away, unwilling to be hurt

again.

Why is he doing this to me?

She fought back the tears threatening to spill over. "Let's pretend it never happened." She allowed her mind to drift to the day he had left her. The hurt. The excruciating pain in her heart. How she cried for hours. He was right. It was best to stop the insanity before history repeated itself.

"It's getting late," she mumbled. "You should probably go."

The air grew thick with awkwardness and uncertainty as he left without looking back.

TEN

Andi forced herself not to think about Luke after he left. Out of habit, she picked her iPhone up off the dining room table to check her emails. Instead, she discovered Meg had left a message. Her perky voice sounded louder and even more excited than usual.

"Andi, you have to get over here! Harry egged our garages and Roxie is out for revenge. She's going to destroy his back porch and I can't stop her!"

"Oh no," Andi moaned. No matter what the anti-board did, Harry blamed her. He would probably flatten her condo with a bulldozer after Roxie messed with his porch, and she would never be able to prove he was guilty. He was always careful not to leave evidence. She shrugged on a black sweater and rushed out the door to stop Roxie before it was too late.

Andi crept behind Harry's building, keeping close to the bushes. The moon slid behind the clouds, making it difficult to see, but the sound of hushed conversation gave away Roxie and Meg's location. She ran from tree to tree until she reached the bushes behind the HOA president's porch.

"Psst. Meg! Roxie!" she whispered.

Roxie scooped something out a bucket and slung it at Harry's porch. Andi could see only small, dark objects.

Curiosity and the need to stop Roxie forced her from her hiding place. She ran to the eccentric woman and grabbed her bony arm before she could launch another scoopful.

"Stop!" Andi glanced at down at . . . worms. The fish bait slithered on top of one another in a paint bucket that had to be half-full. "Gross! Where did you get that many worms?"

"Who's out there?" Harry yelled in his usual coarse voice. Lights flipped on in the bedroom, then in other rooms as he traveled through the condo. Finally, the living room lights illuminated the back porch.

Roxie swung the bucket toward Harry's sliding glass door, emptying the contents. Slimy worms flew through the air and then fell. Some hit the glass, most fell onto his patio furniture. Meg took aim with her camera, snapping one picture after another.

Andi could hear the voices inside coming closer. Her stomach lurched. "Let's get out of here!"

Roxie, having thrown the bucket into the bushes, already had twenty yards on them. Andi ran to catch up. Meg sprinted past them both, holding her cell phone high in the air.

The din of their feet pounding the grass made it difficult to determine if Harry was in hot pursuit. A mental picture of him searching high and low for them fed adrenaline to her legs, forcing them to move faster.

Rounding a corner, she ran smack into Meg's back, bounced off, and fell onto the grass. Rubbing her knee, she caught sight of the cowboy ushering Meg and Roxie inside a condo. Andi picked herself up, quickly swiped at any grass that might be clinging to her pants, and then followed the two women.

The cowboy, dressed in his usual faded jeans and long-sleeved shirt, pulled the door shut after her. The deadbolt locked with a resounding clack.

What if he's the killer?

A shudder of alarm traveled up her spine, leaving the hairs standing up on her neck.

The cowboy strode into his living room and over to a bar in the corner. "Can I get you ladies a drink? You must be thirsty after your exploits."

She raised her brow questioningly.

He grinned in response. "I went outside to have a smoke and witnessed the whole shootin' match."

"You mean *Roxie's* shenanigans," Andi clarified.

Roxie looked at her like she was yesterday's garbage. "Wimp. You and Meg are both wimps."

Meg shrugged off Roxie's comment. "Water would be great," she told the cowboy. "Got anything to eat?"

"I'll check."

"Bourbon for me." Grinning, Roxie dropped down onto the sofa.

Andi wasn't so sure eating or drinking anything the cowboy offered was a good idea, but no one else seemed to question their safety. Perhaps because they weren't on the board.

"I'm celebrating putting Harry in his place. It's about time someone did." Roxie pulled a cigarette out of her bra and ran it under her nostrils for a whiff. "Nothing smells better than victory mixed with nicotine. Except for victory mixed with nicotine and a bottle of bourbon. What's taking you so long?"

Andi glanced up at a branding iron and samples of barbed wire proudly displayed on the wall like Picassos.

What kind of man hung objects that inflicted pain like art?

"Nothing for me, thank you."

He poured Roxie a drink from a bottle he'd taken

from his well-stocked liquor cabinet. "You ladies are welcome to stay until the coast is clear. I imagine that polecat is winding his way around the brush searching for you."

Roxie slipped the cigarette back into her bra and then took the glass offered. Andi watched her down it like milk. She felt her eyes widen in amazement—or was it shock? The fact she even had a liver left was a miracle.

"Ah. That took the chill off," Roxie cooed. "I wish I could have seen Harry's face when he saw the worms winding their way over and around his favorite patio chair. Valerie will never sit in those seats again." She chuckled with pride.

Meg slouched into the sofa. "This isn't going to solve anything. Tomorrow we'll wake up to chocolate pudding on our porches, or worse."

"Chocolate pudding," Roxie laughed so hard her drink bounced out of her glass and ran down the side. She stuck out her pointy tongue and lapped it up like a cat. "That's a good one. Next time we'll smear pudding all over his welcome mat, or better yet, his sliding-glass door. What a mess that would be to clean up."

Andi framed her face with both hands pressed against her temples. When she told Meg she wanted to fight back, she never dreamed Roxie would take things this far, or this low. She did like Meg and she valued their new friendship, but she had no control over Roxie, who was taking the anti-board to the dark side.

The cowboy refilled the amber liquid in Roxie's glass, then headed Meg's way.

The nurse smiled up at him, and he froze in place for an uncomfortably long moment.

"One water, coming up." The cowboy handed her the glass and a can of cashews, never once taking his gaze away from her face.

Meg sipped the water, unaware of the attention

directed at her. Her apple cheeks turned a rosy pink when Roxie recounted the events of the evening. With her heart-shaped face and bouncy blonde curls, Meg resembled a cherub. The type painted on cathedral walls or sculpted into buildings.

Was the cowboy mesmerized by her looks, or worse, was he falling for her? What if he is the murderer?

Feeling protective of her new friend, Andi eased onto the sofa beside her.

The cowboy glanced at Andi as if he had forgotten she was there and then returned to his bar in the corner of the room.

"Did you work on a ranch, Mr. Decker?" Meg asked, oblivious to the effect she had on the man.

"*Owned* one, not too far from Benson." He pulled the tab off his beer and a hiss of air escaped from the can. He turned to face Roxie. "Had to sell on account of the arthritis. Too many things I can't do anymore, like mend fences."

"Couldn't you hire help?" Meg asked.

"Already had help." He took a sip of his beer and set it aside. "Trouble is finding someone willing to do the work of two men for the price of one. That's what it would have taken to save the place."

And then he moved to Euphoria and met Harry. The man had not been born under a lucky sign.

Andi could relate. Trouble seemed to follow her as well. Luke had made a point of reminding her of that fact more than once.

Roxie downed the second bourbon. The cowboy watched with concern.

Andi scanned the room. His furnishings were exactly what she would have expected of a retired rancher. A Navajo blanket had been thrown over the back of a worn leather sofa. A framed copy of a John Wayne photograph hung overhead. Oil paintings of horses and cowboys lined the other walls. Steer horns rested on top of the television. The only item missing in this tribute to the old frontier was a saddle in the corner. She turned back to the horns and wondered if they were sharp enough to gore flesh. If she were the killer, she'd save those for Harry.

She blinked, trying to erase the image from her mind. The way her luck was running, she'd go to the dumpster tomorrow and find Harry's naked, branded derriere sticking out of the trash, sprouting those particular horns.

"You just happened to be smoking near Harry's back porch tonight, Mr. Decker?" Andi asked.

"Not at first. Nothing wrong with my ears. I headed that way after hearing all the racket you ladies made."

The three women glanced at one another. Meg appeared worried. Roxie appeared tipsy.

"We need to work on the noise factor," Meg announced.

"How about we come up with a plan of attack that doesn't involve vandalism?" Andi asked, unsure how her question would be taken.

Meg cringed. "She's right," she told Roxie before scooping up a handful of cashews. "How long do you think we need to hide in here?"

Roxie set her empty glass down on the table. "Twenty minutes ought to do it." She turned her nose up at Andi. "Is twenty minutes okay with you, princess?"

Andi sighed. "I don't mean to judge."

"Sure you do," Roxie snapped, returning her own judgment with a glare.

Shivers slithered down Andi's spine. *Were those the eyes of a killer? Or were those the eyes of woman who knew no boundaries and had too much drink?*

"I just don't want to be arrested," Andi said softly. "Meg and I would lose our jobs. Besides, trashing each other's porches isn't going to solve anything. We need one good move that will get rid of him forever. A move that doesn't involve killing him."

"I vote for killing him," Roxie's sarcastic tone filled the otherwise-silent room. "How about another drink, Mr. Decker?"

Andi wanted to protest giving her another drink, but then she noticed he filled the glass with soda before mixing in a touch of liquor. The older woman wouldn't notice after having downed two glasses already.

Meg leaned toward Andi. "I'm always telling Roxie not to mix booze with her pills. She never listens."

Roxie blew the cowboy a kiss when he handed her the glass.

They weren't going anywhere soon. No time like the present to do a bit of investigating.

"I hear you didn't like Bernice," Andi said to the cowboy.

"Not one iota," he shot back. "That woman should have had snakes coming out of her head to warn a fella."

"Medusa," Andi mumbled. "What made you dislike her so much?"

"The same thing that makes you hate Harry."

She nodded her understanding. "Who do you think murdered Bernice?"

"Don't know. Don't care. Unless of course the killer wants another go at Harry. I'll teach him how to finish the job."

"Really?" She didn't know what to make of this man.

"In my opinion, those board members should all be strung up like horse thieves. If I had any strength left in my hands, I would've done it a long time ago."

Andi studied the expression of hate on the man's face.

Did he have enough strength to hit Bernice over the head with a brick? Hard enough to kill her?

"Bernice was bad enough," the cowboy said, as if

reading her mind. "Harry's a nightmare. I can't count how many fines I've paid over the years—and he sent me four more this week. The man's a demon!" He gestured to an empty space on the wall. "I had to sell an original portrait of John Wayne to pay for a stack of fines that blasted board sent me. I refused to pay at first, but they kept sending me late fees on top of the fines."

"You sold The Duke!" Roxie gasped. "Why on earth would you do a fool thing like that?"

"I didn't have a choice. The board could have taken away my home when my debt reached twelve hundred dollars. I owed them three thousand when I sold the painting."

"And now?" Andi asked.

"They can fine me all they want. I overheard Bernice and Harry talking a few years back. They said they'd put a lien on my property if I ever refused to pay, but they wouldn't take the property until after I die. They didn't want the bad press."

Roxie nodded. "HOA steals another home from the elderly. News at five."

"I don't care if the board takes this place after I die. They can have it."

That cut his motive in half. Why kill when he had nothing to lose?

Meg gripped the glass of water with one hand while she munched on nuts and bounced her crossed leg up and down. Either her leg was keeping time with her thoughts, or she was still high from the adrenaline and fear from tonight's adventure.

"How much do you owe now, if you don't mind me asking?"

"At least two thousand. Those late fees add up quick. I send them a check for a hundred or two every once in a while to keep them from changing their mind about taking the place."

"Two thousand more than what you already paid?" Andi couldn't believe it.

Well, okay, I can believe it. Harry walked the property daily.

The cowboy eyed Andi above the rim of his beer can. "From what I hear, they've just started sticking it to you, little lady. It will get worse. The man's obsessed. My poker buddy comes over twice a week and his old car leaks oil. Harry waits for him to back up and then snaps a picture before I even have a chance to clean it up."

"But you got him back," Roxie added, a huge grin revealing her pleasure. "You punched him in the old snout."

"I did. And I'm proud of it." He toasted himself with a beer lifted high. "The judge found reason to drop the charges. He lives in a community with a homeowners' association, too. Said he could relate to my situation. Too bad he doesn't live here. Maybe then someone would stop that varmint."

"Why don't you move?" Andi asked.

"And give that cretin the satisfaction? Not on your life. And don't you go chickening out either. We are all in this fight together now. Thanks to you and that anti-board of yours."

She swallowed hard. "Please don't pin your hopes on the anti-board. I don't know how this is going to end."

His scowl deepened. "I do. In another death."

****

Luke stood with his hands planted at his sides, taking in the view at Mr. Decker's condo. Meg shoveled cashews into her mouth, her crossed leg kicking with nervous energy. Roxie saluted him with her coffee cup. An empty liquor glass nestled against a bourbon bottle on the coffee table in front of her. She appeared to be a fully awake, caffeine-buzzed drunk. Andi avoided eye contact with any of them. She scratched her head while turning the pages of a magazine.

"I hear you ladies need an escort home." He held the door open and motioned for them to exit. His mood hadn't improved since Mr. Decker had called him at one in the morning to explain the situation. Meg had refused to leave, afraid Harry knew where they were hiding and might be holed up outside with a baseball bat—or worse. The cowboy had a bad case of arthritis and couldn't take anyone on in physical combat. "I checked the grounds. No one is lurking outside," Luke stated.

"You sure?" Meg rubbed her arms, her leg still bouncing. If she didn't calm down, she might explode.

"I promise the coast is clear." Luke sent Andi a look of disappointment. He couldn't believe she had helped trash Harry's condo with enough worms to entice a great white shark. She had to know he would retaliate.

Andi stood and ambled to the door, still avoiding eye contact. Once she stood next to him, she whispered. "I had nothing to do with this."

Roxie handed Mr. Decker the coffee cup. "Thanks for the hospitality. The next time you and your friend play poker, give me a call. I'll bring my own bottle."

"And your own cards?" He lifted a brow as if he suspected the woman cheated at poker.

Roxie cackled. "I bring my own dice."

Meg stood and swiped at the salt that had fallen from the nuts and landed on her black sweatpants. "Thanks again. We appreciate your help."

"Anytime." Mr. Decker's gaze followed Meg out the door.

Although the sun wouldn't rise for a few more hours, decorative lampposts and the full moon provided enough light to guide their way. The cool night air ruffled the leaves in the trees and brushed against their cheeks.

Luke caught a glimpse of movement out of the corner of his eye. He spotted a dark figure running around a building and heading toward the pond.

"One of the other neighbors is out late," Meg whispered.

"It could be the murderer." Andi wandered away from the group. "Let's see who it is."

"Are you listening to yourself?" Luke's agitation revealed itself in his tone. "It could be the murderer, so you're going to run after him?" He hurried to catch up with her. "Like I said before—trouble."

Andi waved him off.

Nearing the back of the next building, Roxie swayed. "I see the light."

Meg grabbed the older woman's arm. "Stay away from the light."

"I'm drunk, not dying." Roxie pointed at the building. "Helen's lights are on. I *know* we turned them off after we finished packing."

Luke studied the windows. The light inside flickered and grew. "There's a fire in her living room! Call 911."

He ran over the grass, then scrambled over the half wall surrounding Helen's porch. The sliding-glass door, the one he had locked before, slid open easily.

Photo albums Andi had boxed up for Helen now lay torn and scattered across the carpet. Like newspaper in a small campfire, page after page ignited, blackened, and curled. He spotted the fire detector hanging against the wall. The wires had been cut and the battery removed.

"Quick! Find a fire extinguisher!" Andi ran into the kitchen and began pulling open cupboards.

Meg rushed to another room.

After checking under the sink and next to the refrigerator, Luke rushed out to the garage. He found the red canister propped up in a corner, grabbed it, and ran back inside. When he returned to the living room, he found Meg jumping up and down on a bathroom rug she'd thrown over the flames. She held a container of baby powder in one hand and a box of baking soda in the other. With each bounce, white powder puffed into the air and then drifted down to settle on the rug.

He stood, dumbfounded. "What are you doing?"

"I couldn't remember which powder smothers fire." Meg glanced down and then shrugged. "Doesn't matter. I got most of it out."

Andi stomped on an ember near the sofa.

Roxie dug a cigarette out of her bra. She dropped to her knees beside Meg and crawled up to the ash with the stick wedged between her lips. Finding a smoking photo, the tipsy woman nudged the end of the cigarette toward the corner.

Once again, Luke stared in disbelief. He had thought there was nothing else this woman could do that would surprise him, but he was wrong. "Stand back."

Luke pulled the pin from the fire extinguisher, aimed, and shot. The foam burst out of the hose and Roxie dropped her cigarette while trying to escape the white blast.

"*Now* it's out," he proclaimed.

"We need to open the windows," Meg said, coughing on the chemicals filling the air.

Roxie sat staring at what remained of the fire and her soggy cigarette while the rest of them opened the windows. Andi pulled the chain on the ceiling fan. Once the air began circulating the smoke cleared, but the odor hovered.

"That was close." Luke stood near the open sliding-glass door where the air didn't smell like burned pictures. "A few minutes later and this place would have been blazing."

Roxie narrowed her eyes. "You killed my cigarette!"

Luke couldn't help but smile until he spotted the

writing on the room's opposite wall. He tried to swallow, but his mouth felt as dry as cotton.

Andi pointed to the blood-colored letters. "Look."

Meg read, "You should have died, witch!"

"Hey!" Roxie scowled. "I'm a bit peeved over my cigarette. That doesn't make me a witch."

Meg shook her head. "Not you. I'm reading the wall."

Roxie squinted, trying to read the writing. "I hope that's not blood."

Luke crossed the room to examine the writing. It appeared thicker than blood. He summoned the courage to run his finger along the edge. It felt creamy to the touch. Reassured, he sighed. "It's lipstick."

"I wouldn't be caught dead wearing that color." Roxie dug in her bra, presumably for another cigarette.

"Who do you think did this? And why?" Meg looked to him for answers he didn't have. "Helen rarely went to the board meetings."

Luke picked up the pictures that hadn't been fully consumed by the fire. They were all of Helen and the reverend. He looked like a happy man with his arm draped around her.

Maybe the reverend is guilty. Did he lose his mind after Helen left him? Did he discover his mother was responsible for the breakup?

Luke needed to convince Andi to stay out of the investigation. If Reverend Nichols murdered his mother and set fire to the condo, he wouldn't hesitate to get rid of Andi.

Andi pressed her lips into a thin line while her gaze traveled from Roxie to Meg. "You know I'm working part-time for a detective agency, right?"

"Sure," Meg shot back. "The whole neighborhood knows."

"Well, I need your help," she said. "I want to confide

in you about this case, but you have to *promise* to keep this a secret. Can you do that?"

"I promise. And Roxie's not going to remember any of this in the morning."

Luke's gaze locked on hers. "I think you should drop the case. Let the professionals handle it."

"The *professional* is busy at the moment and needs my help," Andi said.

Why would this Lenny character, who owned the detective agency, let a schoolteacher do his job? Interviews were one thing; detective work was another.

Andi leaned closer to her friends. "Meg, Roxie, you are both plugged into the gossips of Euphoria Lane. I need your help. We all know Tess is missing."

"Yeah. I hope she's okay," Meg answered. "I'm really worried about her."

"Her husband is concerned, too," Andi shared. "He hired my boss to find Tess."

Luke's stomach sank. Andi's involvement in the case kept growing. She was bound to end up on the killer's radar.

"And you want me to help?" Meg bounced on the couch. "That's awesome! Do I get a badge?"

"Nothing like that." A smile tugged at Andi's lips. "Well, a bit like that. I need your opinion. Did Tess appear depressed and . . . a bit off balance to you?"

Roxie leaned back against the sofa, rubbing her forehead as if erasing a headache. "Loony is more like it."

"She had loony eyes. I kept telling her to wear eyeliner." Meg reached for a partially burned photo protruding from the rubble. She held on to one corner. "This is the picnic at the pool. Look at her eyes." She pointed to Tess seated at a table with her husband, Reverend Nichols, Helen, the cowboy, and Roxie.

"Okay . . ." Andi peered closely at Tess. Her eyes

appeared glassy, almost lifeless. "I see what you mean." She tucked the photo into her pocket, just in case she ever needed a picture of the major suspects in the case.

"Tess never looks directly at you," Meg said.

"She is shy," Roxie interrupted.

"She could be depressed," Meg said. "I never really thought about it before, but I've seen mental patients with those vacant eyes. You don't think Tess is the killer, do you?"

Luke leaned against the bar at the edge of the kitchen. "No motive. Bernice was her friend."

"Friends can have a falling out." Andi raised her brows at him. "Just like couples."

Meg bit her lip, then glanced at Andi as if she wasn't sure she should speak. "I saw Tess coming out of Reverend Nichols's condo several times. I asked her what was up. She wouldn't answer. What if they were having an affair?"

"If Tess fell in love with Reverend Nichols, Bernice would have disapproved because she wanted him to go back to the church. Sounds like motive to me," Andi concluded.

"True," Meg agreed. "Tess could have gotten rid of Bernice and then wanted Helen out of the way. But why try to kill Harry?"

Roxie shrugged. "Why not?"

ELEVEN

Andi had slipped away from her condo after Luke escorted her home. She was convinced Tess had been the person in black they had seen running away from the fire. But an hour of combing the property, hiding behind bushes and trees, had turned up nothing. Not one clue to help her investigation. She returned home, exhausted and discouraged.

Jessie trudged in the door looking just as tired. Dark circles shadowed her smudged eyeliner. She tossed her purse onto the kitchen counter. "Let's trade the cars out now, before I fall on my face."

"I don't want you driving into the garage door," Andi said. "Go change, and I'll move the cars."

Jess yawned while dropping the keys into her open palm. "Thanks. You're a good kid."

"Yeah. Yeah." Andi hated when her older sisters called her "kid," but she never said anything, fearing it would become her new nickname. She watched Jessie shuffle back to her bedroom and then headed outside.

She backed her sister's charcoal-colored SUV out of the driveway and parked it next to the curb across the street. She then proceeded to shift her own Mustang in reverse. The rules in the association made no provisions for a single person swapping two vehicles, so no matter where Andi parked during this switch, she'd break a rule. At three o'clock in the morning, she figured the odds were against getting caught.

After parking the Mustang in the fire lane in front of her condo, she reminded herself it would be there only a minute. Keeping her focus on the back wall, she eased her sister's SUV into the garage. Finally she jumped out, climbed behind the wheel of her own vehicle, and parked it in the driveway behind her sister's SUV. Done.

"This is ridiculous," she muttered to herself, staring at the long line of empty spaces in guest parking down the street. "I had more freedom at the apartment complex."

Back inside the kitchen, she found her sister pouring a glass of milk. Andi had been debating over the right time to tell Jessie about the flyers.

No time like the present. She would be too tired to do anything about it and a good night's sleep would give her time to calm down.

"Did you put your gun away?" Andi asked.

"Yeah, why?" Jessie grabbed a gingerbread cookie from the plate on the counter and bit off the head.

Andi handed Jessie the flyer with the picture of her in a plunging neckline and a man handing her money. "Harry paid someone to leave these on all the windshields in the library parking lot. At least we're ninety-nine percent sure that's how they got there."

"What a creep!" Jessie studied the photo. "He must have hired someone to take this. I would have noticed him if he'd shown up wearing his dollar-store toupee."

"Is this going to compromise your case?"

Jessie shrugged. "Can't say for sure." She tossed the flyer onto the counter. "There's always the possibility he might have helped solidify my undercover persona. I look super sexy there." She lifted the cookie, ready to take another bite. "But I feel sorry for you. You'll be known as the sister of *that fallen woman*."

"I'm not worried about myself. All I care about is your safety. As long as your case hasn't been compromised, we can deal with the neighborhood fallout. You're a nun compared to Harry and Valerie."

Jessie bit off the gingerbread man's leg with her front teeth. She barely chewed before swallowing. "The only other problem I can see is if anyone recognizes me from a previous bust. I don't think I've arrested anyone around here, but I haven't met everyone either." She tapped the picture with her pinkie. "On the up side, I'm wearing a ton of makeup. What you *can* see of my face doesn't look like me."

Andi noticed how the photographer had zoomed in on her sister's cleavage. "I doubt any man will be looking at your face."

Jessie grinned. "I'll talk to the detective in charge and see what he thinks. In the meantime, I'm going to shoot Harry where it counts."

"Get in line. He rigged the sprinklers to hit Roxie's bedroom window. If she doesn't get any sleep tonight, she might gut him."

A scraping sound at the door made Andi jump.

Who would be outside my condo in the middle of the night?

With her heart racing, she exchanged a worried glance with her sister.

"Wait here." Jessie opened the coat closet and retrieved her Glock. She eased over to the kitchen blinds, listened, and then peered outside.

Harry had better not be lurking in the bushes, Andi thought. *If Jessie spots him now, she just might make good on her threat to shoot him.*

172

"Whoever was outside left in a hurry," Jessie said, sounding disappointed. She closed the blinds and then opened the door.

Andi stepped around her sister and snatched up the manila envelope leaning against the building. It had to be from Harry.

"You're right, the chicken ran off!" Yelling into the night made her feel better—even if it meant waking up her neighbors. "Coward!"

A moment later, she dumped the contents of the envelope onto the dining room table. Along with two violation letters, each fining her a hundred dollars for continuing to break the parking rules, she found pictures of her sister's SUV parked in guest parking and her own car parked in the fire lane, taken not more than five minutes earlier.

Jessie stepped back inside. "Doesn't that toad ever sleep?"

"I looked around before I swapped the cars. I didn't see anyone." Andi marched toward the door and leaned her head out. "Chicken! Get back here and I'll tell you what I think of your stinking rules." Her anger boiled in her veins. She held her hand out to her sister, palm up. "Give me that gun. I'll shoot his toupee off."

"He isn't worth the trouble." Jessie waited for her to move before closing the door. "But I *do* think it's time to hit him where it counts. I'm going to do some digging into Harry's past." A mischievous smile flitted across her face. "This creep could be jeopardizing my undercover assignment by handing out these flyers. And, since he managed to get a picture of me, his involvement with the owner of the diner may be more than what we had previously thought. He needs to be taken in for questioning."

Andi grinned. If her sister could make Harry's life miserable for even a minute, she would consider it a huge victory.

"Come to think of it, he told Valerie he's rich. *He* could be a drug dealer. That would explain why he used to hang out at the diner on a regular basis. You should look into this, Jessie."

She tapped her chin with her pointer finger as a new plan spun into formation in her mind. "Drug dealers don't usually file tax returns. I wonder if Harry does. Are you still friendly with that IRS investigator?"

Jessie gave a sly nod. "And she owes me a favor."

****

The next day, Luke was just wrapping up his weekly inspection of the property when he spotted Andi walking toward her Mustang with her purse strap hanging over one shoulder. She opened her car door and then pushed her sunglasses into place.

Memories of long drives they had taken together caught him off guard. While sitting next to him in the passenger seat, she used to run her hand over his arm, maintaining physical contact throughout the ride. Her touch made him feel wanted, connected, loved.

He was beginning to think he had made a terrible mistake when he broke up with Andi.

Isn't true love supposed to conquer all obstacles? What if I had tried harder back then?

Once his hidden camera proved Harry was vandalizing Andi's property and the situation with the homeowners' association was resolved, he would be in a position to ask for another chance.

His thoughts wandered to the root cause of their problems: Andi's insistence on keeping him in the dark where her family was concerned. Knowing Jessie was working undercover could work in his favor. Once Andi saw that he could keep her sister's secret, she would know she could trust him to keep others as well. It would all work out. He covered the ground between guest parking and her driveway with long strides and renewed hope.

When he was almost upon her, he noticed the car was rejecting her efforts to turn over the engine. Her Mustang sounded like a hacking smoker. He pictured Roxie blowing perfect smoke rings and destroying them with her gravely coughing.

Andi twisted the key and then pushed open the door with too much force. Realizing Luke was standing near her trunk took her by surprise for only a second or two. "That jerk messed with my car!"

"You might just be having car problems."

What were the odds Harry was responsible for everything that went wrong in Euphoria?

"I know he vandalized my car, and I need it today." Her hair fell forward in soft waves as she bent forward to check her tailpipe.

"I trust your instincts." It was his experience that she was right more often than wrong. "After you get it towed, I can chauffeur you around. I didn't have anything important planned for today anyway."

She stood, hesitating. "Thanks," she said, finally giving in. "I'll take you up on that offer for a ride. My father can take a look at the car." She opened the passenger's side and reached in for her purse. "I'll pay you back with dinner."

"Sounds like a plan." He sat on the driver's side of her Mustang, leaving one leg hanging out the door. "By the way, when did you learn how to cook? I know you bake, but I didn't know you can prepare an actual meal."

She glared at him for a long, uncomfortable moment. "I *choose* not to cook. There's a difference. As for dinner, don't worry—it won't come from a packaged meal with 'hamburger' in the title. We both had enough of that in college."

Afraid he might put his foot in his mouth again, he silently nodded his agreement. She called her father while he tested the Mustang's engine. It sounded like a huge, old, dying animal. He should have placed a camera in the front of the condo. Somehow he had to catch Harry and stop this war before Andi lost every cent she owned. He felt somewhat responsible.

It's my job to help the community's affairs run smoothly, and I can't even find a way to remove Harry from the board. At least not yet.

"Dad is on his way over. He requested I not be here to get in his way." Before Luke could respond, she added, "And I don't care if fixing your car on the property is against the rules."

"I didn't say a word." When they reached his silver Chevy, Luke waited for her to buckle up before pressing the gas pedal.

"You're going over the seven-point-five-miles-per-hour speed limit," she warned.

"I don't live here." He regretted the words the moment they tumbled out of his mouth.

****

"The Lancaster is up the street on your right," Andi said.

If she wanted to hide out, she would pick a small motel away from the major streets. One known for being discreet. No credit card or identification necessary if paying cash.

Luke braked at a traffic light. "Why are we going to The Lancaster?"

"I'm searching for the vet's wife." Andi reached into her purse and revealed the picture of Tess at the neighborhood picnic. "I have reason to believe she is still in town, but not staying at home. The Lancaster is the closet low-cost motel on my list."

He lifted a brow. "You think she left her husband?"

"She was angry." Andi caught the concern in his eyes. "To tell you the truth, I'm glad you're with me. You'd recognize her before I would. I've only seen pictures—you know her."

The Lancaster turned out to be a dead end. They visited ten hotels and motels before they found anyone who could help. The manager behind the desk of a sleazy, pay-by-the-hour establishment recognized Doctor Owens in the picture. He held a hand magnifier close to the glossy print.

"Yep, that's him." The manager peered through the lens once more. "He was here last night. Paid for one night's stay in cash." He handed the photo back with a hairy, liver-spotted hand while he ran the other over his bald head. "I don't remember names, but I never forget a face."

"And the woman?" Andi asked, wondering if the manager had mistaken Doctor Owens for someone else.

"She stayed in the car." He pointed toward the parking lot next to the empty swimming pool, both a good distance from the office door. "Same blonde hair in the photo. Cut the same, too." He rolled a newspaper and slapped a fly investigating cookie crumbs on the chipped Formica counter. Without hesitation, he swept the dead bug onto the linoleum floor on his side of the lobby.

So the vet hooked up with his own wife. Why drive to a sleazy motel?

Luke handed the man a twenty and his business card. "Please call me if you see the woman again."

On the way out, he pulled the front glass door open for Andi. The bell overhead rang, announcing their departure.

"I'll pay you back," she said quietly.

"Consider it my contribution to the cause."

"What cause?"

"Finding the killer."

She stopped before reaching the asphalt parking lot. "I never said Tess killed anyone."

"You didn't have to. Doctor Owens thinks his wife is the murderer. He told his bookie, who told Roxie, who told me this morning. She's going to tell you later today," Luke said matter-of-factly.

Andi angled her head, mouth agape. "The doggie doctor has a bookie?"

"Buddy. He's Roxie's son." He chuckled. "I'm surprised no one told you."

"Let me get this straight. Roxie's son is a bookie and the vet places bets with him? Do you know if he owes him a lot of money? Does the reverend owe Buddy money? Did Bernice owe him money?"

"Not to my knowledge. And word would have gotten around if anyone owed an unusual amount. Roxie can't keep a secret." Luke removed his car keys from his pocket and unlocked the doors. "The murder had nothing to do with the bookie. He wouldn't hurt an ant."

"How can you be so sure?"

"Buddy is not your movie-type bookie. His business isn't big time, not even close. He works only with people Roxie knew from her beauty-shop days and a few of her neighbors." He climbed inside his Chevy and waited for Andi to buckle up before continuing. "You could say Roxie is the muscle behind the operation. Buddy is a five-foot, hundred-pound, amateur botanist. The man loves his plants. His mother is a different story. She got so angry at this one guy for not paying that she broke his kneecap with a rolling pin."

"I don't believe it."

Luke turned the engine over and backed up. "What part don't you believe? That Roxie's son is a wimp, or that she's his enforcer?"

"The part where Roxie owns a rolling pin."

Luke pulled into the complex to drop Andi off. He reached the end of the street and was about to make the wide curve to turn the car around when he spotted Doctor Owens at the mailboxes. He gestured with his head, and Andi straightened in her seat.

"Let's have a talk with the good doctor," she said. "I want to know why he's keeping secrets from me."

Not sure what to expect, Luke rolled to a stop in front of the curb near where the vet stood. Andi was the calmest Stevenson sister—unless she was extremely angry. At the moment, he wasn't sure if she was upset or confused. He would soon find out. They both climbed out of the Chevy, anxious to hear what the man had to say.

Andi walked right up to him like a woman on a mission. "When was the last time you saw your wife, Doctor Owens?"

Luke leaned against his car, studying the veterinarian's expression for signs of deceit.

The man had spent the night with his wife and hadn't bothered to tell the detective he supposedly hired to find her. Why?

Doctor Owens shut and locked his mailbox door, taking his time, as if deciding whether he should admit the truth. "Late last night," he conceded.

Oh, no. She is not going to be happy.

Luke remained close to his car, waiting for the explosion.

Andi stiffened her stance, anger set in her jaw. "Is there a reason you didn't call and let me know you found your wife? I could have followed her. Found out if she was working alone or with a partner. Instead, I wasted hours—hours I will bill you for—searching for her when you'd already met up with her."

Doctor Owens calmly removed the Wednesday ads from his stack of envelopes and placed them on top of the massive metal box where the entire community received their mail.

"She threatened to kill me if I told anyone that I met up with her. All she wanted was money and a place to spend the night. She swore I would never see her again if I didn't give them to her."

"So you spent the night with her at a motel?" Andi crossed her arms over her chest.

"Certainly not," he spat. "I paid for the room and dropped her off." He stepped off the curb and turned back to her. "How did you find out about the motel?"

"I work for a detective agency." She slid the abandoned stack of ads off the top of the mailboxes and into her waiting hands.

"Tess needed a place to stay. I told her not to come home because the police are investigating the murders. I thought for sure she'd say it didn't matter, that she was innocent, but she didn't."

"You have to tell the police," she demanded.

"I can't. She will kill me if I turn her in."

"Helping her makes you guilty of aiding and abetting." She shot an unsure glance toward Luke, as if asking if her comment was true.

He wanted to shrug, but couldn't without Doctor Owens noticing, so he merely lifted a brow in answer. Luke had no idea what the justice system would call the actions of the vet, other than highly suspicious.

"I was afraid for my life." Doctor Owens stiffened his spine. "Bernice is dead and two other people almost joined her in the cemetery. That has to count for something. It's not like I *wanted* to help her. She made me. Besides, I don't think I can legally be compelled to testify against my wife."

Andi paused for a moment, and Luke wondered if

that was the end of her questioning. If it were up to him, he would press the man for more. He had to know something that would help the police find Tess.

Andi's gaze locked on the doctor like a hunter about to strike its prey. The vet's dominating demeanor did little to intimidate her. "What did you do to help, other than arrange for the room?"

"I sold her engagement ring. I found it in my car, next to the garage remote." He pulled a business card out of the pocket of his tailored slacks. "This is the name of the man who bought her ring."

Andi took the card he offered. After she perused the print, Luke held out his hand for the card. She took several steps in his direction to hand it to him.

Doctor Owens raised a brow in his direction. He obviously wondered what Luke had to do with the investigation.

"I'm giving the lady a ride," Luke admitted.

"Thanks to Harry," Andi snapped.

The vet nodded as if the mention of Harry's name explained everything strange that went on in Euphoria.

Luke peered down at the business card. It belonged to a dentist named Sid, in Peoria. The card promised a pain-free smile. He had the feeling he already knew the sleazy answer to the next question he couldn't help asking. "What is a dentist going to do with a used engagement ring?"

"His new fiancée doesn't know it's used." The veterinarian's brow furrowed. "Don't look at me like that," he demanded. "The guy paid ten thousand for a ring worth twice that much."

Luke wondered if the man's fiancée would consider it a great deal, especially if the previous owner turned out to be a murderer.

"Did you give Tess the whole ten thousand?" Andi asked. "Or did you use part of it to pay off your bookie?"

Doctor Owens ran his hand through his hair. The vein near his temple throbbed. "How do you know about the bookie? Did Roxie squeal?"

"Nope. Not a word." She angled a smug look in the vet's direction. "I told you—I work for a detective agency. I'm good at my job."

"Too good." His gaze locked with hers. "Be careful, Miss Stevenson. Tess is dangerous."

"Where is she now?" Luke asked, wondering how close he should stick to Andi. He couldn't lose her before they even had a chance to start over.

"Tess said she was leaving town. I didn't ask any questions." He played with the mail in his hand. "I was thinking. If you find Tess and I get my money back, your agency can keep it. I heard Reverend Nichols was offering a reward to clear his name. My life is worth more than ten thousand and your fee. Besides, I won't feel safe until she is behind bars."

That's a lot of money for just snooping around and asking questions. No wonder Andi joined the agency.

In his line of work, Luke never saw a bonus anywhere near ten thousand.

"Don't worry, Doctor Owens," she said. "It doesn't matter where your wife went, we have resources. We'll find her and turn over her location to the police. It's just a matter of time now."

"You and your boss have proven you can handle the job," Doctor Owens admitted. "But you had better let Lenny take the reins from here. The woman I spoke to is no longer the woman I once loved. She's lost her sanity." Anguish revealed itself in his gloomy expression. "Her eyes are vacant. She has no conscience."

"I'm not afraid," she said, her jaw set with determination.

Doctor Owens shook his head. "You should be."

****

Sunday evening, Andi sat across from Luke in a dimly lit Italian restaurant. Candlelight flickered, casting dancing shadows over the red-and-white checked tablecloth.

Seated in a corner booth near the front windows, she observed the small gathering of customers across the room and the occasional couple walking past on the sidewalk outside. Those old feelings for Luke stirred deep inside. During their time together, back in college, she had considered herself lucky to have him in her life. Every day after class, she would freshen up in her dorm room and anxiously await his arrival. She didn't care if they ate out, watched television, or studied together.

"There's that smile I remember."

His voice yanked her out of her thoughts.

"Smile?" She felt a blush sweep over her. "Was I smiling?" Unwilling to discuss *why* she was smiling, she chose to change the subject. "I'm glad you accepted my dinner invitation. I wasn't in the mood to cook, and I did promise you a meal for driving me around today."

"I agreed to come—I haven't agreed to let you pay," he said dryly.

"But you drove."

He covered her hand, resting on the table, with his. "It was fun watching you play detective. Besides, I remember your cooking. Eating out is safer."

She chuckled. "Since you have chosen to insult my cooking again, I *will* let you pay for dinner."

"That was my plan all along." He removed his hand from hers to reach for his glass. "Here's to our paths crossing again."

Paths crossing?

She joined in the toast, trying not to overanalyze the statement.

Sauvignon blanc swirled in his glass as he lifted it to his lips for a generous sip. He swallowed and set it down. The mood suddenly shifted, becoming more serious.

"I was shocked when I realized you had moved to Euphoria," he admitted. "What are the odds of you moving into a community I manage?"

Considering her luck lately, the odds seemed good that she'd see him again under the worst possible circumstances. If she were lucky, she'd be living in a community where the homeowners' association was run by group of do-gooders who helped their neighbors.

"I was shocked to discover you were the property manager. I never expected you to walk through my door again."

When he scooted his chair closer to the table, she caught a whiff of his earthy cologne. It reminded her of the countless times he had held her in his arms. She closed her eyes and drew in a deep breath.

"You'll love the lasagna here," he promised. "It's almost as good as my grandmother's."

"I could have made you lasagna."

He grinned and wisely chose not to say a word.

"My cooking's not *that* bad," Andi protested, trying to forget the burned hamburger she once served him.

They both burst out laughing.

"Okay, it's that bad," she conceded. "But my baking is better than ever. I'll make you a plate of assorted cookies to prove it."

Her mind wandered to the first time the realtor had showed her the condo. Her thoughts had filled with daydreams of baking cookies on lazy weekends during the fall, decorating with twinkling white lights for the winter holidays, sitting on the porch with a warm cup of coffee on crisp spring mornings, and reading mystery novels near an open window during summer rain showers. It would have been truly euphoric—if it hadn't been for Harry.

Luke leaned back, making room for the waitress, who wore a bright-red polo shirt and white slacks. The employees all matched the tablecloths.

Andi imagined how life could have been different. Say if Luke didn't manage Euphoria, and if they had run into each other at a grocery store instead of the day he showed up on her doorstep with a violation letter.

Reaching for her fork, Andi was grateful for the chance to eat and not talk. She shoved a bite of cheese-and-sauce-covered pasta into her mouth. She needed a moment of quiet to strategize, to come up with a plan to convince Luke he should forgive her once she told him Jessie owned Lenny's Detective Agency.

Her mind began to wander as she chewed. He had done a lot to help her out lately. She should tell him the truth. Tonight. Before it was too late to salvage their new, growing relationship. But she couldn't. It wasn't her secret to tell. Her heart thudded in her chest. Keeping secrets was the exact reason he had left her before.

Can I convince him that it isn't horrible to be keeping this secret?

"I would hate to be the president of the United States, wouldn't you?" Andi resisted the urge to slap herself on the forehead. She knew better than to speak without a clear-cut plan.

He cut his lasagna with the side of his fork. "Where did that come from?"

"Oh . . . the red-and-white tablecloth and . . . my blue dress." She glanced down at the sundress she'd chosen because it slimmed down her hips.

"I forgot how funny you are sometimes." He smiled, lifting a forkful of lasagna to his lips.

"You didn't answer my question. Don't you think it would be difficult to be president? You know, deciding who gets assistance and who doesn't, which turkey gets pardoned on Thanksgiving and which ones get the . . . you know." She imitated slitting her throat.

He lifted a shoulder. "I guess."

"Sometimes there are no good choices. You simply do what you believe to be right under the circumstances."

"Okay . . ." His brow furrowed with obvious confusion.

"I'm glad you see my point, because speaking of not having a good choice, I have something to tell—"

He pulled off a tiny piece of breadstick and fed it to her. "Haven't you heard you aren't supposed to talk about politics or religion when you are trying to have a relaxing evening?" He eyed her over the rim of his wine glass. "I was impressed with the way you handled yourself with Doctor Owens. You could be a real detective if you wanted."

She thought about the way her knees buckled every time she passed by the dumpster. "Thanks, but I think I'll stick to teaching. I'm helping out only because Lenny is in Hawaii."

"Oh?" He played with his fork. "I didn't know you and Lenny were friends."

She needed to tell him the truth; she just didn't know how. "Lenny recently sold the agency. I'm helping out the new owner."

Luke paused as the wheels turned. "You know the new owner?"

"Yes . . ." she admitted, agonizing over what to say next.

"Your sister is a police officer, she's busy working undercover, and you suddenly have to help a detective who owns an agency?" Obviously still putting the pieces together, he narrowed his eyes and then took a swig of his wine. He swallowed and stared at the half-filled glass. "In all the time I knew you, I never saw you go way out on a limb for anyone other than a relative." He set the glass down and then met her gaze. "Jessie isn't a cop anymore. She works for a detective agency, doesn't she?"

There was no point in denying the truth. It would only make matters worse later. "She *bought* Lenny's Detective Agency, but she can't resign from the police department until she finishes her undercover assignment. You can't tell anyone, Luke."

"It's not your secret to tell." He rubbed his brow. "How many times have I heard that?"

"This is a matter of life and death. Harry once frequented the diner where she's working undercover. He might go back there and tell everyone she's a detective. We're talking about drug dealers here. If her cover is blown, they could kill her."

"Some secrets need to be kept." He frowned, understanding registering in his eyes. "This is why you were asking those presidential questions that made no sense." He tapped his finger on the rim of his glass. "Okay, I will keep your secret. I also won't hold that secret against you."

Andi's shoulders relaxed. "Thank you." Comparing her other sisters' secrets in the past to Jessie's made them pale in comparison. "I should have trusted you back in college. We had plans to marry. That should have meant treating you like family. I'm sorry."

"Me, too." He shoveled the lasagna into his mouth in silence.

She watched his strong jaw move as he chewed. An emotional wall had been erected between them. She didn't need to see it; she could feel its presence. Up until that moment, she hadn't been positive she wanted Luke back in her life. Now that she might have lost him, she couldn't imagine her life without him.

TWELVE

Luke took several hesitant steps forward. Charred wood and blackened steel lay in a heap on the abandoned lot while families resided in homes on either side. The house before him had completely burned to the ground. Only a birdbath, placed in the center of the gravel yard, had escaped the flames.

Andi stepped onto an abandoned brick and he protectively placed a hand on her arm to keep her steady. When she called him earlier that morning, asking for another ride, his first instinct was to claim he was too busy. Scanning the grounds, he was glad he had given in. His curiosity was getting the better of him.

He glanced down at the numbers Andi had hastily scrawled on the back of an old envelope and confirmed the address. This was indeed the last known residence of Doctor Owens and his missing wife, Tess.

"Can I help you?" A young woman in the neighboring yard lifted a tricycle by the handle. The smudge of food on her pale-pink tank top and faded jeans said she might not mind an adult conversation.

Luke forced himself not to answer; this wasn't his

case. He hadn't realized how often he took control of situations until he started driving Andi around.

"I was looking for the woman who used to live here," Andi explained.

"Tess?"

Andi gave her best I'm-a-nice-person smile and walked toward the young mother.

"What do you want with her?"

"Her husband hired me—us—to find her."

"Sorry, can't help you." She turned abruptly, swinging the tricycle wide with the sudden move.

Andi stepped closer. "Please. She could be in danger."

If she isn't the killer, Luke mused.

"Danger?" It came out more a whisper than a question. The woman eyed the both of them with a healthy dose of skepticism.

"Tess is missing and . . . there was a murder in her neighborhood."

The woman gasped. "Who are you? You don't look like cops."

Andi pulled one of Lenny's cards from her pocket. "Andi Stevenson. I work for the detective agency searching for Tess." She glanced back at Luke. "This is my associate."

"I'm Stacey. Tess is my friend. At least, I *was* her friend before they moved." She gestured toward the house. "The kids are inside. Come on in. I have a pot of coffee brewing if you want some."

Andi paused as if unsure.

Coffee meant conversation. That meant they were making progress. "Thanks," Luke said, gesturing for Andi to follow the woman. This young mother was no threat.

Entering the ranch-style home, Luke noted the dusty oak furniture and wall-to-wall toys—enough to fill a store. A toddler with wispy blonde hair dragged a stuffed bunny by the ear. Then, twirling the rabbit in circles, she smacked the chair of a young school-aged girl holding a porcelain teapot. Water sloshed over the side, landing on the miniature cup and saucer neatly arranged on the table below.

"Mom, make her stop!" The older girl, with the height and rounded face of a first-grader, stomped her foot. "I'm having tea with the queen of the mermaids and we need peace and quiet."

Luke suspected the child's mother begged for "peace and quiet" often.

Stacey grabbed the stuffed rabbit and tossed it onto the sofa. "Play nice or I'll put you both in the naughty chair."

Both girls pouted. The older one stomped her feet while the younger one ran to retrieve her toy.

Luke followed the women into the kitchen. He stood behind Andi and in front of the sliding glass door. Glancing out back, he searched for signs of Tess. If they were friends, she could be hiding on the premises. What he did find was a backyard full of children's toys: swings, sandbox, colorful hula hoops, and dolls. The only sign of adult existence was a gas grill that needed to be cleaned.

Stacey swept a purple plastic cup into a sink filled with dirty dishes and then took three clean mugs down from a cupboard. "Tess and I used to share a pot of coffee every weekday morning after her *husband* left for work." Her voice dripped with disdain on the word. "My George always left earlier. He works in Mesa, on the other side of the valley."

"You sound like you don't like Doctor Owens much," Andi noted.

"Not much is right. The man's a control freak. He demanded a spotless house, his dinner waiting for him the moment he walked in, and sex whenever he felt the urge." She lifted her brow in Luke's direction as if he might be guilty of the same. She poured the coffee and set both steaming mugs, along with the sugar bowl, onto the table.

Luke glanced into the sink and spotted two coffee mugs, two juice cups, and four plates. No coffee mug for Tess today. Luke waited until Stacey and Andi sat before joining them at the table.

"If he was so horrible, why did Tess stay with him?" Andi asked.

"She said it was her duty to obey her husband." Stacey rolled her eyes. "Tess grew up in an extremely religious family that believed the husband ruled the home. Glad my parents were more interested in sleeping in on Sundays. No one tells me what to do."

Luke did his best not to show any response. He swallowed a sip of coffee and was pleasantly surprised by the rich, smooth flavor.

Andi noticed his reaction and lifted her mug. "Did Tess love her husband?"

"At first, but it didn't last long." High-pitched arguing and shrieks came from the other room. "Warning two! Pipe down out there!"

Silence filled the air.

Glad the young mother wouldn't have to stop talking to deal with the girls, Luke glanced out the window toward the charred remains of the Owens's home. The chain-link fence provided an unobstructed view of the destruction. "What happened to their house?"

"I have my suspicions, but I don't know for sure. The morning before the fire, Tess came over with a bruise on her face. He had slapped her because she refused to make him breakfast. She thought she had morning sickness. If I were her, I would have thrown up all over his spotless suit."

"Did her husband know she might be pregnant?"

"No. He didn't give her a chance to explain. He slapped her up against a wall and then stomped out of the house. I would have chased him out the door swinging a chair, but Tess was too nice for her own good." Stacey sighed. "Tess was sure he brought on a miscarriage. I tried to get her to go to the hospital, but she refused. I held her for the longest time while she cried hysterically. Then, all of a sudden, she stopped and got a wild look in her eyes. She swore she'd never carry a child of his again and she would get even with him no matter what it took. I figured she'd finally lost her mind. Frankly, I was surprised it took her that long. If he were my husband, he would have died violently—many times over."

Luke couldn't believe what he was hearing. He knew Doctor Owens was uptight, but he never dreamed the man could hit his wife. He also knew Tess was quiet and easily led around by Bernice, but he never suspected she had deep mental issues. He rubbed his chin, trying to digest this new information. Studying Andi, he could see the story had disturbed her as well.

Andi cleared her throat as if needing the assurance she could speak after hearing the woman's story. "Did Tess tell you what she meant by 'getting even'?"

Stacey shook her head. "No, but that night I woke to sirens and the smell of smoke. There were firefighters everywhere, but no sign of Tess. At first I thought she'd died in the fire. I tried to run into the house to search for her, but two firemen held me back. They swore the house was empty."

"Did Tess confess to setting the fire?" Luke asked, earning a surprised look from Andi.

Stacey shrugged. "I never saw or heard from her again." She leaned close to Andi, as if wanting to make sure the kids couldn't hear. "I always wondered if she set the fire to kill her husband."

"Did you see Doctor Owens that night?" Andi asked, taking back control of the conversation.

"No." She resumed a natural sitting position. "He was gone, too. I assumed he went searching for Tess. You know, when they first moved in next door, they looked happy. It just goes to show how any marriage can tank. I think he sucked the life out of her. She knew she could never meet his expectations."

The topic of marriage had Luke thinking. He took in Andi's appearance. She wore a black skirt with a teal blouse that looked professional, yet her tender smile revealed empathy. He admired her—even when she kept her sisters' secrets. He admired her integrity. Their marriage wouldn't have tanked if she had risked taking him into her confidence.

Andi placed both hands around her mug as if she needed the warmth of its contents. With the air-conditioning blasting, she could be cold. "Do you think Tess suffered from depression?"

"Anyone married to him would be depressed. Don't you think?"

Andi lifted a noncommittal brow. Wise move, considering Doctor Owens had hired her.

All this time Luke was thinking the reverend had lost his mind and gone over the brink, but maybe the vet was right and it was Tess who had jumped the ship of mental stability. If so, her husband may have pushed her off the plank.

Luke studied Stacey's face, prepared to read her reaction. "Has Tess contacted you lately?"

Stacey locked gazes with him as if wanting to make sure her answer would be believed. "No. I wish she would, but then, if she did run away from her husband, my house would be the first place he'd look for her." Her eyes grew wide. "Ohmigod!"

"What?" Andi leaned closer.

"I found my back door open two days ago. I thought my husband forgot to lock it. Do you think it was Doctor Owens looking for Tess?"

Andi shrugged. It was a definite possibility.

Luke told the young mother that they would show themselves out. They walked in silence until they reached the street. "That wouldn't have been us," he told Andi.

She glanced over her shoulder, back toward the house. "What wouldn't have been us?"

"Tess and her husband. Their marriage. I would never have expected you keep a spotless home and . . ."

"I know." She cupped her palm on his cheek. "You're one of the good guys."

Her touch melted the tension from the night before. He didn't know what to think any longer. He wanted to be with her, but he didn't know if they could make it work. She did keep her sisters' secrets, but then she had told him about Jessie despite the fact her sister's life would be in danger if he told anyone. It was a major step in the right direction. A flame of hope ignited.

****

Back at Euphoria, Andi had just asked Luke to drop her off at the mailboxes when they spotted Meg and Roxie engrossed in conversation.

"What's up?" Andi asked the founders of the anti-board.

"We were discussing Harry and Valerie," Meg shared.

One of the women in Valerie's water aerobics class approached with a mail key in her grip.

"We should take this conversation inside," Roxie announced after blowing a series of smoke rings. "Let's go to Andi's. I assume you have refreshments."

Refreshments? She imagined Roxie ate whatever the local bars served. "We have chips and sodas. And maybe some peanuts."

"Sounds good to me." Meg bounced ahead, greeting Valerie's friend along the way. The other woman snubbed her with a lift of her chin into the air. The rumor mill must have blamed the anti-board for the destruction of Valerie's marriage.

Andi stepped around Roxie to avoid a similar encounter with the woman. She rummaged through her purse for her key as they strolled along the private street that circled the property. Reaching the path to her front door, she spotted an object hanging from the knob. "What in the . . ."

Meg grabbed her shoulders. "Don't touch it. It could be a bomb."

Cautiously, Andi stepped closer. A Suzie-Pees-and-Spits doll hung from a noose tied to the doorknob. Red liquid oozed from the rope tied around her neck, down her yellow pajamas, and onto the cement. A note printed on plain white paper stuck to her lace collar with the help of a straight pin.

Roxie marched past the women in her neon pink spandex jumpsuit and bent to read the note. "Stop investigating or else."

"Or else what?" Meg asked.

Andi looked at her in disbelief. "Or else I'll be the one peeing and spitting."

"Oh." Meg tightened her grip on Andi's arm.

Andi stared at the Suzie doll dangling from the front doorknob with drool collecting in its plastic mouth. Her stomach lurched. "I guess I should call the police."

She scanned the area for any sign of the psycho who had left the message. Not seeing anyone, she inserted her house key into the knob, doing her best not to touch the doll.

Meg turned to Roxie. "Get your Taser ready. The killer could be hiding inside."

Andi pictured a dark-dressed man jumping at her in the foyer with a rope gripped tight in his hands. "Maybe we should stay put. We can call the police from out here on a cell phone."

Roxie held her Taser high. "Don't be a chicken. I've gotcha covered."

Andi recognized the look in Roxie's eyes. That woman was going inside if she had to shove Andi out of the way.

"Okay. You two stand back." Andi turned the knob while waiting for Meg to find cover behind bushes. She kicked the door open and yelled, "Private detective! You're under citizen's arrest!" She jumped sideways, out of firing range, and waited.

Meg giggled a whisper. "That should scare him."

Seconds ticked by and Roxie grew more impatient. "If you're inside, you better show yourself!"

"Yeah!" Meg yelled. "I have a screwdriver and I'm not afraid to use it!"

Nothing. Not even the sound of a ticking clock.

Roxie barged in, Taser first.

Meg stuck close to Andi as she searched the main living quarters, the bedrooms, bathrooms, and then finally, the garage.

No one lurked inside. No one besides the three of them. Andi suddenly realized her childhood dream had come true. They were Charlie's Angels. It didn't matter that Roxie was one drink away from a nursing home for the bizarrely dressed and criminally insane. Nor did it matter that Meg was a stress-eating Chihuahua. Nor did it matter that Andi herself was a cookie-baking, part-time detective who was bad at lying. They were three women investigating a murder. Life was good—at least for the moment.

Roxie placed her Taser on the kitchen counter. To keep the good guys safe, Andi snatched the Taser and hid it in the china cabinet before calling 911.

****

After the police took their report and left, Andi opened the freezer door to make lunch for her friends. The threat left by the killer had taken at least five years off her life. Eating would help her think and settle her nerves. Now she understood Meg's stress eating.

It was only a matter of time before Jessie heard about the threat. Her friends at the police station would make it their business to make sure she knew. Andi wasn't looking forward to finally confessing that Doctor Owens had hired them either. That conversation would prove interesting.

Surprise! You have another case I didn't tell you about.

She could already see the look of disapproval on her sister's face. It would resemble the one her father had given her on many occasions.

Jessie would waste no time yanking her off both cases. When she moved to Euphoria, all she had wanted was to teach and bake cookies.

How did I get dragged into the middle of a murder mystery? Oh yeah, I threw the trash out and found a dead body, that's how. And Lenny sold Jessie the agency sooner than expected and she didn't have the time to work cases with her undercover assignment in full swing.

Andi felt sorry for Reverend Nichols. And Doctor Owens was willing to pay a huge reward for finding his wife and his money. One thing had led to the next. Now Jessie would ban her from agency work and her life would go back to normal. Regret spread throughout Andi's chest and her shoulders drooped.

She realized she enjoyed playing part-time detective. Her blood pressure couldn't handle it as a full-time gig, but she wouldn't have minded doing a bit of undercover work during school breaks. Just enough to pay for a vacation every once in a while. Now she doubted her sister would even let her file paperwork.

With her thoughts back on lunch, she moved a container of leftovers aside in the freezer and a pack of hot dogs fell out. They landed on the tile with a clack. Staring down at the flesh-colored links, she was reminded of the sausages littering the vet's garage. She couldn't shake the feeling that both the freezer and the bleach were important clues.

Could Tess have killed Bernice in the garage, hidden the body in the freezer, and then dragged it over to the house after everyone had gone to sleep?

After speaking to the Owens' former neighbor and seeing the house burned to the ground, Andi had a list of questions to ask the veterinarian. Correction, she used to have a list. She would never get to ask her questions because Jessie was sure to pull her from the case.

Andi shoved the hot dog package back in the freezer and grabbed a bag of frozen chicken nuggets.

"So," Meg began, "you must be getting close to figuring things out. The killer wouldn't be threatening you unless you've scared him."

"Or her." Roxie opened the refrigerator and scanned the contents. "You going to hang up your microscope?"

"Magnifying glass," Meg corrected. "Sherlock Holmes had a magnifying glass."

"I don't think I have a choice," Andi interjected, pushing the "Preheat" button on the oven. She still couldn't tell them Jessie owned the agency. "I suppose Lenny will pull me off the case now that there's been a threat made on my life." She dumped the frozen nuggets on a cookie sheet. "I hate just sitting around when I could be helping."

"Better than being dead." Meg opened the drawers until she found the one where the napkins were stored and headed to the dining room table with a handful. "But . . ." she called over her shoulder, "if you insist on living dangerously, there has to be a way you can continue your investigation without the killer finding out. Or your boss."

"You're both wimps." Roxie shook her head in disgust. "Find the killer and Lenny will have to give you a big raise. I'll help. You only live once. Make it a life worth living and do it with a great hairdo." She nudged her teased hair with her fingers.

Meg returned to the kitchen. "I'm in. No spitting and peeing doll is going to scare me off. Besides—we're a great team." She sent Andi a hesitant smile. "But it is your life. It's your choice. We'll respect your wishes."

"No. If you don't stay on the job, I'll lose all respect for you." Roxie leaned against the kitchen counter and glanced from one woman to the other. "Now let me tell you about the treasure I found."

Andi placed the chicken in the oven and set the timer. "Do tell."

Smirking, Roxie reached into her cleavage with her hot pink press-on nails and pulled out a small pastel-pink piece of note paper. "I wrote down this number last night."

Andi stepped closer and read. "Ear pieces. 1-800—"

"They're for eavesdropping," Roxie explained.

"I saw that commercial," Meg chimed in. "You can hear conversations from down the street."

Andi grinned. The possibilities for such a device were endless.

****

"That's it! You are off the case!" Jessie jumped up from the living room sofa.

"That's what the killer wants," Andi argued.

"And that's what the killer is going to get." Jessie marched over to the phone. "Owens must have told his wife that he hired you."

"So you think Tess killed Bernice?"

"Yes, but the detectives in charge still think they can pin it on the reverend." She picked up the receiver. "He had the strongest motive. He inherits over a million dollars between life insurance policies and her assets. Bernice owned five rental homes."

"Who are you calling?"

"Dad."

Andi unplugged the phone cord from the jack in the wall. "Don't! Please."

Jessie snatched her cell phone off the dining room table. "You're my sister. I'm not going to put your life at risk. You're staying with Mom and Dad until this is over. I can't *believe* you promised Doctor Owens you'd find his wife."

"I am *not* going home." Andi knocked the phone out of her sister's hand and caught it high in the air. She was not going to hide out in her old bedroom, hugging her Bon Jovi pillow for comfort. She had to think fast. "Compromise: I'll quit working for Doctor Owens *after* I ask him a few more questions, then you can take over. Those questions will help prove Tess's innocence or guilt. And I won't be able to think about anything else until I have the answers."

"*I'll* ask the questions," Jessie stated, ignoring the fact she didn't have extra time to investigate another case.

"You can't, you're undercover. Besides, I'm not

afraid," Andi lied.

"You've been afraid to throw the trash in the dumpster since you found that woman's body."

"Oh yeah?" Andi pocketed the phone, strode to the kitchen trashcan, and yanked out the bag. Fear rose into her chest, but she refused to let it take control. This time, determination was going to beat her trepidation.

She pulled open the door and stomped to the dumpster.

I will do this. No stupid metal box is going to defeat me.

Reaching the gate, she unlocked the door and swung it open. Shaking with fear, she quickly pushed open the lid and tossed the bag inside. Wasting no time, she returned to the condo. Her sister was waiting outside the door.

"Happy? I threw the trash out. Now let me do this one thing. You owe me. I was there when you needed me."

"I'm sorry. I'm interrupting." Luke stepped out of the shadows.

She'd been so intent on proving she wasn't afraid, she failed to notice his arrival.

Jessie planted her hands on her hips. "You can talk to Doctor Owens one last time, to wrap this up, *if* you take Luke with you, but then you're telling *Lenny* that you're quitting your job. Deal?"

She shot Luke a warning look. He could not reveal the fact he knew Jessie was the current Lenny. Luke rubbed his chin, obviously annoyed that Andi was now keeping secrets from her sister.

Andi rolled her eyes. Why couldn't her sister let her finish what she started without bringing Luke into the mix?

"Deal."

THIRTEEN

Luke persisted as he walked beside Andi. "I heard about the doll. It sounds like Tess may be watching you."

"I started this investigation. I want to finish it." Andi quickened her steps, keeping her notebook close to her side. "Besides, despite popular opinion, I *can* take care of myself."

"You are up against a crazed murderer. It would be prudent on your part to keep your friends close."

"You mean the crazy anti-board?" She slanted a look his way.

"I would put my money on Roxie over Tess any day." He continuously scanned the landscape, searching for signs of Tess. "Are you going to keep your promise to your sister and stop investigating after you speak to Doctor Owens?"

"I'll stop hunting for Tess," she said matter-of-factly.

"What aren't you saying? I remember that look. You have something up your sleeve."

"Nothing," she claimed, not so innocently. "I just plan to keep my eyes open for the reverend's sake. He's innocent."

Luke knew keeping her eyes open would lead to trouble. He stopped and waited for her to turn around. "Andi, please be careful. I just found you again. I don't want to lose you."

She pressed her hand against his chest, then leaned forward and placed a gentle kiss on his lips. "Thank you for caring."

He stood, stunned, watching her march on. He would not allow anyone to harm the woman he loved. Realizing he still loved her revitalized him. He jogged to catch up with her. They exchanged warm smiles that promised more kisses in their future.

Luke pressed the doorbell, and they waited impatiently.

Doctor Owens opened the door a few inches—with the chain still attached. "Miss Stevenson? I wasn't expecting to see you again so soon." He made quick work of removing the chain. "Did you find Tess?"

"Not yet. I'm here because I need to speak with you." She rubbed her temple as if she debated whether she should tell him about the Suzy-Pees-and-Spits hanging from a noose. "Mr. Ryder here was walking the premises and asked to join me."

She shot Luke a look that said, "Don't interfere."

"I wanted to see how you were doing," Luke explained, wondering how long the doctor planned to keep them waiting outside.

"Did something happen?" Doctor Owens motioned them inside, ignoring Luke's comment.

"Someone left me a note telling me to stop investigating. Nothing to worry about."

"I beg to differ. If you received a note, Tess wrote it. I'm sure of it." His facial features twisted in disgust and, possibly, fear for Andi. "I knew it wasn't a good idea to involve you. Where is Lenny? Why isn't he handling my case?"

"Lenny is out of town, but I assure you he's getting a lot done on his laptop."

"I'm not paying him to play games on his computer," he snapped.

"He isn't playing games," Luke added with obvious annoyance. Andi was placing her life in danger to help this man. He had no right to make ungrounded assumptions. He placed his hand on Andi's back, reminding her he was there if she needed him.

"Lenny has checked every hotel, motel, and bed-and-breakfast in the valley," she said, "but so far he hasn't found her."

"I could have done that much."

"Lenny can persuade people to talk," she retorted. "And he's thorough. He'll be back in town soon, but he wanted me to ask you a few more questions before he returns to the office and takes over completely."

"You're stepping down?"

"Yes," she answered, regretfully.

"I'm not so sure I want Lenny working the case either. Tess is dangerous."

Andi pressed her notebook against her chest. "The choice is yours, but I assure you, Lenny is not afraid of your wife."

"He ought to be. The whole world should be afraid of that crazy woman." Doctor Owens ran his thumb over his five o'clock shadow. "What do you want to know?"

Andi stepped inside the foyer. "Could Tess have an accomplice?"

His eyes narrowed as an angry scowl emerged. "You mean a boyfriend?"

"Or just a friend?" Her qualification did nothing to alter his expression.

Doctor Owens sighed and then headed toward the living room. Andi nudged Luke in the same direction as the vet lowered himself dejectedly down onto a floral ottoman.

The doctor rubbed his temples. "I didn't want to admit Tess might be having an affair. I guess it's time for me to face the facts."

Luke studied the spotless condo, remembering what the former neighbor had said about the doctor's expectations. "So you think there might be someone else?"

"I saw a man in a black sedan parked outside the hotel when I gave Tess the money she demanded," Doctor Owens said, wearing a bewildered expression.

Judging by the man's ego, Luke suspected the doctor couldn't fathom the fact that his wife would want to cheat on him.

Andi jotted down a note. "What did he look like?"

"Short, dark hair."

That didn't help much. The mailman had short, dark hair. Ninety percent of the men in Euphoria had short, dark hair.

The loud, shrill ringing of the phone took the vet out of the room.

Andi peered up at Luke. "Let's check out the garage."

"Why?"

"Just follow me."

He grabbed her arm. "I don't think we should do this, Andi."

"You said you want to help, so help already." She quickly walked down the hall and slipped into a room dimly lit by the sun peeking through the cracks between the metal garage door and the outside wall. Luke followed her inside.

"What are you looking for?" he asked.

"Frost." She lifted the lid of the freezer and peered down into its depths. Digging around, she reached the bottom of the stack of meat and pulled out a package of sausages.

The door swung open. "What are you doing out here?" Doctor Owens stepped onto the cement floor.

"Proving my theory," Andi said. "When did you buy this meat?" She held the sausage links high enough for him to see.

"I don't know, maybe a few months ago."

"There should be a layer of frost on these packages," she said smugly.

The vet narrowed his eyes. "Have you lost your mind? What does frost have to do with finding my wife?"

"I believe Tess ran off because she killed Bernice. She stashed the president of the HOA in here, and then later that night, sneaked the body into Bernice's home when you were asleep."

"She's not strong enough to . . ." The man looked stricken. "Oh . . . you think she had the boyfriend *before* she left me."

"I spoke to your old neighbor," Andi managed to keep a neutral tone. "She said Tess swore she'd get even with you."

"I lost my temper *one* time." He shook his pointer finger to help emphasize the word. "Just once. I felt horrible. I promised I would never lay a hand on her again. And I didn't. I swear."

In Luke's opinion, a man should never hit his wife, not even once, but he kept his thoughts to himself for the sake of Andi's investigation. "You might want to take a vacation," Luke suggested. "We're convinced Tess is our killer, and she did threaten to get even with you."

"I'll leave town if Andi and Lenny promise to drop the case," Doctor Owens said. "Let the police find her."

No matter what she said in response to the doctor's statement, Luke knew she wouldn't give up the investigation. She would work to prove the reverend's innocence. She wasn't about to let him fry for a crime he didn't commit.

"I'll tell Lenny his services are no longer required," Andi promised.

"It's for the best." Doctor Owens escorted them to the door. "I don't want to find you dead on your driveway."

****

At ten the next morning, Andi crept out of the condo to meet Meg. Jessie had come home during the middle of the night and gone straight to bed after they had taken a moment or two to discuss the flyers Harry had left on the cars in the library parking lot. So far, there hadn't been any fallout at the diner where Jessie was working undercover.

Not wanting to wake her sister, Andi closed the door quietly and stepped out to the front of the building. On her way to Meg's condo, she spotted a squad car entering the property. It turned in the opposite direction. Too curious to ignore the situation, she rushed to follow.

The police officers parked in front of Reverend Nichols's condo.

What now?

She walked closer, not sure what to do. At this point, hc was still their client.

Should I wake Jessie? What would I say? I really don't have any information to report. The officers might just have returned to ask the reverend more questions.

Scanning the front of his condo, she spotted an open window. Did she dare? Was it illegal to spy on the police? Her curiosity getting the better of her, she crept closer, and then sunk down to the wet grass. Wet pants were a small price to pay for information.

The voices of the officers carried through the crisp, morning air loud and clear.

"But I didn't do anything," The reverend spoke softly, but still loud enough for her to hear.

"Reverend Nichols, a bag of peanuts was found in a bush near the professor's condo. It has your fingerprints on it. We are placing you under arrest for the attempted murder of Helen Matthews."

"No. I would never harm Helen. You have to believe me."

The officer the deeper voice read him his rights.

Andi heard the front door open. Not wanting the officers to catch her eavesdropping, she jumped to her feet and strolled around front.

The reverend stepped off the porch with his head hung low and his hands cuffed behind his back. Nearing the street, he spotted her. "Andi, I swear I'm innocent. Tell Lenny to meet me at the police station."

A lump formed in her throat. *What now?*

Lenny couldn't meet him anywhere. The officers led him to the squad car. She recognized her sister's friend Joe. He ignored her as he opened the backseat of the cruiser.

A sense of urgency gripped her. "Don't talk. Call your lawyer!"

Reverend Nichols nodded his answer just before climbing inside.

The officer with dark hair and a mustache, one she had never met before, glared at her as he slammed the back door shut. Joe shook his head at her. He would have a talk with Jessie, who would have a talk with her. Joe clearly didn't know Jessie had already bought the agency or that the reverend was her client.

Andi stood helplessly by as Reverend Nichols stared at her through the window with sad, defeated eyes, pleading for her to save him. As soon as the police cruiser left Euphoria, she ran home as fast as her feet would carry her. Pushing open the front door, she gasped for breath. First thing in the morning, she vowed, she would start jogging again. Despite the sharp pain in her side, she hurried to her sister's room.

"Jessie, the police arrested Reverend Nichols!" Andi shoved her sister's shoulder to wake her, but got no response. "They think he tried to kill Helen." Still not getting a response, Andi yanked the covers off the bed. "Jessie, wake up!"

"I heard you," she mumbled, turning over and pulling the pillow on her head.

"You have to do something. He's innocent. Tess tried to kill Helen, *not* Reverend Nichols."

Jessie opened one lid. "The evidence says otherwise. The guys are just doing their job. If he's innocent, the truth will come out. Now let me sleep."

Andi bounced on the end of the bed to keep her sister from falling back to sleep. "Come on Jess, you thought he was innocent, you said so yourself. And we both know it would have been simple for Tess to break into his condo and steal a bag of peanuts. She's framing him."

"There is no evidence pointing to Tess."

"You need to do something, Jessie. I promised the reverend I would call Lenny for him."

Now fully awake, her sister tossed the pillow to the other side of the bed and sat straight up. Her disheveled blonde hair, smeared dark-blue eyeliner, and worn garnet-colored lipstick gave her a crazed-hooker look. "You promised to stop playing detective!"

"He made me promise him. I couldn't say no."

"He *made* you promise? Did he hold a gun on you?"

"Ah, come on, Jess. Have you ever seen puppy dog eyes on a grown man? It's pitiful. It's a million times worse if the man is a minister. You *have* to help him.

And since you are working undercover, *I* have to help him, too."

Jessie threw off the covers. "Andi, you shouldn't make promises you can't keep."

"I *know* Tess is involved in this case. She didn't just run off with a boyfriend. I feel it in my gut."

Andi tried the puppy-dog look on her sister, but Jessie only rolled her eyes.

"What about the fires?" Andi tossed out. "Tess burned down her previous residence and someone set fire to pictures in Helen's condo. She has a thing for fire."

Jessie yawned. "The arson investigator said a lit candle caused the fire that burned the house down. As for the fire in Helen's living room, the only prints there were Helen's and yours—along with your cohorts in chaos."

"We had permission to be there. Helen asked Roxie to pack up her belongings for her."

"I know." Jessie wiggled into a pair of red, fluffy slippers. "If it makes you feel any better, I've decided to continue working for Doctor Owens. The detectives are not overly motivated to find Tess since they think it's a domestic dispute. I asked Dad to give the man a call, pretending to be Lenny. Doctor Owens is convinced Tess is going to show up in the middle of the night with a baseball bat. Dad promised him that we would find Tess, so the doctor kept us on the case."

But Jessie was still working undercover. That meant she still needed Andi's help. "What do you want me to do first?"

"Nothing. Dad will continue to play the role of Lenny."

"What?!" *Could Jessie dig the knife any deeper?* "I handed you that case."

"And Dad told me he never went to the mall with you

to interview Reverend Nichols. You conducted the interview by yourself—after I told you I wanted Dad there to protect you."

"The reverend wouldn't go to the mall," Andi mumbled. So much time had passed, she thought for sure she had gotten away with conducting the interview in the reverend's condo-monastery.

Jessie shook her head and then shuffled across the bedroom toward the hall. "You're lucky he wanted our help and wasn't out to kill you."

"He's not the killer."

"The police think otherwise. Now, stay away from the reverend and Doctor Owens. The situation is too dangerous for you to handle." She held onto the frame of the door and looked at Andi with regret. "You were the one that said Tess planned to get even with her husband. Dad is a former solider. He is better equipped to take over. He convinced Doctor Owens to get a restraining order. And Dad will call the process server to deliver that order if Tess shows up on the property."

"Dad is going to stake out Doctor Owens's condo?" Betrayal hit Andi like a bullet.

"Yes." Jessie pressed her lips into a flat line. "If she refuses to leave or shows up again, after receiving the restraining order, he will call the police and have her thrown in jail."

Andi stared at her sister, dumbfounded. After all of her efforts, she had been pushed aside.

Jessie angled her head. "Don't look at me that way, Andi."

"Like what?"

"Like I just arrested your kitten and threw it in the slammer with Jack the Ripper." Jessie continued to shuffle down the hall toward the bathroom.

Andi suppressed a grin. Her sister felt guilty. That could work to her advantage. She didn't say a word;

allowing the guilty feelings to simmer.

"This is for the best. You'll see." Jessie stood in the doorframe of the bathroom. "Dad will scare off Tess, and her husband can go on with his life."

Andi watched her sister grab her electric toothbrush and apply toothpaste, still waiting for the guilt to take hold.

"I'll make sure the reverend gets a decent lawyer," Jessie continued.

Andi remained silent.

Jessie looked at her in the refection in the mirror. "Come on! What else do you want from me?"

"Let me work for Reverend Nichols. I want to ask him why Tess was seen coming out of his condo on several occasions. And if she could have taken the peanut bag with his fingerprints out of his condo."

"What?" Jessie spit out the toothpaste and spun around on her slippers to glare at her. "Tess was frequenting Reverend Nichols's condo, and you didn't tell me?"

"I was getting around to it. You're usually asleep when I'm awake and vice versa."

"If Reverend Nichols kept the peanuts in his pantry, Tess had access to them." Jessie appeared to consider the implications. "Okay. You can talk to Nichols."

Andi felt a spark of satisfaction ignite within her.

"But only if you take Luke with you."

She could handle seeing Luke again. The mention of his name brought back an overwhelming feeling of affection, maybe even love. She could love the man, even if there was no certainty that they would be together. It was a feeling. Feelings were safe as long you kept your head together.

"I promise I will take Luke with me."

FOURTEEN

"Let's see if this really works." Standing at the front door of Meg's condo, Andi placed the receiver in her ear and watched her friend cross the room.

The nurse bounced over a bright floral-print area rug, and walked along the length of a red leather sofa with shiny orange- and lime-colored throw pillows until she reached the corner. She stood in front of floor-to-ceiling striped curtains containing the same color scheme. No wonder she always acted as if she'd downed a dozen energy drinks—the annoyingly bright room could give anyone a sensory overdose.

Her nurse's uniform that day added to the feeling. It sported an overcrowded fabric petting zoo containing an abundance of baby deer, goats, and llamas. "Is this far enough?" Meg whispered.

The sound played loud and clear in Andi's ear. "Fantastic! We now know we'll be able to hear Harry and Valerie if they are whispering at a board meeting, but we need to know what the range is in our complex."

"All right, Miss Teacher, it's time for a field trip." Meg ushered her out the door. "I'll stay here. You keep walking down the street while talking. Once you're out of earshot, I'll raise my hand."

"Are you sure this listening device is legal?" Andi asked.

"Of course. They wouldn't advertise it on national television if it wasn't."

"Yeah . . ." Andi still had her doubts. She'd have to check with Jessie later. The cardinal rule was not to break the law. "What do you want me to talk about?"

"Tell me about when you and Luke dated in college."

Andi felt a blush spread from her chest, up her neck, and over her cheeks. "There's not much to tell."

"Come on, tell me," Meg urged. "I haven't had a date since Britney Spears kissed Madonna on stage."

Andi blocked the mental image. At least twenty yards away now, she reached into the pocket of her jeans and removed the picture of Luke she'd placed there that morning. Her sister had said to take Luke with her if she continued to investigate, but never specified he had to be there *in person*. If he was too busy to go with her, she could honestly say she took Luke along, even if it was only in photographic form.

Running a finger over his silly grin in the picture, she remembered the good times. Hopefully, they would have more of them in the future, after Harry was thrown off the board and the killer was thrown in jail.

Andi slid the photo back into her pocket and thought back to when she first met Luke. "We both attended Arizona State. It wasn't one of those unforgettable meetings where you look into each other's eyes and know it's love at first sight. No fireworks or angels singing. Just two college students standing next to each other in line for a hot dog. Or maybe it was pizza."

Meg pointed to her ear and nodded, signaling she could still hear her. Just then one of the neighbors walked past with her poodle. The nurse placed her hand over her ear. Loudly, she sang the words to "Like a Virgin" as if listening to an iPod while opening the back of her van.

An unexpected giggle burst from Andi's mouth. Meg sang so far off key she was surprised the neighbor's dog wasn't howling. Once the neighbor passed, she stopped singing.

Andi suddenly realized she should be pretending to be doing something normal, too. She felt her keys in her pocket. She could check her mail. Walking toward the complex's mail center, she waved as the neighbor passed. The older woman waved back. She obviously wasn't a friend of Valerie's, or she would have snubbed her.

Reaching the community mail center, Andi let her mind wander back to that first meeting. "Luke was having lunch with his roommate," Andi said, going on with her story. "His roommate happened to be dating a friend of mine. The tables in the student union were all filled. I was about to leave when Luke's roommate recognized me and invited me to join them."

Andi sighed. There was no doubt about it, Luke was a handsome man. Back then, he was tall and cute. Now he had broad shoulders and a smile that could melt the coldest heart. "I had seen him around campus before—always with a different girl. I labeled him a player before getting to know him. When his roommate later told me Luke wanted to go out with me, it took him at least twenty minutes to convince me Luke was really a nice guy."

Andi turned to see if Meg had signaled that she was out of hearing distance yet.

No. Not yet. She was pretending to clean the back of her van by holding a plastic grocery bag with one hand and playing with objects in her vehicle with the other. About every fifteen seconds she glanced in Andi's direction and gave the thumbs-up sign.

"Later that night, Luke found my number in the campus directory and asked me out to a movie. I remember changing my clothes at least twelve times before our date. I wanted to look perfect. He always did. Still does.

"He smelled great, too. Calvin Klein cologne. I couldn't pay attention to the film. I don't even remember what was playing. All I remember is that whenever I leaned close to him, I couldn't think straight. I let myself fall for him."

Andi opened her mailbox to find it half-filled. She rummaged through the collection of envelopes and junk mail, but her mind refused to focus on the present. "I desperately wanted him to kiss me. I gazed up into his eyes, hoping he would get the hint. He only smiled and made me wait until he dropped me off at my dorm." She closed the box and leaned against it. "That kiss was worth the wait. *Heavenly* doesn't begin to describe it."

"What was heavenly, dear?" A smartly dressed woman stepped around Andi to get to her box. They'd spoken at the last homeowners' association meeting when she offered her services as an accountant if they wanted to request a copy of the financial statements from the board.

Andi jumped. "I'm sorry. I didn't see you standing there."

"Then who were you talking to?"

"Who was I talking to?"

Who was I talking to?

"I was just reminiscing. Is it strange to talk to yourself?"

She hadn't fibbed. She didn't say she was talking to herself.

The woman looked her up and down with a smile that said she thought Andi had issues with reality. "No, but if you answer yourself with an unusual accent, call a professional."

Andi laughed even though she wanted to melt into her surroundings. She waved good-bye to the neighbor and caught Meg doubled over in a fit of laughter.

"Keep it up, Meg, and *you* can play the crazy lady talking to herself next time."

"I'm friends with Roxie," Meg said. "The neighbors already think I'm crazy."

"I see your point. I'm going to keep walking down the street. Scratch your head when you can't hear me." Andi reached the corner and spotted Doctor Owens at Harry's door with a man she didn't recognize. Quickly, she hid behind a car in a neighboring driveway. "Meg, get over here, but don't let anyone see you."

The nurse ran to the closest tree, grabbed hold of the trunk and searched for witnesses before rushing to the next tree and then to the next. Andi shook her head at the ridiculous scene, hoping no one had seen them moving in a similar fashion on their way to catch Helen washing her car.

Meg ducked behind the sedan next to her. "What's up?"

"Harry has company. Doctor Owens and a man I don't know."

Keeping low, Meg peered around the corner of the car. "That's Roxie's son. He's Harry's bookie. I think he lives near the mall."

Andi put her hand out for the listening device. Her friend wasted no time in giving it to her.

"I'll give you your money by the end of the week," Harry promised. "I'll give you another hundred if you can dig up the goods on this witch."

Andi peered around the corner. All three men perused a bright-yellow paper. She'd be willing to bet it was one of the flyers Harry had placed on everyone's windshields.

What was he up to now?

"Looks like she's a stripper, or maybe a hooker," the bookie said. "What else do you need to know?"

"Anything that will embarrass her enough to move. I want her and her trouble-making sister out of this complex—and my life—*today*."

It was the flyer!

Andi and the anti-board had made Valerie angry, and now for revenge, he was going after her sister again.

Roxie's son spit on the grass. "Don't know about the today part, but if she's hiding anything, I'll find out what it is."

Andi waited for the men to leave before coming up with an excuse to rush home to call Jessie. She had to warn her sister about the bookie trying to find the goods on her.

How easy would it be for him to discover she was a police officer?

"Hold the line a minute," Jessie said.

Andi listened to silence, wondering if her sister was discussing the matter with the chain of command.

Would they yank her off her undercover case? Would they go after Harry?

"I'm back."

"And?"

"I wanted to talk to my friend at the IRS while I had you on the line."

"And?" she repeated.

"Harry is nowhere near being a millionaire. At least not according to his tax returns. Aside from his retirement, he made forty-three dollars in interest income last year. There isn't anything to indicate he has any stocks or bonds."

"Then where is he going to get the money to pay back the bookie?"

"I'm willing to bet he'll trick Valerie into forking over the money," Jessie said.

Andi sighed. "In the meantime, he's going to blow your case, Jess. I should have just paid the fines and kept my big mouth shut."

"You had to fight him. He's a tyrant." Jessie paused for a few seconds, but it seemed like an eternity. "We're too close to making a bust for me to pull out of my undercover assignment right now. We'll have to try to contain the situation."

"What does that mean?" Hopefully something painful for Harry. Visions of water tortures danced through her head.

"I'll deal with it from this end. You try not to worry."

"That's like asking me not to breathe," Andi said with a sigh.

"Do it anyway."

****

The next evening, Luke marched into the crowded library meeting room and found Andi perched on the edge of a metal chair in the front row, near the table. Her tight expression spoke volumes. He leaned close, catching the scent of sugar cookies. She had been baking again.

"Are you all right?" he asked, knowing he was about to get an earful.

"No." Anger sparked in her eyes. "Harry hired the bookie to dig up dirt on my sister and Roxie hasn't been able to reach him to call him off."

Luke wanted to tell her everything would be okay, but he wasn't sure how much damage Harry could cause. If Roxie's son started showing Jessie's picture around, he might discover her true profession. He might also figure out she was undercover. He could even discover she owned Lenny's Detective Agency.

"What's the emergency meeting for?" Andi asked.

"Harry won't say, but he's all riled up." Luke lifted a pile of papers. "He just gave me copies of violation letters he handed out this morning. I haven't told him yet, but this is my last meeting."

"What about your mother's retirement cottage?"

"I'll come up with some way to convince my boss to drop this account without firing me."

Andi didn't appear convinced. "I didn't receive a violation letter like the others. Maybe because he wants to give me a false sense of security before he hits us with whatever he digs up on my sister."

"You're one of the lucky few who didn't receive a letter." Luke hefted his briefcase onto the table and tossed the papers inside. "There are at least fifty letters here. He got his hands on a radar gun to catch anyone going even a mile over the speed limit."

Luke took in the sea of red "Anti-Board" shirts filling the meeting room. More than half of the community had joined their cause. Those who weren't already members most likely would be after the meeting. The heightened tension thickened the air like a low-rolling fog.

Andi followed his lead and checked out the crowd. "I'm willing to bet Roxie and Meg will get the number of signatures they need to get Harry tossed off the board now."

"If they don't toss him off a bridge first."

"You know Harry brought this all on himself," she said, as if checking to make sure he was still on their side.

"I know, but the fallout is getting ugly." The community was spinning out of control and he couldn't stop its building momentum. He didn't think anyone could.

"Speaking of ugly, how is Harry paying off his

bookie?"

"He has money. Everyone knows that crotchety old man is worth at least a million."

"Not according to my sources. Is there any way Harry could be receiving kickbacks from any of the companies the association has been hiring?"

"I hadn't thought about kickbacks. I did check into the possibility that he could be pocketing fine payments without me knowing it, but I didn't find anything." Luke could kiss his job good-bye if they uncovered that Harry was taking kickbacks right under his nose.

Harry stormed down the aisle toward the table where they were standing. His clenched fists could barely be seen beneath the long sleeves of his puke-green suit jacket. If he wore a suit thinking it would give him an air of authority, he needed to think again.

Noting the man's scowl, Luke wondered if he had been taking kickbacks and Bernice found out. That had been Andi's theory before she decided Tess was responsible for Bernice's death.

What if she was right? If Harry was guilty, he would want to get rid of Andi and her sister.

A sense of dread overwhelmed his senses.

"Good luck with the meeting." Andi said, leaving out the obvious "you'll need it."

Meg tossed her a red shirt. "Wear this."

Luke watched her pull the cotton shirt over her head. Instead of tucking it into her jeans, she let the bottom hem ride along her hips. She almost blended into the crowd. The thought made him wish she could disappear from Harry's view, even his memory. Maybe then he would leave her alone.

Harry banged the gavel. "I call this meeting to order."

Andi sat next to Meg and Roxie in the front row as the other neighbors ended their conversations and settled in for the meeting.

The other board members joined Harry at the table. Owens held onto his business-as-usual demeanor while Valerie's perpetually smug expression reminded everyone who pulled the HOA president's strings.

Luke chose a seat at the opposite end of the table, keeping his distance from the others. He wasn't an active participant in the meeting. The job of the property manager was to answer questions if the board or homeowners directed any his way.

"I'd like to address the board." The cowboy stood, his eyes narrowed.

"Too bad. We aren't taking comments from the floor." Harry banged the gavel again. "I called this meeting to take a vote of the board. I make a motion that we give the current property management company thirty days' notice and contact three new companies for bids."

"I second the motion," Valerie promptly replied.

Doctor Owens didn't look surprised.

He knew ahead of time. But was he in on it?

Luke tightened his jaw, not saying a word.

Harry shot Andi an evil glare.

They were firing Luke because of his relationship with Andi. She met his gaze, her eyes wide with anger.

Luke mouthed, "It's okay."

"All those in favor say I," Harry stated loud and clear.

"I," all three board members answered in unison.

Luke resisted the urge to respond, despite the growing murmur in the crowd. He wasn't surprised by the board's actions. He only wished he could have helped remove Harry from his position before he had the chance to fire the company. Luke lifted his phone to text his boss. They needed to talk.

Andi borrowed a spiral notebook from Meg and ripped out a blank piece of paper.

"Harry is making a fool out of you!" she mumbled the words as she scribbled them down on paper. Thanks to their father's childhood obsession, every Stevenson girl could make an impressive paper airplane. Before you could say, "You aren't going to get away with this," her plane sailed over the empty space between her row of seats and Valerie's table.

Just as the crowd began to point and whisper, it hit its target: Valerie's nose.

"What in the . . ." She wasted no time in opening the note. Her eyes grew wide as she ripped the paper several times and then tossed the remains at the crowd. "You witch!"

Andi crossed her arms over her chest and nodded. "And you're being used!"

Harry glanced at Valerie, but continued to address the audience. "Next, I would like to address the violation situation."

The cowboy jumped to his feet. "We would like to discuss those violation letters as well!"

The crowd roared their agreement.

Harry pounded the gavel. "Many of you are late in paying your fines. You owe us thousands of dollars."

"You mean the association," Luke corrected. "They owe *the association* thousands of dollars."

The word "embezzlement" repeated in the crowd like a broken record.

Harry cleared his throat. "We've been generous in not taking your homes to compensate for the money you owe, but that may soon change. In the meantime, we can prevent you from using anything maintained by the association. If you owe us *anything*, and I don't care if it's a nickel, you *cannot* use the pool. We have hired a guard. If you insist on swimming after he tells you to leave, you will be arrested for trespassing."

"You can't do that!" a teenager in the back of the

room yelled what most of the crowd was thinking.

"Watch us." Harry's evil grin distorted his face. "Also, if you owe money, you cannot use guest parking for your visitors. In fact, you cannot drive your vehicles over the roads paved by the association."

"Then how are we going to get home?" Roxie yelled.

"Drop your car from the sky onto your driveway for all I care." Harry narrowed his gaze at Meg. "If you owe money, your code will be removed from the entrance gate."

Anger turned Meg's face scarlet. She gripped her soda can, wound up like a baseball player, and threw it straight toward his forehead. He ducked just in time. The caramel-colored soda splattered against the library's faded white wall.

Andi's stomach clenched as she watched the turmoil percolate.

Harry laughed like Santa's evil twin. Valerie peered over her shoulder at the mess on the wall, then at the threatening crowd rising to its feet. She quickly slipped out the side door. The security guard followed. Andi hoped he intended to get backup and not flee the scene like a coward.

Watching his girlfriend abandon him, Harry stopped laughing and clenched his fists again. "If you park in your driveway, instead of the garage like you're supposed to, your car will be towed at your own expense."

Roxie screamed obscenities and grabbed a skein of yarn from the lap of the woman sitting next to her. With perfect aim, she tossed it to the cowboy. "Hog-tie him!"

The cowboy tugged long strands out of the skein and wrapped each loop around his leathery hands. Pulling it taught, he threatened bodily harm with each silent move.

The board president backed away from the table. When his shoulders bumped into the soda-splattered wall, he turned to Luke.

"Do something!"

"Who, me?" Luke answered calmly.

"You still work for me for thirty days."

"No, I don't. I quit this account hours ago." Luke wasted no time reaching Andi. He gently held her hand and guided her toward the aisle. "Let's get out of here."

Andi had seen friendlier crowds in zombie movies. A sense of urgency took over. They needed to get out of the library before a riot broke out.

"Come on!" She urged Meg to join them.

Meg followed reluctantly. "Roxie, we're leaving!"

"Not me! We're going to have ourselves a lynching."

****

Luke followed Andi back to Euphoria. He wanted to make sure she arrived home safely after the heated meeting, and he wanted to sit and talk about their relationship. Now that he was no longer working for the board, he could date her without worrying about the complications.

He watched Andi ease her Mustang up to the gate and punch in her code. She waited a moment and tried again. Suspecting the worst, Luke climbed out of his convertible. He hurried up to the gate and read the rectangular screen, "Access Denied."

"Harry removed my gate code before the meeting even began," she spat.

He entered his own code. "Access Denied. Harry erased my code, too. So much for the thirty days' notice."

"That evil little man!" Andi slammed her car door and rushed up to the metal gate door available for walkers. She tried her key. It slipped in, but wouldn't turn. "He rekeyed the lock. I can't even get in on foot!"

"I'll take care of this," Luke said. "He can't lock people out. There are children who live in this complex. They need access to their homes regardless of whether their parents pay their dues."

Andi stood on the sidewalk as he popped open his trunk. Meg crawled out of the backseat of the Mustang and joined her. Both women exchanged surprised looks when he revealed a crowbar. He pushed it beneath the gate, then scaled over the top and jumped to the asphalt ground on the other side. His knee ached on impact. Ignoring the pain, he marched on.

Within minutes, other homeowners arrived and parked behind them. All of their codes had been removed as well. The gate wouldn't open for anyone. The growing crowd reminded him of why they left the library. He needed to get that gate opened before the mob took control of the situation. Luke examined the box containing the gate's motor. He inserted one end of the crowbar into the slight opening behind the lock and pulled.

Mr. Decker, the cowboy, kicked the pole holding up the keypad with the heel of his boot. It barely budged. He turned to a tall man about twenty years his junior. "You should have let me hog-tie that weasel back at the library."

"Next time." The man patted him on the back and pointed to Luke. They both scaled the gate to join him. The cowboy needed less help over than one would have expected for a man his age.

When Luke finished prying open the box, he noticed that the cowboy's friend held a pair of wire cutters in his hand. He stepped back to let the man do his thing. He watched him snip away the way a beautician would with scissors, but nothing opened the gate.

Ready to lend a hand, several men said they'd be right back and scaled the gate as well. They returned shortly from their homes with blowtorches, sledgehammers, and drills. They ran an orange electrical cord from the closest neighbor's porch and strung it over the wall for any tools that needed to be plugged in to obtain electric power. The small army of men not only managed to remove the gates from their hinges but totally destroyed them. Harry should be thankful he hadn't shown up before the task was complete. They might not have stopped at destroying metal.

The cowboy eyed the mangled mess. "Maybe we should put it back on the hinges and tie that varmint up to it spread-eagle. The kids could take turns pushing the gate back and forth like one of them there amusement rides."

"The older kids could throw tomatoes at him," his friend added. "Or baseballs."

"It would be better if we find a nonviolent way of dealing with Harry—and one that doesn't involve children," Andi said, the protective teacher in her taking over.

"Missy, you do things your way and I'll do things mine," the cowboy snarled.

Luke thought about *his* way of doing things. "I was impressed with the way you scaled the gate," he told the older man. "I almost took out my knee on the landing."

Andi studied Mr. Decker. "How's your back feeling?"

"I was so mad, I didn't even think about my back." The cowboy stretched and groaned. "To tell you the truth, I wish you hadn't reminded me. It feels like nails stabbing at me again."

Luke watched Andi. Something was going on in that pretty head of hers. He made a mental note to ask about it later.

The group headed back to their cars at a leisurely, content pace—the way dockworkers might after putting in a long day.

After parking in her garage, Andi leaned toward his open car window. "Are you going to be okay? I feel bad that you lost the account."

"Don't. I already feel like a boulder has been lifted off my back." He glanced up at the night sky. The expanse of tranquil blue reflected his mood. "Whatever life has in store for me, it has to be better than working for Harry."

"I hope I'm going to be a part of that future."

"The best and biggest part of my life." He touched her cheek with the palm of his hand and then kissed her full on the mouth. "It's been an *interesting* night. I better let you get a good night's sleep. Your fight with Harry isn't over yet."

"True," she answered, a hint of disappointment in her voice.

"How about dinner tomorrow night?"

He wanted to cheer when her face lit up like the stars above.

FIFTEEN

Still unable to sleep, Andi stayed up watching television. The late-night movie, *Harper Valley P.T.A.*, reminded her of the anti-board and the Euphoria Homeowners' Association. In the movie, a single mother sought revenge against the school board that treated her and her daughter unfairly because she dressed provocatively. Harry treated her and her sister unfairly because he assumed Jessie was a drug-dealing hooker. He had appointed himself the morality police of Euphoria at the same time he was pursuing a married woman.

"About time!" Andi shouted when Jessie entered the kitchen through the garage.

Her sister strolled through the condo to the living room. Old movies must have been on the minds of many: the theme at the restaurant that night was *Star Wars*. Jessie wore a short white dress with gold ribbon trim, white go-go boots, and the famous Princess Leia hairdo with buns pinned over each ear.

"I noticed the front gate. Looks like a tornado hit the complex."

Andi recounted the events of the evening, starting with the homeowners' meeting and ending with the rougher men in the neighborhood waiting out front of Harry's condo with wrenches ready.

Jessie shook her head. "If he's smart, he'll stay away until things calm down around here." She plucked the pins from her hairdo. "Did you tell Valerie her man is not a Rockefeller?"

"I let her know he's been playing her for a fool. If she cares, she'll try to find out what he's been lying about."

"I have more information," Jessie said. "I made a call and discovered Harry's credit cards are maxed out. He also applied for a loan using the equity in his condo. Other than what the man receives from his retirement account, he's broke."

"Great detective work." While Andi watched her sister yank off another boot, her thoughts turned back to Tess and the reverend. "Speaking of detective work, when are you going to wrap up your undercover case so you can run your newly acquired agency?"

The reverend needs a professional to prove his innocence.

"We finally found a hooker at the restaurant who is ready to talk. With her help, we can catch the owner in the act of pimping out the girls. We haven't been able to tie him to the drugs yet, but if we can make a prostitution arrest, he might hand over his drug connections for a deal. If all goes well, we should make an arrest within the next day or two."

"That means Harry can't discover the truth between now and then." Still sitting on the sofa, Andi pulled her knees up to her chest and wrapped her arms around them.

"I forgot to tell you—the guys arrested the bookie. Turns out he had an outstanding warrant. He won't be digging up dirt on anyone as long as he's in jail. That means Harry isn't going to find out anything about my undercover work until the job is done."

Andi felt a wave of relief rush over her. "Anything new on the reverend?"

"Sorry, no. The evidence keeps pointing to him."

Andi checked her watch. "It's after three. I guess you want to go to bed."

"I'm not totally exhausted," Jessie answered. "I wouldn't mind watching TV with you until I pass out. If you'll make hot chocolate and bring out a plate of those sugar cookies, I'll change out of this ridiculous outfit."

"Sounds like a plan." Andi shuffled toward the kitchen.

"Do you have any lotion?" Jessie asked, rubbing her elbow. "I'm as dry as the Sahara."

"Under the sink in my bathroom."

"Thanks."

Andi opened the kitchen cupboard and found two dark-blue ceramic mugs. She filled them both with water and placed them inside the microwave.

"Andi!" Jessie's voice, coming from a back room, sounded terse.

"What did Harry do now?" Rage started to build in her gut. If he left another violation letter already she was going to . . .

"Grab a knife from the drawer and stay put."

What?

"Grab a what?"

"You heard me. Grab a knife and stay put!" There was no mistaking that the barked order came from Jessie the police officer, not Jessie the sister wanting her hot chocolate.

Andi silently slid open the drawer and selected the biggest butcher knife she could find. Touching the weapon brought images from slasher flicks to mind. Listening intently, she heard her sister opening and shutting doors in the bedrooms. Not knowing whether she should speak, she stood, leaning against a counter, holding the knife, blade out, in front of her body.

Please don't let anything bad happen.

She repeated the half plea, half prayer over and over again.

After what seemed like an eternity, her sister emerged from the bedroom holding the backup pistol she kept in her dresser. "It's clear," Jessie reported flatly. "Whoever was here is gone now. You can put the knife away."

"Someone was here?" Andi squeezed the handle of the butcher knife.

Jessie gently took the weapon away with her free hand. "It's okay. But you need to come take a look."

Andi followed her sister into the master bathroom. A message had been left in red lipstick on the mirror. "I told you to stop. You better watch your back," she read, then dragged in a much-needed breath. Searching the area for signs of Tess, she felt faint. "That woman was in our home, in my bathroom."

For some inexplicable reason, she was glad she had cleaned the tub that morning. She assumed the reasoning fell along the lines of making sure you had clean underwear on in case you ever had an automobile accident. Not that her granny panties would stay clean if she were ever in a head-on collision.

Was there a saying about making sure your house was clean in case you were burglarized or threatened with lipstick on the bathroom mirror?

Knowing she might be losing her grip on sanity, she turned to her sister. "How did Tess get in?"

"I don't know, but we're getting an alarm tomorrow." Jessie kept the gun in her hand at her side. "And you're *assuming* it was Tess. You stopped working for her husband and she would have no way of knowing Dad is working for me. I told him to stay away from our condo until this is over. I don't want anyone connecting the dots."

"Who else could it be? Reverend Nichols is in jail. I don't understand why she thinks I'm still working the case. I haven't spoken to her husband since . . ."

When was it?

She thought back to the board meeting. She hadn't said anything to him there. Earlier, she saw him in front of Harry's condo, but she hadn't spoken to him because she was spying on him.

"Oh, no."

"What?"

"Meg and I were testing a listening device in front of Harry's place and the doctor was there with the bookie. You don't suppose Tess saw us and thinks we were spying on her husband and trying to find her, do you?"

"Where were you when you were playing with this device?"

She hesitated before answering. "Hiding behind a car."

"Andi. . ."

"I looked around first. There wasn't anyone around to catch us."

"So you thought. Leave the spying to the professionals. It's what we get paid for."

"I am a professional. Sort of."

Jessie rolled her eyes.

****

Alone in her condo the next morning, Andi double-checked her bedroom window to make sure it was shut and locked. The night before, the police determined that's how the intruder had entered. Embarrassment had washed over her when the officer, one she hadn't met before, said the window hadn't been shut all the way.

Live and learn.

Andi shuffled into the living room and slid open the blinds covering the sliding-glass door. She breathed a sigh of relief when she didn't find trash or birdseed covering her porch. The cameras Luke had installed had done little to prevent Harry's shenanigans, but. . . She turned toward the laptop she had left on her coffee table. She hadn't thought about the cameras the night before because the intruder, Tess, had climbed in through her window. But there was a possibility Luke's second camera caught her sneaking toward their condo.

She sat on the sofa and booted up the computer. Within minutes, she had the monitoring site up and running. With a click of a few keys, she rewound the feed to the previous night. She pushed "Pause" when she spotted someone in a black sweat suit jogging around the back corner of the building. Strands of blonde hair protruded from the black hood that conveniently hid the jogger's face.

Leaning back against the sofa, she studied the picture on the screen. The blonde hair had to be Tess's. Andi spent the next few minutes watching the footage again and again. Something didn't feel right, but she couldn't place her finger on what bothered her.

Finally giving up, Andi closed the site and thought over the events of the past few days.

"Harry, you went too far when you locked everyone out of the community."

She typed "AZ Homeowners' Associations" into her search engine and waited.

Scanning the results of her search, she found, "Homeowners Associations adversely affect real estate sales." She clicked on the link and waited. An article dated 2009 appeared. "Realtors report lower sales in locations where neighbors report problems with their homeowners' associations." Andi scoffed as she read. "Problems? Try an outright war."

After printing a copy of the report, she jotted down the name of the reporter and dialed Information. She had promised her new friends she would find a way to solve their problems that did not involve vandalism. After several calls, she was given the number for the reporter's voice mail.

"My name is Andi Stevenson, and I have a follow-up story for you."

****

Luke arrived at Andi's during his lunch break. "I brought burgers and shakes. You interested?"

"A handsome man bearing gifts." She stepped aside. "Do enter, sir."

Placing the food on the dining room table, he caught the scent of her strawberry shampoo. Before she could reach for her lunch, he pulled her into a full embrace. She felt so good in his arms, he couldn't let go.

"I have thought about this moment all morning."

"I feel much better now that you are here." She hugged him tighter. "Tess left another threat."

Luke pulled back. "What?"

"She broke in and wrote a message on my mirror with lipstick. She warned me to watch my back."

"I don't understand. I thought you stopped working for Doctor Owens."

"It's a long story," she said. "Why don't we sit down and eat? I'll tell you every sordid detail."

Meg rushed through the open door. "There's a huge crowd marching down the street. I think they're going to lynch Harry!"

"I guess Harry didn't come home last night, or he would be dead already." Luke joined Meg at the door.

"We had better stop them before they end up in jail. That's where Harry belongs, not the neighbors."

If it wasn't one thing in this place, it was another.

Andi locked up and joined them. Nearing Harry's condo, they found a TV news van and camera crew among the growing crowd.

Roxie handed out picket signs to the neighbors while an attractive reporter interviewed her. After chanting the quotes on the signs, "Ban HOAs," "Abolish HOAs," "Protect Your Wallet from HOAs," Roxie pointed to Harry's condo. "The man who lives there is the president of our homeowners association and he's a—"

"He has been interpreting the rules in such a way that it is nearly impossible not to break one," Meg interjected before Roxie could finish her description of Harry. "And the board is nothing but a group of puppets who follow his lead. Instead of limiting his power, they keep adding to the rules."

"And the board spies on everyone daily," Andi said, wanting to add her two cents.

"No matter how hard you try to follow the rules, you can't." Meg took over the conversation. "They make them up. They send you violation letters for having a broom on your porch or feeding a pet outside. They'll decide these actions are against some vague 'no nuisance' rule or a vague 'keep your porch clean' rule. After paying all of these fines, we don't have the money to take them to court. And if we do, and lose, we have to pay their fees as well as our own. If they lose, then everyone here will just be given an extra assessment to pay their lawyer fees. It's a lose-lose situation. At least for the neighbors."

"What do you think should be done?" the young reporter asked, flicking her hair off her shoulder like the popular girls did in high school. The move detracted from the seriousness of the situation and, from the reporter's pose, it was obvious she cared more about how she would look when the segment aired than their plight.

Meg took it in stride and continued to push the cause. "Homeowners' associations should have limited power. Aside from maintaining the roads and landscaping, they should be allowed to control only the color of the buildings."

"What about homeowners who want to fix cars in their driveways?" the reporter asked. "Many associations ban that. Are you worried that grease and car parts could detract from the overall look of your complex?"

"Communities should get together and decide on no more than a dozen rules," Meg said. "The rest should be abolished. You don't need to micromanage your neighbors to maintain property values."

Impressed with her speech, Luke and Andi clapped. The rest of the crowd applauded her as well.

The reporter turned toward the camera. "Are you hoping your demonstration will persuade the state legislature to reduce the power of associations?" She handed the microphone back to Meg.

"They already have in some situations, but it isn't enough. Instead of depending on politicians to solve the problem, communities can take it upon themselves to limit their own power at annual homeowners' meetings."

Andi beamed with pride. "Who would have ever thought Meg had it in her to be so articulate?"

"Not me," Luke said.

A loud, shrill scream brought the interview to a halt.

Andi and Luke ran in the direction of the screams—toward the pond. Andi tried her best to keep up while questions raced through her mind.

Did someone fall in? How deep is the water anyway?

Spotting one of the neighbors sitting on the grass with her head down between her legs, Andi jogged to a stop. Meg, and the others following, slowed behind her.

The young woman, who couldn't have been more than twenty, lifted her head. The greenish hue of her face warned Andi to tread carefully. She surveyed the scene, not sure she really wanted to know what had brought on the screaming. Closer to the water's edge, the cowboy held a fishing pole with a burgundy ribbon hanging from the hook. Bent at the waist, he appeared to be studying a large object floating near the surface of the pond.

"Stay back, little lady," he ordered.

Little lady?

Andi didn't appreciate the title, but remained still. It didn't take a brain surgeon to know there was something in the pond the younger woman saw and, as a result, was about to puke up her guts. Andi's own gut told her it was a body. She hoped it wasn't human, but she knew better.

The rest of the crowd reached the grassy area and Luke held up his hands to keep them back. "Let me take a look." It took him less than a minute to investigate and return to her side. He rested his hand on her shoulder. "It's Tess. You don't want to see this. It's much worse than Bernice."

"Tess is dead?" Her mind had trouble accepting the news.

A murmur traveled through the crowd. The bravest, or the most curious, inched closer.

"Please stay back!" Luke held up his hands again. "She must have been in the water for more than a few days. It is not a pretty sight."

The young woman on the grass confirmed his statement by vomiting. One of the older women pushed through the crowd to assist her by holding her hair back. A few neighbors backed away. Many stayed in place, straining their necks to get a better view of the body, but they didn't move forward per Luke's request.

As Andi watched the poor girl heave again, she

thought about the body in the pond and what it might look like. A sudden wave of nausea overcame her, and she gripped Luke's arm for support. "If Tess has been dead, then who—"

"Left you the threatening message?" He glanced back at the pond. "I don't know."

The reporter and cameraman rushed to the pond. Judging by the determined looks in their eyes, no one could stop them. Luke must have known better than to try. He placed his arm around Andi and led her away.

Andi remembered seeing a burgundy ribbon recently. "Luke, please ask Mr. Decker where he caught the ribbon attached to his hook."

She forced herself to release the grip she held on Luke's arm and immediately missed the stability his strength had offered. The realization that she had been missing him for years began to take hold. She had never wanted to face the truth before. Crossing her arms over her chest, she hugged herself for comfort while she watched Luke talk to the cowboy.

He returned a moment later. "He says it was wrapped around a necklace hanging from her body. He yanked it off by accident when he pulled Tess toward shore."

"Does it have a cross at one end?"

Luke lifted a brow. "How did you know?"

"Reverend Nichols was holding on to a bookmark just like it the day I interviewed him."

More proof of his guilt.

The sound of more commotion caught her attention. The crowd parted and Jessie marched over the grass. The two uniformed officers following her set about securing the crime scene.

Luke nodded at Jessie. "I'm glad to see you're here to take over, Officer Stevenson."

Jessie's eyes widened.

"*Officer* Stevenson?" Roxie repeated. Surprise lit up

her face.

Andi recoiled as if slapped. This wasn't happening.

Jessie grabbed onto Luke's forearm and leaned close. "I'm not with the police. They just happened to show up when I did."

Andi caught Valerie rushing away. She glanced back at them with a grin before running off. "You think she heard him?"

Jessie looked at her like she was slime floating on the pond. "She heard all right, and she's running straight to Harry."

Andi wanted to crawl in a hole. She should have told Jessie that Luke remembered her attending the police academy. She had avoided the conversation because she didn't want to explain how he had figured out that Jessie was Lenny. He had promised he wouldn't say anything.

Luke's jaw fell open, and he blinked before speaking. "I'm sorry, Jessie. You walked over here with the other officers. I thought your undercover assignment was over and you were back to regular duty."

"My undercover assignment?" Jessie turned to Andi. "I trusted you. Now I have to call my boss and tell him my little sister blew my cover. Excuse me."

Andi's heart sank. "Jessie, I . . ." She watched her sister walk away, feeling like her world had ended.

Family comes first. I betrayed my sister for a man.

"It was a mistake, Andi," Luke said. "I didn't mean to say anything that would compromise her work."

Andi thought back to college and the times she had kept her sisters' secrets from him. It had been the right thing to do. She should have continued to keep her mouth shut. Her sister would never forgive her. She would never forgive herself.

"I have to leave."

"Andi," Luke called after her. "Talk to me, please."

She couldn't even look at him. "I can't. I have to fix

this."

Roxie planted her hands on her bony hips and laughed. "Who would have thought the hooker was a cop?"

SIXTEEN

Andi found her sister storming out of her bedroom, buttoning up her police uniform.

"Jessie, I'm sorry. Luke remembered you were a police officer."

"You told him I was working undercover."

She nodded. "He guessed that you owned Lenny's agency. I didn't want him to tell anyone."

"You told a secret to force him to keep a secret? That doesn't even make sense." She rushed back into her bedroom, where she grabbed her gun belt from the queen-size bed.

"I realize that now." Andi sat on a corner of the bed, watching her getting ready for work. "Now what?"

"The rest of my team is making the arrest as we speak."

Andi remembered Jessie telling her they were hoping the owner of the diner would reveal his drug source. "Do you have enough evidence to get the owner to talk?"

"I don't know." Jessie pulled her hair back in front of the dresser mirror. "I really don't want to talk about this right now."

"You mean you don't want to talk to *me*." Andi ran her hands over her face.

"I can't deal with this right now, Andi. For your own safety, I need you to stay out of everything that involves me and my job." Jessie marched out the door.

"I'm sorry," she mumbled. "I let you down." Andi flopped back onto the bed and stared at the ceiling for more than half an hour.

Emotionally spent, she ambled into the living room and turned on the television. A mystery movie played on her favorite channel. Settling into the sofa, her mind wandered back to hearing the woman scream at the pond.

Tess is dead.

The police would look for evidence linking Doctor Owens to his wife's death. The husband was almost always the primary suspect until proven innocent. She doubted there was any evidence linking him to either death or the attempted murders. He had no motive.

Who killed their wife during an argument over a golf membership at the country club? And why would he cut Harry's brakes? The doctor made good money; he could pay the HOA fines. He also had no reason to plant peanuts in Helen's creamer and frame the reverend.

Andi watched the bad guy on the television break a vase over his wife's head.

Assuming Doctor Owens killed his wife—why? What was his motive?

She rubbed her temple as if the action might help her think.

What if Tess came home wanting more money? Doctor Owens could have killed her, knowing everyone would assume Bernice's killer was responsible. He might have wanted to frame the reverend by stealing his bookmark ribbon to tie to her necklace. The reverend was a natural choice since he was already a suspect.

Her mind turned to hiding the body. The freezer would have been the perfect hiding place. When the coast was clear, he could have dumped her body into the pond. He could have cleaned up any mess back home with the bleach that killed the fish.

She sighed and slumped farther into the couch. She knew there were two problems with her possible scenario. First, it would mean there was still another killer living on Euphoria Lane.

What were the odds?

And second, the fish were already dying the first time Tess asked Owens for money.

The idea of solving mysteries no longer appealed to her. She flipped off the television and sat in silence, allowing feelings of despair to overwhelm her. There were over a dozen nice neighborhoods she could have chosen.

Why did I have to move to Euphoria? HOA hell. And the very same community managed by Luke.
Luke . . . We were so close to finding our way back to each other. Why did he have to say anything? Why did I have to say anything?

She fell onto her side, wishing she could sleep for a week. Everything was such a mess. Her sister probably hated her. Andi couldn't even think of continuing her relationship with Luke when he expected her to share her sisters' secrets. She had learned her lesson.

She rolled onto her back and stared at the ceiling.

If everything happened for a reason, why did Luke come back in my life just so I could lose him again? Perhaps I needed closure.

Sometimes when she felt lonely, she would reminisce about the past, about the good times they shared. If nothing else, this disaster taught her they were not meant to be together. At least this time she was older and could handle losing him. An unsettling feeling in her heart told her she was lying to herself. She sat up straight.

No. I will not suffer all over again.

Swinging her legs off the couch, she stiffened her resolve. She was much stronger now than she was during college. She was also stronger now than when she first discovered Bernice's body, thanks to Harry.

She was tough, and it was time to prove it. After slipping into her tennis shoes, she tightened her laces. "I'm going to face danger head-on."

That meant throwing out the trash—without tossing it on top of the dumpster and power-walking away. She opened the lid to the kitchen trash can and yanked out the bag. A paper plate fell to the floor. Undaunted, she shoved it back inside, tied the bag, and set her course to the dumpster.

Taking long, deliberate steps, she closed the distance to the metal receptacle where she had found Bernice's dead body. Despite the memories, she felt no need to turn back. She had a mission to accomplish.

Reaching the wooden enclosure, she unlatched the lock and pulled open the gate. There before her stood her nemesis. The dumpster. A huge metal box full of coffee grinds, milk jugs, and pudding containers. The trash Harry had tossed on her porch. A sense of calm spread throughout her body. She no longer felt afraid. Dealing with Harry had made her stronger. She had faced that demon and survived.

Andi casually pushed open the lid and took a long, deliberate look. White trash bags, cardboard boxes, and a broken television set littered the cavern inside the metal bin. She held her own bag high and dropped it inside before gently lowering the lid back down. Triumphantly, she slapped the dust from the lid off her hands and onto her jeans.

The hum of an engine grew closer as she closed the gate. Valerie was driving her way.

Feeling brave, Andi marched to the middle of the street, planted one hand on her hip, and held the other out straight in a "halt" position.

Valerie drove her gold sports car closer and closer, as if she didn't see her.

Andi stood her ground. She was a new woman. Not afraid of anything or anyone—other than her sister's wrath.

The car rolled closer, until it was just yards away.

She could see the indecision flicker across Valerie's face. Andi lifted her hand higher, keeping her legs straight as a board and her feet planted firm.

The car slowed but continued on its course to run her over.

Andi refused to budge. Refused to picture her mangled body in the hospital.

Ten feet separated them. Nine feet, eight feet, seven feet, six, five, four . . . Valerie slammed on the brakes.

Valerie pounded her hands against the steering wheel. She shoved open the door and practically fell out of the car. "Are you crazy?" Holding on to the door frame, she tugged her stiletto heel out of a crack in the asphalt before continuing. "I could have run your fat butt over and saved us all a lot of trouble. You are so stupid!"

"If you had driven away, I wouldn't have been able to warn you."

"Warn me? About what?"

"Harry's been lying to you. He's broke. He doesn't have a million dollars."

"You're the one lying. Not that it matters. I love Harry for who he is, not for his money."

"Of course you do," Andi tossed back, her words dripping with sarcasm. "He's still lying."

"Is not!" Valerie stomped her feet like a toddler.

"His credit cards are maxed. Look for his financial records and you'll see I'm telling you the truth."

"I don't believe anything you say. You are a mean, hateful person."

Andi almost laughed. The pot was once again calling the kettle black. "I'm warning you because even *you* don't deserve to be suckered in by that man. If you truly love him, even if he's poor, then good for you. But if you threw away your marriage because you think he's going to bankroll your future, he's played you for a fool."

"What's going on?" Harry strode down the street, ready for a fight. "You leave Valerie alone!" He pointed at Andi like a parent scolding a child.

Valerie spun on him. "I want to see your financial records when we get home."

"What? Why?" He took Valerie's hand in his own. "Don't believe anything that witch has to say. She's just trying to break us up. But she can't." He glared at Andi before escorting Valerie back to her car. "Now, don't you go worrying your pretty head over money. I've got it all taken care of." His voice softened. "I know—let's go out to dinner. I'll take you to your favorite place at the mall."

"He's going to buy you dinner at the *mall*?" Andi held both hands up in a gesture that said Valerie must be able to clue in. "Sounds like a rich man to me."

Valerie turned to Harry. "Are you going to show me your financial records or not?"

He shook his head. "I'm not going to do anything *they* want me to do, and neither should you."

"Show me your financial statements."

"No."

"She's not the one lying. You are!" Valerie yanked her arm away from Harry. Apparently not his girlfriend for long, she wasted no time in climbing back in her car. She slammed the door hard, gunned the engine, and turned the wheels in the direction of the man who had been lying to her.

Not entirely without brains, Harry shuffled backward onto the grassy common area. Valerie gunned the engine once more for show and then spun her wheels. She headed straight for him. Terror-stricken, Harry ran. He ran over the grass, then back onto the street. His toupee tilted, then fell to the road. It looked like a dead rat.

"Stop!" Andi sprinted after them, not sure what to do. "I didn't mean for you to kill him! Just kick him in the butt with your stilettos. Run over his toupee!" She pumped her arms harder to catch up. "He's not worth going to jail!"

Valerie continued to chase Harry, gunning her engine and spinning her tires for effect. He flailed his arms about wildly, running for his life. Reaching the mailboxes, he grabbed hold of the top and hauled himself up and over. Before he could reach the other side, she slammed into the side of the mailboxes with the front end of her car. The jolt sent him flying like an old, bald, badly dressed crash-test dummy. He hit the dumpster gate full force and then slumped to the hard asphalt below.

****

Luke's meeting with his boss had gone better than expected. He had entered the man's office positive he would be fired, but Mr. Miller said the Euphoria account wasn't worth losing a valuable employee over. Unfortunately, Luke did have to promise that he would attend the emergency homeowners' meeting since no one at the company had time to take the account until the following week.

When he arrived at the library, Meg spent ten minutes telling him about Harry's "accident."

"Valerie was so overcome with guilt she volunteered

to drive Harry to the hospital. While loading him into her car, she prepped him on what he was allowed to tell the doctors. If he dared tell the truth, she promised to have him tied to a tree before she sold baseball bats to any neighbor who wanted to pulverize him."

"She would have customers lining up down the street," Luke said. "I wish I had been there to see the look on his face when Valerie tried to run him over."

"As soon as she dumped him off at the hospital, she drove back and put out notices alerting everyone to an emergency homeowners' meeting."

Luke read the flyer Meg handed to him: "If you want a say in how things are run around here, you will want to be there." He searched the crowd for Valerie, but she hadn't arrived yet. "I can't wait to see what she has up her sleeve."

Andi entered the library and sat in the front row. She met his gaze and quickly turned away, obviously not wanting to see or speak to him. His whole world had turned upside down since she moved to Euphoria and now that he had messed up everything, he felt like he had lost his balance—or worse, his foundation.

Once Valerie arrived, Luke took his place at the front table and Meg joined Andi and Roxie in the front row. Mr. Decker kept sneaking glances over at Meg.

What's up with that?

Luke remembered Andi asking the cowboy about his back. He had appeared in good health the night he helped destroy the front gate.

Did she think Decker could have killed Bernice? He had motive. He hated the entire board.

Watching the man sit close to Andi gave him the creeps. He wanted to step down from the table and take her away, but she would resist. He had lost the right to play the role of her protector when he slipped up and told everyone within listening range that Jessie was a police officer. A wave of guilt washed over him.

Valerie smacked the gavel down at exactly seven o'clock. "Thank you for coming to this emergency meeting."

Harry's former girlfriend was the only board member in attendance. The reverend was still in jail for a crime he may or may not have committed, and Doctor Owens was home grieving over his wife. According to the rumor mill, he'd shot himself full of dog tranquilizers. He told neighbors he wanted to escape reality.

Luke scanned the library meeting room. Despite the short notice, word had gotten out that this was going to be the event of the year, and most of the community made sure to attend. Once again, the red "Anti-Board" T-shirt was the costume of choice. The room was a sea of red. Blood red. The thought reminded him that there was still a murderer out there.

Or in the room.

He watched Roxie and the cowboy laughing together. A feeling of unease settled in his gut. With what he knew about the both of them, he wouldn't be surprised if they had committed the murders together.

"I've called this meeting to appoint new members to the board," Valerie announced. She held a paper high. "I have proxies from both the reverend and Doctor Owens, and since Harry is in the hospital, he can't come."

A few yahoos encouraged the crowd to clap.

"Harry will be okay," she continued.

The crowd booed.

Valerie raised a hand for silence. "Despite the rumors, I am here to tell you it really was an accident, and I would like to thank Andi Stevenson for telling everyone it was an accident."

The crowd's opinion divided. Some cheered. Some booed.

Andi slumped down in her seat.

Valerie, the new acting president, tapped on the microphone to regain everyone's attention. "Since Harry's not here to veto anything, I want to appoint Andi and Meg to the board."

The crowd jumped to its feet in an overwhelming show of support. Andi turned to her new friends and lifted a questioning brow. Roxie and Meg grinned in response. She realized they must have known ahead of time. Luke motioned for her to come to the table. She hesitated at first, then slowly made her way up front.

Once seated at the long table, Meg spoke first. "As a newly appointed board member, I would like to make a motion that all fines owed to the association be forgiven." More clapping and yahoos followed. The motion passed unanimously.

Their next official motion was to change the number of board members to add Roxie and the cowboy, which stacked the board against Harry if he chose to return.

Roxie stood, and with her arms stretched high in a sign of victory, she yelled, "Next we are going to get rid of those blasted rules!"

This time the crowd stomped its feet along with more clapping and chanting. Luke shook his head in pleasure and disbelief. If he wasn't seeing it with his own eyes, he would have never believed these events to have been possible.

Once the celebrating settled to mumblings in the audience, every rule was discussed, debated, and then voted on. Enough residents stayed to maintain a quorum of homeowners—otherwise they would not have been able to vote away most of the rules. The library director happened to be a resident of Euphoria Lane, so he gladly kept the building open for them. The meeting officially ended at one o'clock in the morning.

The newly appointed board chose to keep three rules: No one could change the paint color of their building, no one could add on to the structure without permission from the board, and no one could leave car parts overnight on the driveway. Harry would return home a pitiful, powerless former president. Valerie officially took over the position of president. Luke had to admit that a tiny part of him felt sorry for Harry—he had lost the woman he loved. Luke knew how that felt. A dark void grew in his chest where his heart had been.

****

Andi opened the lid to the plastic container securing her cookie cutters. After selecting daisy, tulip, and rose cutters, she sprinkled flour over the kitchen counter and then removed cookie dough from a glass bowl. She heard Jessie open the front door as she dusted the rolling pin with flour.

"You will never guess what happened," her sister announced with an I-told-you-so attitude. After closing the door, Jessie placed her badge and gun on the table, and then leaned over the counter that divided the kitchen from the dining room.

Andi was so glad her sister was talking to her, she almost forgot to answer. "I'll take the bait. What?"

"The reverend signed a confession to both murders an hour ago."

"What!?"

How could I have been so wrong about the man? The whole monastery in his condo was creepy, but he had sounded intelligent and sincere when he asked me to prove his innocence.

"You're right, I am surprised. I can't believe this. Why did he kill them?"

"He didn't say."

Andi shook her head in disbelief. "Wow! I was in a room alone with a killer and that fact doesn't even bother me. What does that mean?"

"That you are stronger than any of us give you credit for. If you want to work for me again part-time, let me know. I promise to assign you to less-dangerous cases."

She shook her head in disbelief. "You want me to work with you after I betrayed you?"

Jessie clasped her hands together on the counter. She allowed herself a moment of calm contemplation before speaking. "Andi, you didn't betray me. You never would. As you explained, Luke guessed what was going on."

Why is she being so forgiving?

"Ah, you must have arrested the owner of the diner."

A chuckle gave away the truth. "You know me too well." Jessie slapped the counter with one hand. "He flipped on everyone involved in the drug ring. We made over twenty arrests. Right after we booked them all, I gave my two-week notice. The boys are throwing me a farewell party tomorrow night and you, my dear sister, are invited."

Andi still couldn't believe her sister had forgiven her so easily. "That's wonderful!" She pushed the rolling pin over the dough on the counter. "I'm so happy for you. I'm just not sure I should continue working for you. I was convinced Reverend Nichols was innocent."

"Don't beat yourself up. We all make that mistake at least once." Jessie entered the kitchen and patted Andi's shoulder. She grabbed herself a bottle of water from the fridge. "I'm off to the gym. It feels like an eternity since I worked out. This case consumed my life, but not anymore."

It was good to see her sister smiling again. Andi doubted Reverend Nichols would ever smile again.

But she still wasn't convinced he was guilty.

Several hours later, she dabbed pastel-pink frosting on the last of her edible roses and then licked the remnants off her finger. "A masterpiece, if I say so myself."

While creating her cookie flower garden, she couldn't get the reverend off her mind. Back in college, her philosophy professor had once said a person knows the truth when he hears it. If that was true, then why didn't she feel like she heard the truth when Jessie told her Reverend Nichols was guilty?

But then, if he was innocent, why would he sign a confession? Perhaps his lawyer convinced him to take a plea bargain because there was so much evidence stacked against him.

She mentally combed through the facts. Trials were usually won and lost over motive. Nichols may have had motive to kill his mother and Helen, but not to cut Harry's brakes or kill Tess. He wasn't receiving violation letters like the rest of the community. On the other hand, that meant almost everyone else on Euphoria Lane had motive to try to kill the board.

The same board I'm now on. Not a settling thought.

Doctor Owens had convinced her Tess was guilty. For about a minute she thought he might be guilty, but he was one of the few who didn't have a motive to kill the board.

He wasn't receiving violation letters because Tess was on the board. Did he need to believe Tess was the murderer because she left him? Was his ego that fragile? Had Tess run into the killer when she came onto the property to demand money from her husband? What if Doctor Owens was right? What if Tess had lost her mind, killed Bernice, and hid the body in the freezer until after her husband took the sleeping pills that night? She could have tried to kill the others because she thought they might suspect her, or she might have blamed them for something they hadn't uncovered yet. Later, she decided she couldn't live with what she had done and committed suicide at the pond. Perhaps she stole the cross attached to the bookmark, hoping God would forgive her for taking her own life. She could have thought it had a stronger connection to God because it belonged to the reverend.

Andi's theory was all conjecture, she knew.

But then who else could be the murderer?

This was a puzzle she needed to solve to her satisfaction. If Doctor Owens still thought Tess was guilty of Bernice's death, he might let her spray the garage with Luminol to search for signs of Bernice's blood. No matter how well a person cleaned up a murder scene, traces of evidence would remain.

SEVENTEEN

Luke had just wrapped up a last-minute meeting with the landscaper when one of the neighbors reported that Reverend Nichols had been arrested and signed a confession. He had to admit he never saw that coming. Andi had been convinced of his innocence, and her reasons sounded compelling. She wouldn't take the news well. He wanted to stop by her place to talk, but he figured she would probably slam the door in his face.

On his way back to his Chevy, he stepped out between the buildings across from Andi's and found her placing a bag into her Mustang. She quickly closed her trunk when she spotted him. He knew that undeniable look of guilt.

"What are you up to now?" he asked, knowing she might not answer.

"None of your business," she snapped.

"I deserve that, but I'm worried about you. I heard about the reverend and I know you well enough to know you are not going to let this go."

She shrugged. "I have an idea. It's nothing for you to be concerned about." She rolled her eyes when he waited for her to explain. "I think Tess killed Bernice and hid the body in their freezer. I'm hoping Doctor Owens will allow me to spray Luminol in his garage."

"Where did you get Luminol?"

"Jessie had a bottle at the detective agency. I was just adding gloves to the bag when you arrived."

He knew she wouldn't listen to him, but he had to try to dissuade her from investigating further. He still cared—he still *loved* her.

"Someone left a message on your mirror, remember? Reverend Nichols was in jail the night it happened, so unless he hired a thug he met in his cell, someone here is trying to scare you off. If he or she sees you talking to Doctor Owens, you might be next on the hit list."

A sparkle lit her eyes. "The reverend *was* in jail when that message was written! The police were so glad he confessed they overlooked that fact. He should not have signed that confession."

Luke sighed. "You're missing my point. Investigating could be dangerous to your health."

She stared at him as if he was her archenemy and, at that moment, he knew he probably was.

"Then come with me." She snatched the gym bag from her trunk. "I don't have all year!"

Resigning himself to the inevitable, he took the bag from her and shrugged it over his shoulder. It was a lot lighter than he had expected.

"Andi, promise me you will not go anywhere near the doctor without me or Jessie. The killer is watching his condo. The killer is watching *you*."

She quickened her steps. "I promise this is the last time I'll visit the doctor's home. Now let's go see a man about a murder."

The veterinarian didn't take long to answer the doorbell. His appearance was shocking; his eyes were framed by huge dark circles and his five o'clock shadow left him looking dirty. He was taking his wife's death hard. He let them in and offered them a drink.

"No, thank you. I hate to bother you so soon after . . ." Andi grimaced.

The doctor sank on a corner of the ottoman. "It's no bother. How can I help the both of you?"

"I was wondering about the cross bookmark your wife had wrapped around the necklace she was wearing. I believe it belonged to Reverend Nichols. Did she have it with her the last time you were together?"

"The last time I saw her alive?"

"I'm sorry. I didn't want to say the wrong thing." Andi lowered herself to the sofa.

Luke placed a gentle hand on her shoulder. She shifted away.

So much for hoping she was on the road to forgiving me for betraying her trust.

"It's almost impossible to say the right thing when a man has recently identified his wife's body." Owens ran his hand through his dark hair. "Please don't worry yourself. I'm on so many medications, I doubt I'll remember this conversation in the morning."

"We are truly sorry for your loss," Luke offered.

"You wanted to know about the bookmark. No, I don't remember seeing it before. Reverend Nichols must have placed it around her neck when he killed her." He gnawed at his lip while glancing out the window, then back at her. "He signed a confession."

"I heard," Andi said softly.

"So why are you here?" Doctor Owens asked, confusion registering on his frail features.

Andi stood. "I shouldn't have come. I'm sorry I bothered you."

On the way to the door, Luke and Andi both noticed boxes stacked at the end of the hall, near his bedroom door. Was he planning to move, or was he wasting no time in removing his wife's belongings?

Andi's gaze traveled to the dining room table. Luke's followed the same path. A pile of paperwork and a cup of coffee covered the flat wooden surface. For a man on tranquilizers, he appeared to be getting a lot of work done.

Once the door closed behind them, Andi took slow, deliberate steps toward the sidewalk.

"I thought Tess committed suicide, but I don't think so any more. And I don't think Reverend Nichols killed her."

Luke knew the boxes and paperwork in the condo had something to do with Andi's new line of thinking. "Promise me you will not go near Doctor Owens again."

She glanced back at the door as if pondering his statement.

"Andi, promise me."

"I already promised," she offered reluctantly.

****

Soon after the sun set, Andi stood in front of her condo, pretending to shoot the breeze with Meg and Roxie while they waited for the veterinarian to leave. They knew he would because Roxie's son, currently out on bail, had called his after-hours emergency service. His pet Doberman had "eaten a poisonous plant" and needed immediate attention. He refused to let anyone other than Doctor Owens treat his dog. Andi had been amazed at how the bookie took orders from his mother without question or explanation.

She had heard Doctor Owens took his job seriously. Living up to his reputation, he soon emerged from his garage. He carefully backed his black SUV out onto Euphoria Lane. Although the streetlamp shone down on his windshield, it was difficult to make out more than his shadow from half a block away. Meg waved to him as he left through the gate like she normally would have. Andi pointed toward Harry's condo as if complaining to Roxie about the former HOA president.

The second the vet was out of sight, Roxie handed her the universal garage door remote with a flourish. "You hurry up and do your thing. We'll keep an eye out for the doggie doctor."

"What should we do if we see him?" Meg asked.

"Text me." Glad her friend had inadvertently reminded her about the possibility her cell phone could ring during her Luminol test, Andi set it to vibrate. She nervously slipped the phone into the pocket of her tan shorts. She had never broken into anyone's home before. If caught, she could go to jail and lose her job.

But I have to take the risk. Lives are at stake.

She pointed the remote toward her condo and the garage door lifted. In the back trunk of her Mustang, she found the Luminol and black light where she'd left them in the gym bag.

"This should take only a few minutes. If I'm not back in fifteen, call my sister. She's at the police station filling out paperwork."

Meg patted her on the back. "I wish I were as brave as you. I wouldn't want to be all alone in that garage if a body had been stored in the freezer. What if it's haunted?"

"Thanks. Now I have something else to worry about." She shrugged the bag of equipment over her shoulder. "Remember, fifteen minutes."

Keeping out of the light of the streetlamps, she sneaked over to the vet's condo and pointed the remote. The garage door lifted with more noise than she'd anticipated. A quick glance around confirmed there were no witnesses, other than her friends. She could feel her pulse racing. No one at her school would ever guess she was capable of committing a crime.

Hopefully, they'll never find out.

She halted the garage door when it reached the halfway mark, bent under to enter the dark room, and then sealed it shut with another press of the remote. For a second she thought about Meg's fear of a ghost and shuddered. Not willing to give in to paranoia, Andi dropped the remote into the bag and felt for the flashlight. She pulled it out of the bag and pushed the switch to the "On" position. A small circular spotlight hit upon a dark-colored suitcase and a set of golf clubs resting against the far wall. The clubs cast eerie shadows resembling alien creatures with odd-shaped heads. Near the door leading to the condo, she found several paint cans and a pole attached to a roller that had been left in a spotless silver tray. They hadn't been there the last time she had checked out the garage. Doctor Owens was planning to paint.

Is he hoping to cover up any trace evidence?

Andi set down her bag and removed the Luminol. She attached the spray nozzle and took aim at the walls, the cement floor, and the freezer lid, both inside and out. After returning the bottle to her bag, she removed the black light. Once she was ready to flip on the switch, she summoned the courage to face whatever she might find.

Taking a deep, grounding breath, she slid the switch into place and found only the circle of light from her flashlight shining on the wall behind the freezer and on the cement floor. If he had killed Bernice or his wife and dragged them to the freezer, there should have been evidence of blood.

Feeling a bit disappointed without knowing why, she scanned the room again and eyed a couple of spots that appeared to be glowing on the wall near the door. Not sure what to make of that, she continued to turn slowly to the right. On the opposite side of the garage, the wall lit up with glow-in-the-dark blood spatter. Evidence someone may have been killed in that very room made her stomach lurch. Her knees threatened to give out from under her.

The door creaked open, and Andi's heart jumped. She stared into the face of the cowboy peeking out from behind it.

"What . . ." she couldn't find the words needed to finish her thought.

"I was going to ask you the same thing, girly." He stepped into the room and stared at the wall, the floor, and then back at her. "The freezer used to be on that side. It needed to be moved to clean the walls properly."

How would he know that? Are the two men working together?

She'd fainted enough times to know the tunnel vision she was currently looking through was not a good sign. She blinked, forcing it away. Her life depended on her remaining lucid.

"How did you get in here?"

"I have a key." He held it up for her to see. "I've had it for a while now. I watch the house when Chris, Doctor Owens, leaves town with the missus."

Were the two men working together to knock off the board?

He stepped closer to the golf clubs, which were spotted with glowing blood spatter.

"This here would be the murder weapon, I suspect."

"How cleaver of you, Mr. Decker." Doctor Owens flipped on the light switch. He held a gun pointed directly at Andi. "I knew something was up when I reached the clinic and my 'emergency client' was running happily around the parking lot. I immediately smelled a setup. Creating a diversion could only mean you needed me out of my condo." He waved the gun toward the cowboy. "I didn't expect to find you both here."

"I spotted this one sneaking into your garage and decided to check it out." Still holding the golf club, the cowboy sidled up to Andi. "Now, Chris, you know you can't shoot us both here and get away with it. Guns make too much noise."

He tapped the barrel. "Not this one. I had it modified. No one will hear more than a couple of pops like champagne bottles opening. With so many people squeezed into a small location, people don't investigate a faint noise here or there."

"I see your point." The cowboy nodded glumly. "They don't notice noises like this one." He pulled a set of keys out of his pocket with his free hand and tossed them at the far wall.

Doctor Owens followed the motion with his eyes, and the cowboy swung the golf club with the strength of a man half his age. He batted the gun out of the doctor's hand. The weapon flew across the room and skated across the cement. In a complete rage, the veterinarian jumped the older man and yanked the golf club away. Before the cowboy could react, Doctor Owens clubbed him over the head. Mr. Decker fell forward, sprawling out over the pavement. Blood dripped down his gray hair.

Andi stared at the body slumped on the cement floor.

I'm responsible for the cowboy's death. He wouldn't have come over if he hadn't seen me sneaking into the garage.

The veterinarian turned toward the gun. Andi had to act fast. Running ahead of him, she kicked the gun high. It slammed against the wall behind the hot water heater and fell out of reach. Having bought just seconds of time, she ran to the garage door button, pushed hard, then ran to the bag containing the golf clubs. She pulled one out and spun to face him.

He hit the button on the wall, forcing the garage door to stop lifting. He pushed it again, and the door closed. Reaching to the side, he turned on a radio on top of a cabinet.

Andi knew the radio meant her fate had been decided. He didn't want anyone to hear him killing her with the club. She should have screamed when the garage door was open. If she tried now, no one would hear over the radio. Her only hope was that Meg and Roxie had seen the door opening and closing.

Time was running out. She couldn't let the vet win. Their gazes locked, each holding a golf club ready to do as much damage as possible. Empowered by the adrenaline rushing through her body, she shifted her balance back and forth like a wrestler.

"My friends know I'm here."

"But they don't know I am." An evil grin lit up his face. "I parked outside the gate and sneaked inside the complex."

"I see." Her jaw clenched. She needed to hold him off for as long as possible. Her friends would call Jessie after fifteen minutes. "You killed your wife."

"Took you long enough to figure that one out, detective," his words dripped with disdain. "I can't blame you for not putting the pieces together earlier, though. I did plan it all quite well."

"Your wife's death was premeditated?" That she hadn't suspected.

"No, you idiot, the cover-up. Although I did warn Tess if she ever tried to leave me again, I would kill her." He gestured to the suitcases with his club. "We had a fight over me playing golf, just like I told the cops. She annoyed me, and I slapped her. She claimed it was the final straw and came out here to grab a suitcase." He shook his head. "I told her she could never leave me. She should have listened. Just like you should have stayed away while you could."

He took a step forward.

She took a step back.

The cowboy lifted an eyelid, but didn't move. He was probably too weak to be of any help, but Andi was glad he wasn't dead.

"Bernice," she muttered. "Why did you kill her?"

"I had no choice. She heard us fighting on her way back from the board meeting and knocked at the door. Her mistake was noticing the blood on the cuff of my shirt. I told her Tess had fallen off a ladder and I needed her help. She fell for it and rushed to the garage. I was forced to kill her, too."

He took another step forward.

Andi took another step back.

"You used bleach to clean up the garage, and it killed the fish." She knew she had gotten that much right.

"I do regret killing the fish." His tone said otherwise.

"You took Bernice back to her house and dropped her out of her window."

"True. And now you know too much."

He lunged at her and she jumped to the side, out of his reach.

"Why try to kill Helen and Harry?" She had to know the whole truth.

"I wasn't sure how this was going to play out until you found Bernice's body in the dumpster. Everyone assumed a deranged killer was after the board. I decided to keep the myth alive. When they find your body, and his," he pointed to the cowboy, "they will think the killer is going after the newly appointed members of the board as well."

"But the motel manager saw Tess."

"He saw a hooker in a blonde wig. I needed you to think Tess was alive."

She suddenly realized what was odd about the person

who had walked past her security camera. "*You* left the note on my bathroom mirror. You dressed in a black sweat suit and wore a blonde wig so I would think it was Tess."

A sinister smile spread over his face. "Everyone in the complex heard about Luke hiding cameras for you to catch Harry. I used them to make Tess look guilty, and you fell for it."

The garage door jerked to life and lifted.

Not understanding why, or how, she took advantage of the sudden distraction and swung her club at the veterinarian. The impact to his stomach left her hand feeling the force of the strike. Doctor Owens doubled over and dropped to his knees. She swung the club down over his back before he could recover.

The garage door continued to lift and Andi's heart lifted as well when she spotted Luke standing in the center of the driveway with a remote in his hand.

She ran into his arms. "Luke, he killed Tess and Bernice."

The cowboy swayed as he tried to stand. Doctor Owens recovered and pushed him back against the wall with a thud that echoed throughout the small room.

Luke took the golf club from her hands and stormed inside. He swung hard, connecting with the vet's chin. The man slammed into the wall and slid to the ground, next to the cowboy. The older man rolled to his side as if wanting to get as far away from him as he could. Doctor Owens's eyes rolled up to the ceiling, and he passed out cold.

Four squad cars descended on the scene. Officers jumped from their cars, guns extended.

Luke dropped the club with a clank.

Jessie ran to Andi's side. "Are you okay?"

"I'm fine. Arrest Doctor Owens. He's the killer, not the reverend."

"I heard everything," the cowboy mumbled. "He's guilty. He admitted everything."

The older sister raked a glance over her. "You sure you're okay?"

Andi nodded.

Meg ran up to her. "We did what you said! We called your sister after fifteen minutes."

Roxie sashayed up the driveway in her spandex pants and stilettos. "We called Luke, too. He had my other remote. I figured we'd need it to get inside."

"I am so happy to see you two." Andi hugged them both at the same time. It felt so good to be safe and alive. The reverend would soon be released, and the real killer would be tried and convicted.

Luke walked away without saying a word.

Panic rose in her chest. "Don't go!" Andi left her friends to run to the man she still loved. The man who had risked his life for her. She couldn't read his serious expression.

Is he angry at me?

"You saved my life." She stepped forward, but her efforts did little to close the distance physically and emotionally.

"You had the situation under control," he answered. "You didn't need me."

"You opened the garage and distracted him. If you hadn't, I would be dead." She leaned close and planted a kiss on his cheek. His posture straightened.

"You broke your promise," he accused. "You swore you would stop investigating and that you wouldn't go to Owens's condo again. I can't trust you."

"You can't trust *me*?" She couldn't believe he had the audacity to say such a thing. "You betrayed *my* trust! You told half the neighborhood that my sister was a police officer."

"It was an honest mistake. She walked up to the pond

with two police officers following her. You, on the other hand, made a conscious decision to break a promise."

He was right. She should have never made a promise she had no intention of keeping. She just didn't want him to interfere. Words failed her as he walked away. Her heart broke all over again.

NINETEEN

The next board meeting a long, lonely month later, didn't draw the usual crowd. Half of the seats were left empty, and no one wore a red "Anti-Board" T-shirt. Valerie took over Harry's position as board president. After learning he had been removed from the board by the petition started by Meg and Roxie, Harry decided to visit relatives in Maine. Andi hoped he'd move there for good, but Valerie doubted he would.

The cowboy was recovering nicely from his injuries and explained he had stared at Meg the day they hid out in his condo because she reminded him so much of his late wife during her younger years. Andi regretted thinking he might be a killer because of his bad temperament. In fact, now that Harry was out of town, the cowboy smiled frequently.

Andi stood near the door, holding a platter of homemade sugar cookies in the shapes she had first intended to make when she bought her condo on Euphoria Lane: small cottages, an assortment of flowers, and colorful butterflies. She pulled back the plastic wrap and offered them to her friends and fellow board members. Valerie took one and then sashayed up to the front table.

Meg reached for one and smirked. "What? No gingerbread cookies? We could still chomp off Harry's cookie head for the fun of it."

"With Harry no longer a threat, I have decided to focus on happy things," Andi said.

"I'll second that." Luke stood in the open doorway.

"What are you doing here?" Roxie asked.

"What *are* you doing here?" Andi echoed. "We were expecting the new property manager."

He shifted his briefcase to his other side. "I *am* the new property manager. With Harry officially off the board, I decided to take back the account." Amusement played with his expression. "Although I hear the new board can be quite a handful."

His smile sent a shiver up her back. Andi tried not to let it show.

Does this mean he has forgiven me?

She had forgiven him. He was right—he had made an honest mistake when he revealed Jessie's undercover status. Anyone would have thought her assignment was over when she showed up with two police officers.

"I believe this board can be quite reasonable, when working with the right man," she said.

Meg and Roxie both smirked. They obviously had high hopes for their relationship.

A most grateful reverend reached for a cookie. "I hope this board will remember to love thy neighbor and to treat others the way they wish to be treated."

"Amen to that, reverend." Roxie snapped a flower cookie in half, ready to pop one end into her mouth. "You can start by making nice with Helen. She's coming home now that the real killer is behind bars."

Reverend Nichols nodded. "There are many changes I need to make. I'll start with Helen."

"Andi," Luke said softly, "can I speak to you in the hall?"

"Sure." She hoped this was a good sign. If he gave another "I want to be friends" speech, she would scream.

After glancing around to make sure they were alone, Luke placed his briefcase on the tile and took both of her hands in his. "I miss you."

She resisted the urge to cry. "I miss you, too."

He stared down at their joined hands and rubbed his thumb over her knuckle. "I did a lot of thinking, and I understand why you didn't feel the need to keep your promise to me. I broke my promise to you."

"It was an honest mistake. I get that now."

He nodded his understanding. "This morning, I remembered how I felt when I realized you were almost killed. I decided life has handed us an opportunity to give our relationship one more try. That is rare. We shouldn't throw this chance away."

She sniffed back her tears. "I agree."

He stepped back, straightened his posture, and then reached out his hand to shake hers. "Hello, I'm Luke Ryder, the property manager. It's nice to meet you."

Her heart warmed, wanting to explode. They weren't getting their second chance—it was their third, maybe even a fourth.

"It's nice to meet you, too," she managed to say despite the lump forming in her throat. "Would you like to join me for coffee after the meeting?"

His gaze met hers. His eyes darkened with emotion and unspoken promises. "I would love to."

He brushed a tender kiss on her lips. Every worry she ever held about their relationship melted away.

"I love you, Andi."

Her heart exploded with joy.

"I love you, too." She jumped into his arms and planted a long, firm, passionate kiss on the man she intended to keep for the rest of her life. The sound of the door opening forced her to her feet, back away from Luke, but not before Meg caught them.

"Sorry." Embarrassment flickered across Meg's face. "I didn't mean to interrupt a private moment. Valerie wants to start the meeting."

"We'll be right there." Luke waited for the door to shut before he gingerly placed the palm of his hand on Andi's cheek. "I guess it's time to get to work."

She touched his hand and gazed into his eyes. "This is one board meeting I don't mind attending."

"I'm looking forward to the part where the meeting ends and we can be alone again." He winked, then opened the door and followed her up the aisle to the table where the rest of the board waited for them.

Judging from the murmuring in the small group gathered for the meeting, Meg must have announced what she saw when she opened the door. Their grins said they approved of Andi's romantic relationship with Luke. A smile tugged at her lips. She approved, too.

"Speaking of the neighborhood," Roxie said, watching Andi and Luke sit at the end of the table. "I hear Mrs. Spitzer has been acting strange lately."

"I bet her ex-husband is threatening her again." Meg's eyes narrowed. "He's a horrible man."

Meg passed the plate of cookies around while exchanging glances with Roxie, Valerie, and Reverend Nichols. They all turned to watch Andi.

Their unspoken words asked if she planned to investigate.

"No. No. No." Andi shook her head and held her palms out in gesture that said "back off." "I am hanging up my detective shoes. Spring break is over Monday. I will be too busy grading papers and planning lessons."

Ignoring their looks of disappointment, she bit off a piece of cookie and wondered how long the woman had been having trouble with her ex.

A giggle escaped her lips. "Summer break is only two months away. I might have time then."

Roxie and Meg both offered their assistance.

Luke took a cookie she offered and added, "I have vacation time coming. Perhaps I could help."

Andi grinned, wondering if she had ever been this happy before. She had finally found her euphoria.

ABOUT THE AUTHOR

Tina Swayzee McCright is a multi-award winning author of romantic mysteries. Her writing was influenced by watching hours of *Murder, She Wrote* and *Diagnosis: Murder*. She lives in Arizona with her wonderful husband, in an HOA community where she once served on the board. She has a BS in Communications and an MA in Curriculum and Instruction. Although she has been an educator for over twenty years, she believes her greatest accomplishment was raising an amazing daughter. You can read more about Tina at www.booksbytina.com.

Reviews of Euphoria Lane are greatly appreciated.